When Promises are Broken

When Promises are Broken

A River Wild Romantic Suspense Novel

Chrissy Garwood

Chrisolite Books
Sorell, Tasmania, Australia

I dedicate this book to my sister Julie Garwood.
I praise God for the support and encouragement
she has provided to me over the years.

Contents

A Sister Scorned 7

A Chance Conversation 15

Five Friends 21

Rooftop Retreat 29

Racing the Rain 35

The Weeping Woman 43

Miserable Monday 47

A Confidential Consultation 53

Destiny Delayed 57

Tuesday's Tempest 61

A Dangerous Descent 69

Wednesday Worries 75

Friend or Foe? 83

The New Nanny 89

Three Telephone Calls 95

Gypsy's Goodbye 101

Confirmation or Confusion? 113

Piper's Plan 121

Secrets and Suspicions 129

A Hopeful Heart 137

When Dreamers Dream 143

A Timely Test 147

A Dangerous Decision 151

Stressful Surprises 161

Seeds of Suspicion 167

An Anticipated Arrival 173

Change Is Coming 179

Morning Messages 187

Bitterness and Betrayal 195

An Isolating Incident............ 201
Scandal and Sorcery 205
Disrupted Dreams 209
Waiting and Watching 215
Jungle Jeopardy 223
Rescue of Recovery? 231
Eager to Escape 237
Hearts and Hands 245
Trials and Temptations 251
Funeral and Family 257
Reunion Revelations 265
An Inspired Invitation 269
Secret Strategies 275
A Possible Proposal 281
The Commitment Celebration 291
Character List 299
Timeline............302
Acknowledgements 303
Have you read Book 1? 305
Fantasy River Series 306

A Sister Scorned

༄ ☼ ༄

James 3:13 WEB
Who is wise and understanding among you?
Let him show by his good conduct
that his deeds are done in gentleness of wisdom.

༄ ☼ ༄

Sofia Fontana sat with her back to the bar, enjoying the rare opportunity to be a guest in her family's restaurant. As the *Ristorante di Fontana* manager, Sofia had worked tirelessly on preparations for her younger sister's wedding. It had seemed an impossible task to accomplish everything in seven weeks, but her team had proven themselves worthy of her praise. Though she kept her professional smile carefully in place as she watched the festivities, she wondered what would happen when Evie's infatuation faded.

She cast a critical eye towards the staff serving drinks this evening. The girl Sofia was training to be her deputy hurried over to refill her glass. Sofia accepted the champagne with a smile. "Excellent work, Danielle. Keep an eye on the others. Make sure they offer everyone champagne – the bridegroom is paying." She smiled as the girl relayed her message.

Resplendent in their new uniforms, they were working efficiently. Sofia sipped her champagne, savouring the taste. She listened to her team's playful banter as they greeted familiar faces. Many longstanding patrons of the restaurant were among the two hundred guests. More than one family friend had paused to congratulate Sofia on her contribution to this memorable occasion. Her parents seemed determined to make sure everyone knew that Sofia had made all the major decisions.

Sofia turned to look in the large mirror behind the bar. It was easy enough to find the bridegroom, who stood tall above the crowd. He was surrounded by a throng of people eager to congratulate him on his unexpected marriage. The invitation had been to his betrothal, so all but her family had been taken by surprise. Sofia knew Evie would not have escaped Romano's arms since the ceremony, so she adjusted her position and was rewarded with a glimpse of her sister. The bride seemed radiant with happiness, and oblivious to how unequally matched she was to the giant she had married. They were an unlikely couple. Beside her intimidating husband, Sofia's sister resembled an innocent child.

Sofia had done her best to dissuade her sister from making this mistake, but the bride refused to listen. The tension between them had intensified as the wedding day drew closer, until Evie had announced she had chosen someone else to be her matron of honour. Sofia had kept to herself the intense pain of being relegated to the role of spectator. Now, she felt her colour rising at the memory, and shifted her gaze to stare at her reflection. She smoothed her shoulder-length dark hair and banished her frown. Her practised smile erased all trace of negative emotions.

Sofia tilted her head, taking advantage of the bright lights above the bar to check her makeup. Satisfied she looked her best, she was about to turn when a memory from her childhood pierced her heart. Her sister Evie had loved the story of Snow White, and would tease Sofia for caring so much about her appearance. Sofia recalled the long-ago taunt: 'Mirror, mirror on the wall, who is the fairest of them all?'

Her eyes lingered on her reflection a moment longer. The blue, knee-length cocktail dress she wore clung to her generous curves. She had purchased it from one of her favourite city boutiques after her parents insisted she have something new. She suspected her mother was trying her hand at matchmaking, as Sofia had already refused more than one amorous man's invitation to dance this evening. Her mother seemed to have forgotten that Sofia had survived two failed marriages and was never without admirers. If she sat here alone, it was her choice. Sofia's smile strengthened.

Turning from the mirror, Sofia sipped her champagne as she surveyed the L-shaped dining room. The refined table settings accentuated the Mediterranean décor that Papa favoured. Romano's generosity had allowed her to purchase new table linen, and no expense had been spared on the floral decorations.

Many of the guests were seated, enjoying the Italian feast. She watched the wait-staff weaving between the tables. As if aware of her attention, an enthusiastic young man headed in Sofia's direction with a selection of her Mama's famous pizza. She deflected him with a wave of her hand, having already partaken enough. It was essential to save room for dessert, which would quickly be followed by the wedding cake.

Laughter drew her attention to the corner of the room where Romano's employees were seated. Sofia straightened on her stool. After Romano's five years of restaurant patronage, she knew each of them by name. Sofia sighed, weighing up the consequences of what she was seeing. Danielle appeared beside her. "Is there anything you require?" the girl asked.

Sofia shook her head. "I'm debating whether I should talk to Matilda before Papa notices," Sofia said. "That teenager is too much like me at the same age."

Could she dissuade her daughter from flirting with one of Romano's apprentices, without making things worse? The situation was further complicated because the young man was a friend of her eldest son, who was seated beside the besotted couple. There were no words for her disappointment that Leonardo preferred employment with Romano over working in the family restaurant. She tossed back the last of her drink, wishing earnestly that Romano had never walked through her door.

Just when she thought things couldn't get any worse, Sofia's youngest son ran past, chased by the flower girl and her brother. "Marco!" Sofia cried as she leapt to her feet. Her sudden movement put her directly in the path of one of the guests, and the small collision was sufficient to pitch his drink over his jacket.

"I'm sorry!" she said, holding out her hand towards the bar. Someone handed her a cloth. "Let me help you."

As she dabbed the damp patch on his jacket, Sofia noticed the white rose boutonniere pinned to the lapel. Sofia had ordered only three buttonhole decorations for the wedding party, so this man must be the minister who had officiated at the ceremony.

Her hand trembled as snatches of his wedding address replayed in her mind. Pastor Edwards had spoken eloquently. At first, she had been captivated, until she realised his pretty speech underlined the mistakes she had made in her own matrimonial choices.

None of the sermons delivered by her Catholic priests had ever wounded her like his words. Her sister's Protestant conversion was yet another of Sofia's concerns, and she had determined to have nothing to do with this man. These thoughts raced through her mind, while her defensive response was to babble about the possibility of stains.

"Send me the dry-cleaning bill," Sofia concluded, finally raising her eyes. In her high heels, she looked directly into his brown eyes, which shone with amusement. His mouth turned up in a genuine smile, and she blinked at the unexpected physical attraction.

Pastor Edwards was approximately her age, with short wavy brown hair. He wore his suit with the comfortable air of someone used to formal occasions. Her practised assessment took only a moment to declare him trustworthy and reliable. The kind of man who would be excellent husband material. Sofia took a step backwards. She presumed he would already be married. She readily admitted many faults, but stealing another woman's husband was not one of them.

"Thank you, but there's no need," he said. "This suit was going to the dry cleaners anyway."

To Sofia's chagrin, Pastor Edwards settled on the stool beside her. She threw another glance towards her wayward son.

"The children are having fun," Pastor Edwards said. The laughing trio was now running rings around a harassed waiter. Her thirteen-year-old son's love for food often got him into trouble. "I apologise for delaying you from your mission, but it looks like someone else is going to deal with them, anyway."

The matron of honour wove through the crowd in pursuit of the unruly flower girl. Sofia nodded, settling back on her stool.

Returning her attention to Pastor Edwards, she wondered about his motives for sitting with her now. Sofia decided to go on the offensive. "Before you say anything, I need to warn you that I won't welcome any advice about my sister. She has been away for twenty years, and nothing can undo the past. Evie talks about forgiveness and restoration. I haven't seen any evidence, and this wedding reinforces my concerns."

He seemed genuinely surprised. "You disapprove?"

"Why am I the only one who sees through Romano's facade?" She leaned closer, not wanting other guests to overhear. "Everyone ignores his criminal past. No-one questions the source of his wealth. And he put my sister in hospital the day she met him."

"Evie told me it was an accident."

Sofia's hand jerked, and she blushed. Thankfully, her glass was empty.

He didn't seem to notice how close he had come to a second drenching. "Isn't it possible he's reformed?" Pastor Edwards asked.

Sofia snorted. "I suppose you believe in miracles too?"

He laughed. "This is a contentious topic! You might not approve of the relationship, but you must be satisfied with the reception? Your sister said you organised everything. Congratulations."

She smiled with satisfaction. "Our restaurant will benefit from hosting this event." One day, the family business would be Sofia's, and her standards were high. This restaurant was her future. There were many competitors, and she must secure their good reputation. "Everyone's enjoying the refreshments. It was my idea to dispense with a set menu, and to offer our guests multiple serves from a selection of our restaurant's favourite dishes. Our staff are well trained. No-one will leave here without eating their fill."

Sofia glanced towards the bar, where her employees were especially busy. Another bottle of expensive French champagne was being opened. Sofia's smile broadened. Romano had told her to increase their cellar for the wedding, and she had taken full advantage. She had added some exceptional wines and spirits to their already superb drinks menu. It had been a pleasure to present the groom with the bill. Not even Romano's unflinching payment diminished this triumph.

"Would you like a refill? Orange juice? Are you not allowed alcohol, or are you driving?"

"Orange juice will have to do. My boys have soccer in the morning. As Pastor, I can't risk being pulled over for drink-driving."

"Your wife isn't with you? Is she at home with the children?"

Pastor Edwards shook his head. "One of the teenagers from Youth Group has bravely volunteered to watch my two boys. I expect to arrive home to chaos and discover they've raided the pantry for sugary treats. No-one will sleep tonight. But I mustn't bore you with my complaints about parenting. I understand you're raising three children alone?"

Sofia fumed that someone had told him about her domestic situation. She waited for him to ask about her children's fathers, but he changed the subject. "You're nothing like your sister."

Why would he be comparing her to Evie?

"My sister has lived a sheltered life, in isolation, with older relatives in Sydney. While she's innocent and pure, you should know I'm neither." Sofia leaned even closer. Pastor Edwards gulped his drink, averting his eyes from her cleavage. She felt vindicated and withdrew. He was the one who had made the conversation personal. "I don't need you or any other religious do-gooder to bring me to account for my sins."

"I wouldn't dare." His smile wavered. "I didn't mean to offend you."

Sofia took pity. "Do you like our restaurant? I can organise a discount for your church meetings."

"I'm impressed with what I've seen. My leadership team have been looking for a city venue for one of our fellowship gatherings. I'll make a recommendation."

"Thank you. We'd welcome your fellowship gathering." Turning, Sofia discovered her deputy had anticipated her request. The young woman must have been eavesdropping. Sofia took the restaurant business card and passed it to him. Pastor Edwards read the information before placing it in his jacket pocket. He offered her his own business card. Why would he think she needed his card?

"In case you ever need to talk." He retreated quickly.

She glanced at the card: John Edwards. Sofia passed the card across the bar without comment.

CHAPTER 2
(Tuesday 29th August)

A Chance Conversation

ℰ ☼ ℭ

1 Samuel 16:7b
"Don't look on his face, or consider his height,
for he has been rejected;
Don't judge a man by his outward appearance,
because the Lord looks at the heart."

ℰ ☼ ℭ

The weather was perfect for a walk in the city. Sofia held a sturdy carry bag in one hand, and her stylish handbag in the other.

Her weekly lunch date with her best friends was an event she never missed. For Sofia, it was a working lunch – it counted as research into her competitors. The 'Tuesday Girls' rotated their venue each week.

Her high heels clicked briskly on the pavement. She wore her new dress because her friends hadn't been at the wedding to see her wearing it. She brought pieces of wedding cake to share, and photos of the bride. She had rehearsed what to say; her storytelling should satisfy their curiosity.

Arriving early, she entered *La Vita è Bella*. Her friend Guiseppe Amorosi looked up from behind the bar as she strode through the door. He dressed the part of a Romany traveller with flair. An absent-minded teacher had once

15

labelled him 'that Italian gypsy boy'. The nickname had stuck.

Gypsy wore his black hair long, with a bandana securing the shiny ringlets away from his face. He was a pretty man. Today he wore red: a brocade waistcoat over a bright paisley shirt, matched with tight black pants. Gold medallions hung around his neck. Hoops in his ears completed the picture.

"La vita è bella, Gypsy."

"Life is good," the small man translated in reply.

Sofia placed the carry bag on the counter, and retrieved from it a bottle of French champagne. He looked at the label and grinned. "Sofia, you shouldn't have." She laughed as he opened the bottle, filling two glasses.

"Be a good boy, Gypsy, and chill the other bottles."

"Your wish is my command, oh Queen."

"Gypsy's blessed to receive such a gift," a deep voice remarked. Sofia glanced towards the smartly dressed man seated at the other end of the bar. If her friends were here, they would tag him as Tall, Dark and Handsome. TDH. She suppressed a broader smile.

"Only my beloved Sofia would bring such an extravagant gift," Gypsy informed the stranger, raising his champagne flute in a salute before taking a sip. "Dear Sofia is celebrating. Her little sister has married Sebastian Romano." The broad-shouldered man nodded.

"Not celebrating, Gypsy," Sofia corrected him. "But the bridegroom did pay a premium price for the champagne. It would be a shame for it to go to waste."

She raised her eyebrow at Gypsy's matchmaking attempt – not his first. Gypsy was a renowned gossip, and later she would question him about this new acquaintance. Gypsy smiled, filling another glass with champagne. He placed it on the counter beside her and beckoned to TDH. Sofia admired the stranger as he approached her.

"Sofia Fontana, may I introduce Valentino Horatio?"

Valentino sat on the stool beside her, raising his glass. "I'm delighted to meet you, Sofia. Congratulations on your sister's marriage."

Gypsy leaned forward. "She doesn't think the marriage will last. The bride insisted on a white wedding, but there's no denying Romano's true nature. By the time the honeymoon is over, her innocent little sister will understand why Sofia warned her not to marry him."

"You don't like your new brother-in-law?" Valentino said. "If your sister's half as attractive as you, then Romano's a lucky man."

"Do you know Romano?" she asked, glancing away to conceal her intense interest in his answer. A friend of Romano's would be no friend of hers.

"I know *of* Romano, through his business dealings with my older brother. Romano has a reputation for being secretive and violent. And for controlling the people in his circle of influence. I can understand your concerns for your sister."

"What kind of business is your brother in?"

Valentino and Gypsy exchanged glances. Her old friend tapped his fingers on the counter. Then he raised his arm to encompass the whole room.

"He owns this restaurant?" Sofia asked in surprise, for she knew Gypsy held the licence.

Her friend shook his head. "He owns the building – the entire city block."

"That's one of his enterprises," Valentino added. "He has diverse interests, here in Australia and overseas."

"Are you involved in your brother's business?"

"I prefer to limit myself to property management and leave the empire building to him. Sometimes he asks me to help, but mostly I'm an independent man."

"Independently wealthy too," Gypsy added, pouring himself another glass of champagne. "He's an excellent catch if the right woman were to show interest."

Sofia shot Gypsy a warning look, but he laughed.

"I have to tell him you're single and looking for Mr Right. It's been months since you've dated anyone, Sofia. When your sister arrived from Sydney, you shut yourself away to care for her. She repaid you by falling for the first bad man who crossed her path."

Sofia frowned. "Gypsy, you know I'm not looking for Mr Right or anyone else at the moment. I have a disastrous record for finding Mr Wrong. Valentino, I've been married twice. I work nights in my family's restaurant, and I have three teenage children living at home. My life's complicated."

"So is mine," Valentino admitted. "Gypsy will tell you after I'm gone, so I'd better confess. I'm divorced, too. I married too young, and my ex-wife has the children. She said I was married to my work. She especially resented all my evening meetings. It sounds as if our schedules match perfectly. Perhaps you would have lunch with me one day?"

Sofia gazed into Valentino's green eyes. Her heart beat faster, and she looked away. She didn't normally resist temptation. Something was happening in her soul, an unfamiliar struggle. Was this due to her sister's recent folly, or something more?

She sipped from her glass. "How do you know Gypsy? He's never mentioned you before, and you can see he's an impossible romantic."

"From time to time my brother asks me to call in and check on his Melbourne investments. It's my loss that our paths haven't crossed before. Perhaps I should be asking how well you know Gypsy? I'm surprised he's willing to share you with anyone."

"Gypsy and I are old friends. Nothing more. I value his friendship too much to fall for his flattery."

"Oh, cruel Sofia!" Gypsy feigned distress. "You break my heart all over again. Valentino, may I tell you the romantic tale of how my beloved Sofia won my heart?"

"Tell all, Gypsy."

"Sofia and I were at school. She was three years older, and I worshipped her from afar. Her sister was in my year, so I knew all about Sofia. She was beautiful, with many admirers.

"One fateful day, she rescued me from the toughest playground bullies. Teasing a small boy about his Italian culture was easy. Except they tried in front of the most popular girl in school. Sofia came charging in with her eyes blazing. Her girlfriends backed her up. Her fiery tirade drove those bullies away.

"From then on I followed Sofia everywhere. I moped, reciting dreadful poetry until she took pity on me. I made myself useful, and she grew fond of me. Then I persuaded her to let me work in her restaurant. I served her for ten years, and then Sofia launched me out on my own. That's how I came to be here. So, you can see I owe her everything."

Gypsy finished his monologue with a dramatic bow and then drained his glass.

The phone on the counter beside Valentino began to vibrate. He finished his drink and smiled at Sofia. "I have an appointment I can't avoid. I'll be interstate for the rest of the week, but I'm free for lunch next Monday. If you let me know where you'd like to go, I'll make the arrangements? Here's my number."

He produced his card. When Sofia reached for it, Valentino took hold of her small hand as he gazed into her eyes. Boldly he stroked her wrist with his thumb. "I'll wait expectantly for your call."

He didn't linger for a reply. Sofia watched him leave. Through the window, Valentino turned towards her, raising a hand in farewell.

Sofia's friends hesitated outside the door, following Valentino with their eyes.

"Perfect timing," Gypsy said. He appeared from behind the bar with another bottle of champagne.

Sofia smiled in anticipation. Valentino was a fortuitous distraction. She intended to make the most of it.

Five Friends

৪০ ✦ ৪

Hebrews 10:23
*Hold fast to the hope you confess without wavering;
for He who promised is faithful.*

৪০ ✦ ৪

"Someone's pleased with themselves," Melissa remarked.

Sofia grinned and waved Valentino's business card. The other women joined in her laughter.

Together the five friends made a remarkable group. Fashionably dressed and flirtatious. Melissa and Lauren were glamorously dark and curvaceous, like Sofia. Kylie and Natalie were slender blondes. Friends since high school, they were all the same age. Between them, they had experienced twelve marriages and the birth of fourteen children. Only Sofia was unmarried at the moment.

Kylie leaned forward, "Tell us."

"There's nothing to tell – yet. I might be having lunch with Valentino on Monday."

Gypsy filled their glasses and returned to the bar. Sofia glanced after him. Usually, he joined them. Something was wrong. He reached for the brandy, his fourth drink since her arrival. She would talk to him later. Gypsy was one of her favourites.

"Where is Valentino taking you?" asked Lauren, demanding Sofia's attention.

"I haven't decided yet."

The women made suggestions for a romantic rendezvous. Then they speculated about where this might lead.

Sofia changed the subject. "How do you like this champagne?"

"It's excellent. Leftover from your sister's celebration?" Natalie asked. "Did she marry him, or listen to your advice and ask him to wait?"

"Of course Evie didn't listen," Melissa interrupted. "Did any of us listen to warnings before our first weddings?"

"Or our second?" Kylie concurred. "That's why we've had eight divorces between us."

The friends laughed, and empathised over one another's matrimonial mistakes. The lessons they had endured together strengthened their friendship. Each of them was now wiser. Three failed relationships made Sofia more cautious. There was no denying her excitement at the chance of romance, but it would be disastrous if her awakening passion overruled common sense. Sofia reflected on how Valentino had delivered his invitation. A small doubt awakened. Why had this perfect stranger paid her such attention?

Sofia glanced around the table. She vowed to ask her friends for advice. They would warn her if they thought she was heading for another disaster.

"Tell us how you met him," Lauren said.

"Gypsy introduced us. He was at the bar when I arrived. His brother owns this building. I'm surprised Gypsy hasn't mentioned him before."

"Gypsy knows many people," Lauren said quickly. "You said you *might* be having lunch with him? Why are you hesitating? He's good looking and wealthy, and someone like him doesn't turn up in your life every day."

"I don't want to act prematurely. I've criticised Evie for rushing everything, but I'm no better. It's obvious Valentino wants a physical relationship, and the prospect of spending time with him is enticing. But—"

"But what?" Lauren said. "You're an experienced woman. There's no doubt you know how to give men what they want. I don't understand this hesitation. You shouldn't have let him leave without saying yes."

"I don't deny the temptation, but what if there's more to romance than physical attraction. I've always been quick to satisfy a man's desire, but that hasn't been enough. To be honest, I'm tired of short-term relationships."

"But you won't know if this man is your dream match if you don't give him a chance."

"Do any of you know him?" Sofia asked. "He could be like the others, eager to have me for the wrong reasons. He mentioned an ex-wife. If he's so wonderful, why did his marriage fail?"

"Nobody's perfect," Natalie smiled in encouragement. "Don't miss out on this opportunity because of your past experiences. You were too young when you fell for Nicholas. Then you were too traumatised by his abuse to make rational decisions about Sven. You did much better with Theo, and all the blame lies with him and his dishonesty. If you fall in love again, you'll do so with your eyes wide open."

Sofia distracted them by bringing out the wedding photos and sharing the cake.

"Here's Evie wearing the red coatdress for the betrothal ceremony. It was impossible to tell she was wearing her wedding dress underneath. Mama Rosa hadn't warned Papa. I wish you had been there to see the reaction when Romano started removing the red dress. After the ceremony, everyone wanted to know if Papa knew, because his face went red, and they saw how he turned to Mama. She patted his hand and pushed him forward so he could announce the surprise wedding was about to begin.

"Here's a photo of the matron of honour rescuing Evie from Romano before unveiling the white dress. This one is my favourite. Evie made an excellent choice for her wedding dress. The rose coronet she wore instead of a veil suited her perfectly."

Over lunch, the friends shared the everyday details of their busy lives. They offered praise and support in equal measure, along with well-intended advice. This close group of women were raising wilful teenagers. They found strength from sharing their experiences. No-one seemed to notice Sofia was quiet. She let the rhythm of their conversation wash over her.

At two-thirty, Lauren and Melissa stood. They rushed away to collect their children from school. Kylie left a few minutes later. She had a dental hygienist appointment. Natalie and Sofia lingered over their final glass of champagne.

"It's been a delight, Sofia. Do you have time to come shopping with me?" Natalie asked. "My eldest is turning eighteen and planning a fabulous party. Now I need the right dress to wear. You always know where to find the best bargains."

Sofia glanced towards the bar. "I was hoping to chat with Gypsy, but I'll catch him later. Have you tried that new boutique around the corner? There's a dress on display in their window that would be perfect."

After bidding farewell to Gypsy, the pair walked to the boutique. Natalie tried on the dress Sofia recommended.

Both the style and the price were agreeable. While Sofia waited, she noticed a turquoise dress hanging on the display rack. "What do you think?" she asked Natalie, holding it up. The fitted dress was shorter, the neckline more revealing.

"Try it on. It would be perfect for your lunch date."

"I haven't decided if I have a lunch date," Sofia replied with a grin.

It had been a long time since she had felt like this before a first date. Was she more affected by her sister Evie's whirlwind romance than she'd thought?

"Do you have time for coffee?" Sofia asked Natalie, and they went to a popular cafe.

Now Sofia spoke from her wounded heart. "I'm not sure it's a good time for me to start dating someone new."

"Why not? It's been fourteen years since your last serious relationship. The children are old enough to look after themselves. You deserve to be happy."

"Do I? I've alienated myself from my sister because of Romano. Matilda thinks I'm resentful because I'm jealous."

Natalie pounced on that remark. "Jealous about Romano? Never!" Natalie waved her arms emphatically. "Any interest you had in that man was dead years ago." She lowered her voice as she continued, "You were never really interested. It was your Papa who encouraged you to ask him out." Sofia nodded, and dropped her eyes to her coffee.

"The way he turned you down," Natalie hissed, "revealed a lot about his attitude towards women. You knew immediately he was trouble. That's why you're so worried about your sister's involvement with him now. What kind of sister would you be if you hadn't tried to warn her!" Natalie reached across and patted her hand, which unsettled Sofia even more. "We all agreed you should steer clear of him, and that was before we knew about his criminal record."

Finally, Sofia was back on solid ground. "When Gypsy told me Romano had been in prison, I wanted nothing more to do with him. He's too much like Nicholas." Sofia shuddered at the mention of that name. Her first husband had been trouble, and had even assaulted her sister. "I'd vowed never to fall for another violent, controlling monster."

"We have been wondering if you'd noticed the parallels with your first marriage," Natalie murmured.

Sofia sighed. "It was a mistake keeping my feelings to myself. When Leonardo told me he was quitting hospitality school, I was furious. He'd discussed his plans with Papa, and it was too late for me to do anything. He already had the apprenticeship at Romano's automotive business by then. A week later, my sister arrived, and she fell into Romano's hands as well."

"You make it sound like some kind of conspiracy. How concerned *are* you about Evie's safety?"

Sofia shrugged, struggling to put her thoughts into words. "She submits to him in everything, but I can't deny she seems content, genuinely happy. As her love for him has deepened, the changes have been remarkable. Her time in Sydney wasn't kind to her. I had always imagined her happy and enjoying life, so it was a shock to see the shrivelled old maid she had become. Under Romano's influence she regained her confidence. He transformed her into a beautiful young woman again."

"So, what's the problem?"

"Evie chose Marilyn to be her matron of honour. That hurt. If I had kept quiet and pretended I was happy for her, things would have been different. She continued to include me – I helped her select the wedding dress – but my resentment was like a wall between us. During the reception, I sat at the bar alone. I felt as if *I'd* become the old maid."

"But you're an attractive woman, Sofia. There's plenty of time for romance ahead of you. Surely Valentino asking you to lunch tells you that?"

"What if I'm desperate and I've thrown myself at the first available man?"

"Did that happen today? Or were you charming, making the invitation inevitable? Gypsy introduced you, which should reassure you. Besides, this man is handsome and available. Stop worrying and enjoy the adventure. If Valentino turns out to be the right one for you, you'll be glad you took the chance. But if something warns you away from him, you can write this up as another lesson learned."

The two friends picked up their bags and tidied the table as they prepared to leave the crowded cafe. Students from the nearby college jostled in the queue. Bumped from behind, Sofia fell into the arms of a man juggling two milkshakes and a coffee. The hot beverage spilled over his jumper.

"I'm sorry!"

He laughed. "Sofia, we have to stop meeting like this."

Sofia was horrified. Pastor Edwards again! Retrieving a napkin from a nearby table, she dabbed at the coffee stain.

"Sofia, is everything okay?" Natalie asked. She looked from Sofia to the unknown man.

"Natalie, this is Pastor Edwards. The minister who conducted Evie's wedding. He must think I'm habitually clumsy and on a mission to ruin his clothes."

"Call me John, and don't worry about the coffee. I drink too much anyway. At least the milkshakes had lids, or we'd both be a mess. I'd better take these to my boys. Thanks for trying to clean me up. I've plenty of time to get changed before dinner tonight. I look forward to seeing you this evening."

"Hello John, goodbye John," Natalie said to his retreating back. She drew Sofia out onto the footpath. "Dinner tonight? Do you have TWO men interested in you? I don't see why you're worried about becoming an old maid!"

"He meant dinner at *Ristorante di Fontana*. His church group have booked the upstairs function room for the evening. Besides, he's married."

"Girlfriend, open your eyes. That man is interested in more than *talking* to you."

Sofia glanced back, shaking her head. Natalie was mistaken. The words from his speech at Evie's wedding still echoed in her heart. There was no way a married Protestant man would be interested in a Catholic divorcee.

After Natalie left, Sofia went to check on Gypsy.

"Sofia, did you forget something?"

"Gypsy, I'm worried about you. You didn't come and join us. Is something the matter?"

"Oh, Sofia, you're a dear to worry about me. I've had a little money trouble. But something unexpected turned up this afternoon to solve the problem. I'm glad you came back. I wanted to ask you what you thought of Valentino? I've known him for years, and it would be wonderful if the two of you became friends."

"Only friends?" He laughed with her, and she felt relieved. Sofia pressed Gypsy for personal details about her potential date. He told her to ask the man himself. He assured her she wouldn't regret accepting Valentino's invitation. Sofia was almost convinced.

Rooftop Retreat

🙰 ☼ 🙴

1 Corinthians 15:58b WEB
Stand firm. Let nothing move you.

🙰 ☼ 🙴

Grey clouds raced across the sky. Sofia walked briskly to *Raphael Towers*, where she was meeting Valentino at noon. She wrapped her coat snugly around her to ward against the chilly breeze from the water. The Tuesday Girls had recommended *Masterpiece* restaurant for this first date. She had talked to her friends many times by phone, wavering over whether or not to see Valentino.

However, Sofia had no uncertainty about this restaurant. The online menu sounded delicious. Bookings were essential, and she'd only confirmed their date the previous afternoon. Valentino had assured her this wouldn't be a problem. It was commendable if he'd been able to get a table at such short notice.

Sofia was unfamiliar with this riverside development. She walked along the promenade, in the shadow of the mirrored building. She passed other restaurants including the impressive entrance for a popular nightclub. Turning the corner, she came to the apartment building that contained *Masterpiece.*

Warm air and a gentle hush greeted Sofia as she entered the building. Valentino was waiting. He seemed taller and more handsome. Taking her hand, he led her towards a bank of elevators.

"Thanks for coming, Sofia. You made an excellent choice for our lunch date. *Masterpiece* has an excellent reputation."

Where was he taking her? The *Masterpiece* dining room was to her right. Sofia came to a decisive halt. Valentino squeezed her hand, seeming unconcerned by her hesitation. "I wasn't able to secure a table, but I've made other arrangements. The chef has agreed to serve our meals elsewhere. I'm sure you'll be happy with this compromise."

The elevator door opened, and they stepped inside. In the confined space, Valentino's aftershave was intoxicating. She berated herself for hoping he might try to steal a kiss. Until recently, she had been liberal with her favours, but today she wanted to exercise constraint. Her sister's chastity before the wedding had made a strong impression.

"Where are we going? I only agreed to lunch. If you're expecting anything more, you'll be disappointed."

"I'll be content with lunch, Sofia. I have a table waiting for us on the roof."

Valentino used a key card to access the higher floors. The elevator ascended smoothly as illuminated numerals flashed to indicate their progress. When it stopped, the doors parted to reveal the twenty-sixth floor. A young man wearing a red uniform opened a door leading to the roof. Sofia walked up a gentle slope into an unexpected botanical paradise.

She stood on an immaculately manicured lawn, surrounded by greenery and colourful blooms. "This is amazing."

Beneath a blue shade sail, a table awaited them. Gas heaters warmed the area. Valentino helped Sofia remove her coat. Had his hands lingered too long? Taking his place on the opposite side of the table, he poured champagne.

"To an enjoyable lunch, and a promising friendship," Valentino saluted her. "Would you like to see a menu, or will you allow me to choose for you?"

"You can choose." Her curiosity grew as he raised his hand. A waiter appeared bearing two starter plates. She had studied the menu, and this was her first preference. How had he known? "What would you have done if I'd asked for a menu?"

"You would have had a longer wait. Is this dish to your liking?"

"It's delicious."

"I'm pleased you're enjoying it. I know you appreciate good food. You like to check out your family restaurant's competition."

"You've been talking with Gypsy? I hope he didn't tell you all my secrets."

"He's your loyal friend. He only told me enough to capture my interest."

"You had more satisfaction from him than I did."

"I'm a private man."

"That's what Gypsy said."

"What would you like to know?"

"How did you manage this? A private rooftop garden was unexpected."

"My brother owns this building, too. My apartment's here. I'm not above using his assets to impress new friends. Are you impressed?"

Sofia waved her fork. "You've made a good start. The remainder of lunch may be disappointing."

"I hope not." He signalled the waiter who quickly delivered the main course.

"The service here is excellent," she said.

"Coming from an expert, that's a generous compliment. Gypsy said you require high standards from your staff. Of course, you pay above the award rate to keep them."

"Gypsy says too much." She glared at her fork.

"I'd like to have dinner at your restaurant."

"Of course. But I must warn you my parents are hopeless romantics."

"Our families are alike in that regard. I made my sisters promise not to interrupt our lunch today. Would you marry again, if you found the right man?"

"I have to find him first. Would you marry again?"

"My situation's complicated. My family would want to be involved."

"Families are always complicated. Even unimportant ones like mine. I'd better confess, my family is cursed."

"Cursed? That's intriguing."

"My parents believe my sister's marriage has broken the curse, but I'm unconvinced."

"She married Sebastian Romano?"

"That was the name we knew him by. Before the wedding, we discovered his father had changed his name to escape the curse."

"I thought it was *your* family curse."

"The two families were linked in the past. My father and Romano's father were friends in Italy, betrothed to two sisters – my mother and her twin. When Romano's father broke off his engagement to my aunt, she cursed him, and anyone associated with him."

"Romano marrying your sister cancels the debt?"

"That's what my parents believe, but I don't think it's that simple."

"How does this curse work?"

"Tragedy at every turn. Romano's mother died in childbirth. His childhood was miserable. His adolescence violent and cruel, leading to prison. When his sentence was almost complete, his father died. It seemed he would spend his days alone, and then he met my sister. That was tragic too – he almost killed her. Then a few weeks ago, someone abducted her."

"I heard about the abduction. That was your sister? You're fortunate to get her back alive. Did the police find the people responsible?"

"Not officially. Evie believes her husband knows what happened. He said they won't be causing any more trouble. Presumably, his friends killed them."

"Romano sounds dangerous."

"I don't want to talk about him."

"What would you like to talk about?"

"You."

"Okay, I'm forty-three. The youngest son of the youngest son, from an influential Italian-Australian family. I get to choose my path, and I've the money to pay for those choices. I've one brother and four sisters, and too many other relatives. My father's family moved to Melbourne from Sydney. Perhaps they were acquainted with your family there? I'll see what I can find out. They might know about the family curse. I might be your Prince Charming, destined to save you."

"You wouldn't be the first to try, but I turned the other princes into toads."

"You have the wrong fairytale. In mine, the prince kisses the princess, and they live happily ever after."

"This princess has a heart of stone. It will take more than kisses to convince her. She's sold her happiness for kisses before. Now she has three fatherless children to raise by herself."

"Is that why you think you're cursed?"

"I take responsibility for my mistakes." She was serious now. "It wasn't a curse, but my stupidity. I hope I've learned my lesson. It's going to take more than kisses to convince me to trust anyone, even if he's handsome and wealthy."

"I'll accept your warning. I enjoy a challenge. But we've been too serious. Would you like a walk in the garden before dessert, or are you pressed for time?"

"A walk in the garden would be nice."

"Bring your coat. It's much colder in the open."

Racing the Rain

৪৩ ☼ ৫৪

James 1:12a
Blessed is the one who endures temptation,
for when they have passed the test,
they will receive the crown of life.

৪৩ ☼ ৫৪

For an hour, they followed meandering paths across the rooftop of this city tower. There were fountains, waterfalls, rock-lined streams, and shady glens. The garden architect had created open spaces for large gatherings. Sheltered nooks furnished with padded divans catered for more private assignations. At first, Sofia steeled herself for an invitation, but her companion kept his distance. She began to relax.

The weather changed rapidly, dark clouds pressing down on their aerie. Sofia shuddered in her coat. He led her to the edge of the building, and they ascended the steps to stand beside the waist-high wall. A chill wind buffeted them, and Valentino placed his arm around her shoulders. Sofia welcomed the warmth of his embrace.

"There's going to be a storm," he said. "Take a few minutes to enjoy the view, and then we'll find shelter."

Sofia looked across the cityscape as the sky darkened even more. She located her restaurant in the middle distance, and was pointing in that direction when the first drops of rain began to fall. She was taken by surprise by the onset of a torrential downpour.

"Can you run in those heels?" he asked, guiding her down the steps.

Sofia bent down and slipped them off. The blinding rain made it difficult to see where she should go. "Which direction?" she asked. When Valentino indicated the path, she sprinted away. She had been an athletics champion at school and was still agile on her feet. He pursued her. Around the corner, a circular white building nestled amidst a grove of slender trees. Valentino caught Sofia at the entrance. Wrapped in his arms, she was delivered from the deluge as he pushed open the wooden doors. His strength kept them upright. Sofia's heart raced as she turned in his arms to face him. She blinked at the intensity of his gaze. Pushing herself out of his embrace, she stepped backwards.

He closed the door and took off his wet jacket. Droplets of water fell onto the floor before he threw the garment over a chair. Sofia removed her coat and did likewise. Heavy rain pummelled the vaulted roof as the storm lashed their sanctuary.

Sofia assessed her condition. She was relatively dry apart from wet hair, and her stockings had been ruined by running barefoot. Sofia turned to examine the room. It was more spacious than she thought. The furnishings were white. There were chairs set up in expanding arcs around a raised platform that formed the stage for a grand piano. This building must be a small concert hall. Warm air wafted across the room. Sofia looked for the source. There were vents at strategic intervals between the evenly spaced arched windows. The comfortable temperature suggested the heaters had been on for some time.

Against the walls were small tables where elegant lamps provided additional light. A massive crystal chandelier sent shimmering reflections around the opulent room. Valentino disappeared through another doorway, returning with two towels. Passing one to her, Valentino began to dry his hair with the other.

"There's a mirror through there," he advised her, and she took her towel with her. The doorway led to a room furnished with a large divan, dressing table and comfortable chairs. There was a separate restroom. Sofia pushed the door closed before removing her wet stockings. She tossed them into a convenient bin, before slipping her feet back into her shoes. Working the towel through her short hair, she then combed her dark locks with her fingers. Sofia dabbed at her makeup, thankful her mascara was waterproof. Satisfied, she returned to the main room.

Valentino had removed his tie and was leaning against the piano, drinking red wine. Another full glass rested on a dressed table in the space between the chairs and the stage. Sofia picked up her glass. Impressed with his choice, she drank freely.

"I thought you might be ready for dessert," he said.

She eyed him suspiciously. "You're not going to make that poor waiter come out in this rain?"

He smiled broadly and stepped forward to take her free hand. "Come with me. The kitchen's through here. I'm sure I can find something to tempt you."

She hadn't noticed the second door. The kitchen was also white, small potted herbs and edible flowers the only colour. Valentino had already laid out two bowls on the central counter. A row of silver spoons was lined up beside a selection of frozen desserts.

"We have a dozen flavours. Try this one."

He picked up a spoon, scooped out a creamy dollop of gelato and brought it to her lips. Sofia's heart beat even faster, alerted to danger by his confident expression. Without his jacket and tie, his rumpled hair softened his features, and he looked even more tempting. It would be easy to push aside the spoon and kiss him. Sofia took the spoon from his hand and fed herself. He watched her intently, and she lowered her eyes.

Her taste buds tingled with recognition. Lemon, lime and macadamia! Looking along the counter, she recognised all her favourites. "You knew we'd come here!"

"I didn't plan the drenching, and if the rain had held off, we would have returned to our table. But I didn't want the weather to chase you away, so I made provision."

"I haven't changed my mind about only being here for lunch."

He smiled and picked up another spoon. "Are we going to stay here, or will we return to the other room?"

A short while later, they were seated beside the piano. Setting aside the empty bowls, Valentino waited for her to speak.

"Do you play the piano?" she asked.

"My mother wanted me to be a concert pianist. When I reached adolescence, I discovered other passions. I no longer had the desire to practise."

"I wanted to have lessons, but Papa couldn't afford them. Will you play something?"

He carried his wineglass to the piano, where he placed it on a small table. Valentino flashed a smile before focusing on the instrument. He ran his fingers up and down the keyboard. Then he launched into an intricate piece of classical music. She watched in admiration as his hands danced over the keys. Sofia sipped her wine and relaxed again.

As she listened to him play, the afternoon drifted away. She hardly noticed the answers she gave to his casual questions. He asked for personal information while revealing little about his privileged life. She told him details about the recent wedding, and her thoughts about the married couple. Then he asked about her plans for the future.

"What am I doing here?" she asked. "You must have women throwing themselves at you."

His fingers stumbled on the keys. "Six months ago, my mother gave her unambiguous opinion of the women I favoured. The fashion model who was clinging to me took umbrage because I didn't defend her. She stormed off in a huff. At the end of the evening, despite other offers, I slept alone. It hit me that all my relationships were shallow, even my brief marriage. My mother said I needed an independent woman who could stand up for herself. I've been looking, and now I've found you. My mother would approve of you."

Sofia looked down at her empty glass. "I'm flattered you think your mother would approve of me." She made no attempt to hide her sarcasm.

Valentino pushed back the piano stool. "I can assure you, dear Sofia, that I didn't invite you here to please my mother." He laughed as he walked to the side table to select another bottle of wine. He brought two glasses of dark red wine to the table, and placed one before her. "This is a special vintage, and I hope you enjoy it. You won't find this anywhere else." He raised his glass and saluted her. "You asked why you are here, and I gave you an honest answer. Those other women were like cheap sparkling white wine, all fizz and no substance." He swirled the wine in the glass, his eyes fixed on her face. "But you are comparable to this quality wine, Sofia." His confident smile widened. "This dark Italian red has a bold, full-bodied earthiness that promises a greater delight, and has never disappointed me." He savoured the aroma. "A wine like this should never be hurried." He tasted the wine and his dark eyes seemed to draw her closer. "Once I discovered it, I knew it had to be exclusively mine, no matter the cost."

Sofia took a cautious sip as she considered his words. This wine was indeed superior to many she had tasted, and before she realised it, the glass was half empty. A warm glow flooded her body. It suddenly felt imperative to speak her mind. "I'm going to be honest with you," she said. "I'm tired of playing games, and I'm not interested in a casual affair. I'd rather sleep alone than be used again."

An uncomfortable silence followed her words, causing her to realise that the pelting rain on the roof had ceased. She wondered why he made no reply, and found she could not read his expression. He seemed to be waiting for her to say something else. Glancing at her watch, Sofia drained her glass and rose to her feet. She put out her hand to steady herself, surprised at how light-headed she felt. That final glass of wine must have been stronger than she thought. She needed air. "It's time for me to go."

Before she lost her determination, Sofia donned her coat. Valentino accompanied her in the elevator, walking her out to the footpath. With every step, her disappointment grew. She had declared her disinterest but secretly longed for an invitation to stay. Sofia felt sure he could hear her pounding heart. She turned to look at him, surprised at how emotional she was feeling.

"Thanks for a lovely lunch."

"It's been a pleasure, Sofia."

He drew her to him, ignoring the passersby. He kissed her firmly on the mouth until her desire for him fully awakened. Then he released her. She felt dizzy, and breathless with anticipation.

Without another word, he left her standing there. Trembling all over, she watched him re-enter the building and disappear from view. Desperately she longed for him to come back to her. She hoped in vain.

How long did she stand there waiting? The tremors ceased, but she was holding her breath. She gasped for air. Sofia took a shaky step, and was startled to hear a ragged sob escape her control. It had been years since she'd permitted the luxury of tears, and the floodgate opened. She walked away, uncertain where she was going, or why she was so devastated.

She had refused his offer and held out for an elusive dream, but would now have willingly abandoned her new-found principles for half an hour of intimacy. Such was the depth of her loneliness.

The Weeping Woman

ಬಿ ☼ ಞ

Proverbs 4:23
Carefully guard your heart,
because it is the source of everything you do.

ಬಿ ☼ ಞ

John Edwards sat on a bench beside the riverside promenade. He had a takeaway coffee in one hand and his smartphone in the other. It was his day off, but he had spent hours mediating a complicated situation between two church members. An avalanche of emails had made the matter worse. John looked for his boys, and felt a pang of guilt. Whenever he planned time with his children, something arose to demand his attention.

John had collected them from their after-school activity. They had enjoyed a tram ride around the city centre, followed by ice-cream. Soon they would catch a train home. Last time he checked, they had been balancing their way along a low concrete wall that separated the wide riverside promenade from the sloping lawn that led to the river. He scanned the area and couldn't see their distinctive school uniforms anywhere. He leapt up in panic. He was climbing over the low wall when he heard a familiar cry behind him.

"Dad! Dad!"

He spotted his eldest son waving his arms to capture John's attention. Matt had climbed the steps outside the main entrance to *Raphael Towers*. He was alone. Where was seven-year-old Peter? With a surge of adrenalin, John hurried through the crowd to meet the nine-year-old.

This was John's worst nightmare. He glanced towards the nearby tram stop and groaned as he saw the flood of afternoon commuters converging on the area. This promenade was a popular shortcut for people who wanted to access the city's different transport options. He was dimly aware that other family groups, rugged up against the chilly afternoon, were turning to look. Matt continued to cry out.

He momentarily lost sight of Matt when a group of tourists stopped in front of him to discuss their next destination. John dodged around them, only to step into the path of a young jogger wearing headphones. She glared at him and ignored his apology. Finally, he arrived at the steps. "Where's Peter?"

Matt came down to meet him "He's following the weeping woman. Come on!" Matt tugged at his hand.

"What weeping woman?"

"You said you pray for her. Come on!"

"When did I say I was praying for a weeping woman?"

"She wasn't weeping then. It's the woman from the cafe."

John hurried to keep up. A gap opened in the crowd allowing him a clear view of his youngest son. The boy, easy to spot in his uniform, was walking beside a familiar figure.

That woman. Evie's sister Sofia had made no effort to hide her antagonism towards him at the wedding reception. But they kept bumping into each other. It might be amusing, except the dry-cleaning bills were stretching his limited budget. Looking at the remaining coffee in his hand, John took precautionary action. He tossed the cup into a bin.

He increased his pace. Peter's young face showed concern as he talked to the troubled woman, but she seemed to be ignoring him. Neither of them was looking where they were going. If no-one intervened, she would tumble down the bank into the river, taking his son with her.

"Sofia!" he called out. Rushing forward, John leapt in front of her. She blinked, a dazed expression on her face that rang alarm bells. She appeared to lose her balance and as he caught her, she wrapped her arms around him. His coat muffled her distress as she wept on his shoulder. Awkwardly, he held her.

His mind screamed danger, as he considered her condition. This uncoordinated, emotional female bore no resemblance to the confident woman he had met before. What was he to do with her? His mentor had warned that he was particularly vulnerable to gossip. They were out of the main throng here, and he spotted an empty bench seat nearby.

He drew Sofia down beside him. Her sobbing continued as she pressed against him. His sons watched with wide eyes. The boys often asked when he would find them a new mother. He didn't want hope to spring up from this unfortunate encounter.

"Sofia, what's happened?"

His coat muffled her quiet answer. "A terrible mistake – I said no when I should have said yes."

John hesitated. "Who did you say no to?"

"There was a man," Peter said. "He kissed her and then he went into that building. She was standing on the footpath. Then she was crying and walking, and I followed her."

"Sofia, did he hurt you?"

She shook her head. "No, this is my fault. I'm an idiot."

Her confession intensified her tears, and her body shook in his arms. John looked at his boys again and sighed. He was a trained professional and should know how to manage a distressed woman. Did he sense something more sinister at work here? Could he broach the subject without causing her greater distress? He took another deep breath and offered up a quick prayer for the right solution to this difficulty. Prayer! That should have been his first choice. All afternoon, he'd been struggling with another problem, labelling himself an inadequate father. Where was his faith?

"Sofia, can I pray with you?"

He took her silence as permission. "Heavenly Father, thank You for welcoming us into Your presence. Please listen to our prayers. Precious Jesus, Saviour and Friend, thank You for Your love and protection. Thank You that You know everything. Your understanding is infinitely greater than our own. Please pour out Your blessings on this child, and show her how to obtain Your forgiveness. You know what's happened. You know she feels responsible. Please offer her a fresh start. Holy Spirit, Comforter and Guide, please fill her with Your peace..."

As John spoke the words, peace flooded his mind. The prayer continued, as inspiration led him until there was no more to say. A hush fell over the group. Sofia's head nestled against his chest. Perhaps she had fallen asleep? He loosened his embrace. Immediately, Sofia moved out of his arms.

Only then did he think about the boys. They were praying beside him, eyes closed, hands clasped. So often he had prayed with them over their problems. He was proud of their compassion for a stranger. John reached out and ruffled their hair.

Miserable Monday

ॐ ✿ ॐ

Ecclesiastes 3:11
He has made everything beautiful in its time.
He has also set eternity in our hearts;
yet not one of us can comprehend what God has done
from beginning to end.

ॐ ✿ ॐ

When Sofia came to herself, she was almost curled up on John Edwards' lap, and his shoulder was wet with her tears. She couldn't remember any of his prayer but had been comforted by his kindness. John walked her all the way back to the family restaurant, apologising for not having his car. His two boys stared at her with their innocent brown eyes. The youngest one held her hand. The concern on those small faces haunted her.

Sofia expected John to leave her at the staff entrance, but the trio accompanied her inside. The afternoon feast was in progress, and Papa made them welcome. Before their father could say anything, the small boys were seated at the table eating pizza. John hesitated before he joined them at the table. The boys made friends with Marco, more at home with her family than she was feeling. Sofia hurried to the restroom, and her mother followed her.

"Sofia, are you unwell?"

"I don't think so."

There was a pause. Sofia looked up from watching the swirling water in the hand basin. Her Mama's troubled reflection gazed at her from the mirror.

"Did your lunch date go well?"

Sofia searched her confused memories for a clue. "Yes."

"And your date? Has he done something to hurt you?"

She was more certain of this answer. "No, Valentino was the perfect gentleman."

"Then why the tears?"

Sofia shrugged as she reached for some paper towel to dry her face. What could she tell her mother? She told the truth. "I don't know."

"And Pastor Edwards, your sister's friend?" Mama Rosa paused. "Why is he the one who brought you home?"

"I don't know that either!"

When Sofia returned from the restroom, John had gone.

"Sofia, what's going on?" Papa demanded. "I asked Pastor Edwards, but he wouldn't tell me."

"Now is not the time," Mama Rosa said. Papa looked from Sofia to Mama Rosa, who shook her head in warning. Sofia smiled in appreciation, and swiped at her tears. "Sofia needs to go home."

Papa took command. "Matilda, phone Leonardo to come immediately from work. You and Marco will have to go too, so your brother doesn't have to return for you."

Sofia tried to stand tall. "I'm alright."

"Have you looked at yourself?" Papa demanded. "Your eyes are glazed, and you can't stop crying. Go home and rest. Explain yourself tomorrow."

Papa refused to argue with her, and she went quietly when her eldest son arrived. At home, her three children fussed over her. Sofia escaped to her bedroom. She had always protected them from her private sorrows. This weakness clearly troubled them.

Sofia tried to replay her afternoon in her mind. Why was she crying? And why were there gaps in her memory? Her strongest recollection was of Valentino walking away without a backward glance. What had she said or done to offend him? Her shame stopped her from contacting Valentino to find out. The only conclusion which made sense was that she had experienced some kind of breakdown which led to her rejecting his advances. As she seized on this explanation, her anger at herself intensified.

Her phone began to buzz. The playful music signalled an incoming call from one of the Tuesday Girls. Months ago, it had been amusing to program each other's phones to identify their group. Now, the cheerful sound filled her with dread. Sofia looked at the display. It was Lauren. She declined the call, tossing the phone onto the bed.

Immediately, the music began again. Sofia sighed. She should turn the phone off. Immediately the phone pinged with an incoming message. She ignored it. A series of pings followed in quick succession. Sofia realised it was inevitable; if she didn't answer them, one or more of her friends would arrive at her door. It would be easier to talk to one of them over the phone than to confess her humiliation to the whole posse.

"Hi, Lauren."

"Sofia? Where are you? I went to the restaurant, but you weren't there. Your Papa wouldn't tell me anything. Why didn't you answer before?

"I'm at home.'

"Is everything okay?"

"Not really."

"Are you crying? Sofia? Did someone hurt you?"

"Why does everyone keep asking that? I've been an idiot and a fool. I ruined everything."

"Sofia! You're not making any sense."

"I broke down and cried in the street."

"Sofia!"

"I have to go. Can you let the others know I'm okay? Everyone's messaging me, and I don't have the energy to repeat myself."

"Of course I'll tell them. But Sofia, you're not okay!"

"I can't talk about it now."

"Tomorrow then, over lunch?"

Sofia massaged her forehead, finally admitting that she had a pounding headache. "I don't think I'll come to lunch."

"Sofia! You've never missed lunch, ever. If you cancel on us, we'll turn up..."

"Goodnight, Lauren."

Sofia switched off the phone and crawled into bed, pulling the quilt over her head. She cried a river of tears until exhaustion swept her away.

The heartbreak entered her dreams. The wind roared and rain pelted from the sky until a fearful flood came. Sofia tumbled into a river wild and overflowing. The raging current bore her relentlessly away. Sofia fought for her life against the forces of nature. All the stars in the night sky fell, swirling and plunging into the depths with a frightening hiss.

Her terror thrust her out of the dream.

Slowly, awareness of her surroundings came to her. The shadowy darkness of her room brought no comfort. There was intense pain in her chest. Her breathing was ragged, and she struggled against an overwhelming tide of panic.

Fearing for her sanity, Sofia reached for her phone. She rocked while it reactivated. Who would she call? It was four am. When she was a child, nightmares had been frequent. She would wake her younger sister Evie who knew how to talk her through the anxiety. But Evie was on her honeymoon.

Her head throbbed. Sofia turned out the contents of her work handbag, searching for headache tablets. Unexpectedly, John Edwards' business card fell onto the bedcovers. How did it come to be in this old bag?

With trembling fingers, she examined it. Written in blue ink on the back was a mobile number. Why had John Edwards given her this number? Was she desperate enough to ring him?

Sofia's vision blurred. After several false starts, she felt sure she had the number right. Sofia held her breath.

"Hello, this is John Edwards. Do you know what time it is?"

Sofia ended the call with a sob. A few seconds later, John Edwards called her back.

"Sofia? Is that you? Sofia, I'm sorry. I didn't mean to be grumpy. Sofia? You're crying again. I'm going to pray for you, and then we'll both go back to sleep. You can call me tomorrow. I promise you I'll be in a better mood then."

John's calm confidence chased away the fear. She lay down and listened to his voice, and after he ended the call, fragments of his prayer echoed in her mind. The forgetfulness of slumber enveloped her, and she fell into a deep, dreamless sleep. When she awoke, the wretched tearfulness had left her.

Sofia lay listening for the familiar sounds of morning. Her head felt heavy, and her eyes were sore. A raging thirst burned her throat. The house was too quiet. Sofia checked the time. She had overslept.

In the kitchen, she found a note beside the coffee machine. The teenagers had taken care of themselves. They hoped she was feeling better now. Carrying a mug of coffee, Sofia returned to look for her phone. While she slept, she had missed a call from her parents, and another from Lauren. There were messages from the Tuesday Girls, mostly from last night. The ones received this morning asked if she had changed her mind about lunch. Lastly, there was a message from John Edwards, sent at eight am.

Call me after 10 am.

The first call she made was to her parents. Sofia was convincing about her recovery. The next call was to Lauren.

"I'm feeling much better, and I'll see you at lunchtime. There's no need to worry about me. Everything's fine."

Sofia selected John Edward's number.

"Good morning, Sofia."

"Good morning, John. I must apologise for phoning you earlier. I was half crazy and didn't know what I was doing."

"Apology accepted. I don't usually get phone calls from 'half crazy' people at four am, so I haven't perfected my response yet. I'm sorry I was rude. Why did you phone me?"

"I had a nightmare and was looking for some headache tablets when I found the card you gave me at the wedding. Only when you growled at me did I realise how wrong it was to call. Your kindness yesterday made an impression."

"Who do you usually talk to in the middle of the night?"

"I haven't needed anyone for a long time. I'm self-sufficient. It's only since my sister came back that anything's changed. I've been struggling with my emotions. My resentment is impossible to ignore. I've become suspicious of anyone who is kind to me."

CHAPTER 8
(Tuesday 5th September)

A Confidential Consultation

ౚ ✿ ౙ

1 Chronicles 16:11
Seek the Lord and His strength. Always seek His face.

ౚ ✿ ౙ

Two men sat in a suburban cafe, their monthly meeting about to conclude. John Edwards closed his eyes and rubbed his brow. Being a city pastor was a big responsibility. The list of problems he had discussed with his mentor, a retired minister, was extensive. A quick prayer was usually effective in throwing off tension, but not today.

A slip of paper floated off the table as he gathered his case files together. He made a futile attempt to catch it.

The older man picked up the paper from the floor. The page bore a single heading embellished with flowers. John's face reddened. Filling pages with similar decorations began during childhood when his sisters encouraged him to create borders for their drawings. Sometimes, he reverted to the form.

"What's this?" Max Foster asked.

John hesitated. "In the last twenty-four hours, I've prayed with Sofia three times, and she continues to weigh on my mind. Those are my notes from her conversation this morning."

"These aren't like your usual notes."

"There's nothing 'usual' about Sofia. At least she wasn't crying this time. She couldn't talk when she phoned me at four am."

"She called you at home? Don't your calls go through your secretary?"

"Sofia isn't one of my clients. I met her at a wedding I conducted – her sister was the bride. She was unhappy with her sister's choice of husband. And she spilled my drink. I don't know why I gave her my card or why I'd written my private number on it. I never expected to hear from her, especially not at four am."

"Have you seen her since the wedding?"

"She bumped into me last week, and spilled my coffee. My boys heard me muttering about praying for her. Yesterday, the boys found her crying and came to get me. Sofia broke down, and I prayed for her."

"No spilled drinks this time?"

John looked up. His mentor was smiling. "No, but her tears drenched my coat. I've never seen anyone that inconsolable. She clung to me as if I were her only hope."

The expression on Max's face sobered. "Why did she call you?"

"She's Catholic. The last time we spoke, she asked if I'd hear her confession."

"Did she have anything significant to confess?"

"She spoke about her resentment, and she said something about a childhood nightmare, but she didn't go into details. Perhaps she was testing my trustworthiness."

"Are you going to schedule a formal counselling appointment for her?"

"I don't know. I can sense God has a plan."

"You need to be careful. You're a single man, and she sounds vulnerable."

"She wouldn't be interested – she already has someone else. Besides, I'm not her type."

"But is she yours?"

The implications rocked John. He didn't consider himself single, despite being divorced for seven years. Devastated when his wife left him, he had devoted himself to caring for his boys. Then there was his growing church family to consider. He had pushed a relationship from his agenda.

"I've already promised to be available if she needs to talk. What should I do?"

"Make sure she only talks to you in a safe environment, or refer her to another counsellor. But be careful. Someone could get hurt."

"That 'someone' being me?"

"You're the one to answer that question."

Max returned the paper and John looked at it anew. He had written down the details of her life. Her failed marriages and troubled relationships. The challenges with her three teenage children, and the estrangement from her sister. His empathetic response to her loneliness underscored every word. How had he been so blind?

Two topics weren't discussed. The details of the dream; and what happened between her and the man who broke her heart. The nightmare still terrified her – she couldn't face the memory of it. Had John avoided asking about the man, because he feared an intimate confession? He knew she needed help, but what were God's intentions?

Destiny Delayed

❦ ☼ ❦

Proverbs 17:22 WEB
A cheerful heart makes good medicine,
but a crushed spirit dries up the bones.

❦ ☼ ❦

Deliberately late, Sofia slipped into the restaurant and took her place at the table. Her friends were cautious in their greeting. Sofia had dressed carefully, ensuring her makeup and hair were perfect. She wanted to erase the outward signs of her inner turmoil.

This week's venue was a small Asian restaurant, half a block from *Ristorante di Fontana*. The women shared a bottle of white wine as they waited for their meals. Sofia twirled the stem of her wineglass. After some awkward attempts at ordinary conversation, the table fell silent.

"Sofia? What's wrong?"

She blinked back a tear, focusing on the swirling liquid in her glass.

"I'll be fine in a few days," she said. "I've made another poor choice. When I get over the disappointment, I'll pick myself up and go on as normal."

"The date didn't go well?"

"The date was perfect. Valentino was perfect. It was me who was all wrong. I told him I wasn't interested in having an affair and walked out."

Her friends stared.

"But Sofia—" Lauren exclaimed.

Sofia held up her hand to silence her friend. "He said his mother would approve of me," she laughed bitterly. "I can't stop thinking about the mistakes I've made. Why would any mother approve of me? My children have different fathers. None of my relationships has lasted longer than six months. Why should I expect a relationship with Valentino to be any different? I'm better off on my own."

"Did you tell him that? Surely he tried to change your mind?"

Sofia shook her head, and tears began to fall. She turned her head away, searching in her handbag for a handkerchief. John Edwards' card tumbled out.

Lauren pounced.

Sofia's face blanched. "Give it back," she snapped.

Now everyone looked at her. Slowly she extended her hand and Lauren returned the card. Sofia took a deep breath. "I have a confession to make. I've been talking to a counsellor."

It was a half-truth. Sofia's friends responded, speaking over the top of each other.

"Why do you need a counsellor?"

"You can always talk to us!"

"We've supported you through two divorces and multiple breakups..."

"We're your closest friends. We're always here for you..."

With a forced smile, Sofia held up her hand to silence them.

"That's why I can't talk to you now. We have a shared history, and you care too much. You only want to me to feel better."

"That's what friends are for."

"Right now, a stranger is what I need. I have to make some changes. I don't like the person I've become."

"But Sofia, we love you the way you are."

"With you, I feel comfortable and accepted. But when I'm on my own, it's different. I hear the bitterness and suspicion in my voice. I hate myself. I'm driving Leonardo away. He's accused me of trying to control his life. I've belittled and criticised my sister because she wouldn't listen to my advice. Matilda says I'm jealous – perhaps there's some truth in that. Matilda's turning into a perfect copy of me. One day, she'll hate me too. I've had sex with too many men. My life's a disaster. I'm beginning to agree with Papa about the family curse."

Her words faded. At different times each of her friends had been in her situation. Strong and defiant, Sofia had always pretended to be immune to the torment. Now, her friends were struggling to deal with her weakness. Her confession would inspire them to try and fix her problems.

Their food arrived. The conversation turned to whether the meals met their expectations. Sofia poured herself another glass of wine, feeling lighter.

"Can I see that card?" Natalie asked. It was easier to trust Natalie. "Pastor John Edwards? Is he the man you tipped coffee over last week?"

"Yes. I've also tossed orange juice over John. Yesterday, to build on my earlier good impression, I humiliated myself by crying all over him. His small boys were watching. Next time he sees me in public, I'm sure he'll run the other way."

"That'll make seeing him for counselling difficult."

"I talk to him on the phone. That way, he can't see me crying, and I don't have to watch his reaction. Did you know Protestant ministers don't offer absolution? He said if I wanted my sins forgiven I had to ask God directly. He also wouldn't give me penance. After listening to him, I can understand why my sister converted."

"Has he tried to convert you?"

"Not yet. John hasn't said anything about my Catholicism. I've had him pray for me three times now, and each time I've felt better. That's something I haven't experienced in all the years of attending Mass. I usually come away feeling worse than when I arrived – more convicted of my failings."

"My grandmother used to pray with me," Kylie confessed. "I haven't thought about Gran for years. When I stayed with her, I never had any bad dreams. I believed she had special powers."

Sofia's attention drifted as her friends shared stories from their childhood. The atmosphere around the table was normalising, and she was relieved.

Tuesday's Tempest

ॐ ✺ ঙ

Proverbs 19:21
There are many plans hidden in our hearts,
but God's purpose always prevails.

ॐ ✺ ঙ

The gathering storm clouds mirrored Valentino's darkening mood. The late afternoon traffic was tedious, and Raymond was too cautious. This set of traffic lights had already changed three times. Finally, Raymond drove into the underground car park. Valentino was determined to escape his brother-in-law's scrutiny as soon as possible.

Raymond had insisted on being his driver today. It was not unusual for one of his brothers-in-law to accompany him to business negotiations, but Raymond's presence had been especially irritating. The tension between them was bringing Valentino dangerously close to losing control. Today, there had been no time to eat and hunger had compounded the problem.

None of his negotiations had gone smoothly. Raymond kept quiet during the meetings but reprimanded him when they were alone in the car. Valentino's impatience grew. All day, Valentino had tried to find time to satisfy his unanswered questions about where Sofia disappeared to after she left him.

As he stepped from the vehicle, his phone beeped. He looked at the screen and swore in frustration. Raymond stared at him as they moved toward the elevator.

His brother had summoned him.

"I have something to do before I meet Enzo," Valentino told Raymond. "You tell him I'll be there as soon as I can."

"He's not going to be happy. I told you to phone him after the first meeting. Then you dismissed his second call later. You know he only phones when it's urgent."

"I don't have to explain myself to you. Enzo should have left a message."

There was a small crowd waiting for the elevator. Raymond pushed himself inside and stabbed the button for the second floor. He stared at Valentino who remained outside. The doors closed. Valentino ran to the stairs and headed downwards. His angry brother could wait.

Valentino needed information before he could answer his brother's questions about Sofia. It was Tuesday afternoon. Valentino wanted to examine the *Raphael Towers* camera recordings. The men he had sent to follow Sofia after her unexpected departure hadn't been able to locate her. His certainty that she would change her mind had blinded him to any other possibility. His feet pounded on the stairs to match the throbbing pain in his head. Nothing had gone well today. He kept returning to Sofia's family curse. After a restless night, he had overslept, disrupting his crowded schedule. Failure was unfamiliar territory.

He had waited for her to contact him. Then he had visited her family restaurant, but she wasn't there. Despite lingering at the bar, he learned nothing about her whereabouts and drank too much. A visit to her home would have required an awkward explanation. What if she hadn't gone home? Curiosity made him impatient.

Valentino used his key card and pushed through the door to the below-ground security hub. The two guards jumped to their feet, standing at attention.

"I want to see the external recordings for Monday afternoon. Start with the accommodation complex. A woman left through the main entrance at three forty-five. Show me where she went."

They found the timeframe he required, and the scene replayed on the screen. Sofia turned towards him in farewell, and he could see her response to his passionate kiss. But his prediction that she would follow him had been wrong. He was shocked to see her brokenness after he abandoned her. He had seen no hint of weakness at the time, and he had thought she must have some kind of immunity to the potion he had added to her wine. He had missed the perfect opportunity to bring her under his control. His anger intensified when he saw her walk away in the wrong direction. The technicians efficiently tracked her progress, and he was astounded when a small boy approached her and reached for her hand. He cursed loudly when Sofia fell into the arms of an unknown man.

"Stop the recording!" Valentino leaned forward. "Who's that? Cross-reference the other cameras. Get me an image I can use."

The two specialists began their search. Valentino knew they wanted him gone. His older brother was the brains behind the expanding business empire. But Valentino was the enforcer. His reputation guaranteed their obedience.

They found a suitable image, and as the printer hummed, he signalled for the recording to continue playing. He was outraged to see how easily this man had taken Sofia away.

Why had his sources failed to tell him about his competition? He began planning his revenge, assuming that this man had taken advantage of Sofia's vulnerable condition.

As he retrieved the photograph from the printer, the door opened. Raymond entered the room. "There you are! Enzo is waiting."

"I'm busy."

"Is that Sofia? I see your plan failed."

Valentino threw Raymond a warning look before signalling to the security officers that he was finished. They turned back to their monitors, which reverted to real-time images. Opening the door, Valentino stormed into the hallway, with Raymond close behind. "What does Enzo want?"

"The woman involved in last month's abduction has turned up. You're to retrieve her."

Valentino marched into his brother's office. His carefully rehearsed speech became redundant when he saw his aged mother. Elegant in her matriarchal black robes, she stood at the window immediately behind his brother. Silently, he cursed Raymond for neglecting to tell him Doña Gabriella Marcella was here. She was supposed to be in Sydney. As he hastened to greet her, he saw reflected in the window a large gathering. His sisters and their husbands were present, signalling this to be a meeting of importance. That his mother was standing suggested she had convened the gathering. Rarely did she take an interest in business matters. When she did, nobody denied her whatever she requested.

"Mother, I didn't know you were visiting, or I would have collected you. I thought you had no plans for a Melbourne visit until October."

"Enzo said you were busy and couldn't spare the time, so he had to send another pilot."

Valentino's resentment towards his brother increased. Why was he surprised his sibling repaid his loyalty like this? Enzo had already been the established head of the family when Valentino became his deputy. Their mother had been forty-nine when her youngest son was born. Valentino's late arrival had been inconvenient. His mother left for Sydney as soon as Valentino was old enough to fend for himself.

"I hope she was worth it?" his mother snapped.

"What?"

"Your brother tried to cover for you, but it's obvious you disregarded my advice. Instead of answering your brother's calls you were preoccupied with a new woman. Until you moderate this selfish behaviour, you're an embarrassment to the family."

Why had his brother withheld the truth? Pursuing Sofia was part of Enzo's plan. To be rebuked for sacrificing his personal life for the good of the family incensed him.

His mother placed her right hand on Enzo's shoulder. Silver-haired Enzo sat behind his massive desk, a self-satisfied smile on his face. Valentino refused to add to his sense of humiliation by arguing his case in front of the other family members who were seated behind him. While his sisters were sometimes sympathetic, Valentino's ascendancy had pushed aside their husbands. There were no allies for him here.

"Our mother brought a request from our uncle for your specialised assistance," Enzo said. "The woman we transferred to the Sydney organisation evaded the team sent to collect her. Now, you must retrieve her."

"That was weeks ago. Why am I needed?"

"You're the one who organised the transfer."

"My role ended when I arranged her flight. The people in Sydney should retrieve her."

"Our uncle has been inconvenienced by two failed attempts. You must fix the problem. Our family honour is at stake."

"You know I've unfinished business..."

"Sofia? You said she would be easy to secure, and yet you failed. I'm beginning to mistrust your judgement. That makes two women who have thwarted you. Sofia's going nowhere. This other woman takes priority. There's a car waiting."

"If I obey you, I want something in return." Surprise registered in his brother's eyes. "Contact Piper and get him to identify this man."

Valentino laid the photograph on the desk.

His brother frowned. "You want to involve our cousin in this? His loyalty extends only so far. If he has to choose between Romano and our family, I know which way he'll turn."

"Piper came to us for assistance because Romano told him to. It's only reasonable he repays the favour."

His brother's cold laughter followed Valentino from the room. He thought of sending a message to Sofia, but he was uncertain how long he would be out of town.

When he returned, Valentino would talk to Enzo about retiring from his role as family enforcer. He was tired of being sent to far-flung places at his brother's whim. His obedience had cost him more than one relationship. If he decided to pursue Sofia in earnest, he wouldn't make that mistake again.

ॐ ☼ ୭

The afternoon sky seemed ominous when the car delivered him to Essendon Airport. He climbed into the waiting Cessna Citation X, taking the co-pilot's seat. The cockpit lights were the only illumination. The private jet began taxiing onto the runway before Valentino fastened his seatbelt.

In the pilot's seat, Roger Silvania said, "This is Cessna Citation November Zulu Oscar calling Control Tower, requesting clearance for immediate takeoff."

"Control Tower to Cessna Citation November Zulu Oscar, you are cleared for takeoff. Proceed to Runway Four. Be advised there is a severe weather warning for Sydney. Following takeoff, climb to thirty-thousand feet and maintain altitude."

"Roger that, Control Tower. Cessna Citation November Zulu Oscar proceeding to Runway Four. Over and out.

"I've filed a flight plan to avoid the worst of the storm," Silvania said to Valentino. "It's going to be a rough flight. Do you want to take the controls?"

Valentino appreciated the respect this competent pilot was showing him. "You fly. I'd prefer not to be out in this weather, but my brother gives the orders."

"You're angry."

Valentino looked sideways at the pilot, who was rubbing his medallion honouring Saint Thérèse, the patron saint of pilots. That was part of Roger's ritual. Next, he would bring out the cross he wore around his neck.

Valentino moderated his tone. "I drank heavily last night. We both know the alcohol in my system would be a disadvantage in this storm. I don't think my brother would approve if I crashed his new plane."

"No more talk about crashing," Silvania admonished him. "You know I pray to the saints before each flight. I'm going to buy you a talisman as a reminder. I've been flying for thirty years, and I've never failed to arrive safely at the right destination."

Valentino chuckled at the familiar rebuke. For Roger Silvania, this was part of his in-flight safety procedure. A reminder to his co-pilot that flying was a serious matter. Valentino brought out the cross of Saint Joseph of Cupertino which Silvania had given him. The unpredictability of his brother's orders meant Valentino wore it all the time. "You forget you've already fulfilled that promise. You must be getting old, my friend. Now concentrate on flying and fulfil your boast. My brother will be happier with both of us when we arrive."

CHAPTER 11
(Tuesday 5th September)

A Dangerous Descent

ॐ ☼ ॐ

ॐ ☼ ॐ

An hour into the flight the storm showed no signs of abating. Valentino realised today's flight might break the pilot's perfect record. Having to divert the plane became a greater possibility as the storm intensified. They already flew at a higher altitude. Silvania tapped on the console, where a red light flashed.

"What's wrong?"

"It's probably nothing. That light came on several times this morning, but it didn't stay on long enough to set off any alarms. I wanted a complete electrical systems analysis. The engineers only had time for a preliminary check."

As Silvania uttered those words, the control panel started to blink. Whole arrays of white lights flashed red. The emergency siren sounded, then the overhead light extinguished, plunging them into semi-darkness. The plane plummeted, as though pulled from the sky by an unseen hand. Valentino grabbed the steering column in front of him. Averting disaster would require all their skill.

The rapid descent delivered them into torrential rain. Violent winds tossed the plane. A blinding flash sent blue light sizzling over every surface. Valentino's ears were ringing. Every nerve in his body signalled pain. An acrid smell of burning accompanied the panic in the pilot's voice.

"Mayday! Mayday! Cessna Citation November Zulu Oscar, calling Kingsford Smith. We've been struck by lightning and losing altitude. All electrical systems have failed. We need to make an immediate landing. Please direct us to any landing strips capable of taking a Cessna Citation Ten. I repeat. Mayday! Mayday!"

Static was the only reply. The cockpit fell ominously silent. The entire control panel faded into darkness.

"What happened to the backup system?"

"That was the backup system."

Nothing in the training manual prepared them for this.

"We're losing altitude. We're not going to make it."

"Keep trying. My brother will be angry if we lose his plane."

"If we don't slow our descent, neither of us will need to worry about your brother."

Valentino pulled his phone from his pocket.

Crash imminent.

He sent the message and waited. The plane lurched, jolting the phone from his hand. The reply beeped in the darkness. Valentino wasn't undoing his seatbelt to get the phone. The rapid descent continued unchecked. Then suddenly the lights came back on. The control panel lit up as if nothing had happened.

"I have control again. Help me get the nose up."

Another flash of lightning broke the darkness.

"We're too close to the trees!" Roger shouted.

An explosion of noise and light enveloped them.

ॐ ✧ ॐ

Valentino hung upside down, still strapped into his seat. The rain had stopped, but wind howled around him. There was no moon. Tree branches swished nearby. He must be in the open, but how far was he from the ground?

Smoke wafted towards him and the night lightened with an ominous fiery glow. A surge of adrenalin gave him the strength to twist and turn in his seat, desperate for a better understanding of his situation. He only had a limited range of movement, but this was sufficient to confirm his suspicion that he had become separated from the plane. The ground, which must be somewhere beneath him, was obscured by thick undergrowth. His particular tree was a mature eucalypt, and he was more than a metre out from the main trunk, suspended from a thick branch. He reached out his hand and his fingers brushed the tips of the waxy leaves that dangled beside him. Unable to reach anything solid, he looked back towards the ground.

Valentino pressed the release button on his seatbelt. Gritting his teeth, he dropped through the darkness, landing hard. Something pierced his side, and he cried out. He struggled from the undergrowth and came upon the plane's wreckage. It had broken into three pieces. One section of the divided cockpit was a few metres away. How did he survive this? He could barely distinguish his seat hoisted high in a broken tree. He ripped off a shirt sleeve and wadded it against the wound in his side as he moved forward.

The larger rear section of the plane was two hundred metres away, bathed in flickering light. Small flames leapt into the surrounding scrub. Valentino fought the instinct to run. Scrambling around the shattered tree, he discovered Silvania lying motionless over the controls. Valentino shook the pilot, and the prostrate man groaned.

"Silvania? We have to get out of here! There's a fire. Can you move?"

The injured man raised his head. "My leg is stuck. I think it's broken."

Valentino dragged Silvania from the remains of the cockpit, heading downhill. After a few metres, their world exploded. Debris and burning embers showered them as both men were thrown to the ground. Valentino struggled to his feet, tugging Silvania upright. Ignoring the pain Valentino continued onward. The groans of complaint from his lighter companion faded. He kept them moving until his strength began to fail. Now when he stumbled, it took longer to regain his feet. The pilot had become a useless weight.

Valentino pitched headfirst into a narrow ditch filled with running water. He reached out for the other bank, dragging himself from the mud. He stretched forward onto a gravel road. He crawled across, narrowly missing a second fall into another ditch on the other side. The rough track's surface was only a few metres wide. He crawled back to retrieve the unconscious pilot.

Valentino gasped as they lay in the darkness, a jumble of limbs on the track. He pulled himself to his feet and shouldered his burden. The road aided him, and he fell less often. Sparks filled the air, and the glow behind them cast eerie shadows across the landscape. The occasional kangaroo sprang out of the scrub and tore across the road to safety.

Then the bush gave way to a small clearing. Dogs sounded the alarm, and lights flickered in a huddle of buildings down the hill. Headlights appeared, followed by the distant sound of an engine. He watched the vehicle moving through the darkness, and then turn in his direction. Valentino kept to the centre of the road, determined to be found on his feet when help arrived.

To set the world on fire seemed appropriate for his latest failure.

Wednesday Worries

ଷୠ ☼ ଓଷ

Psalm 46:1 WEB
God is our refuge and strength,
a very present help in trouble.

ଷୠ ☼ ଓଷ

"Da-ad! Peter's eating my toast!"

There was no ignoring that wail. John turned to find his sons wrestling at the breakfast counter. He had been preparing their school sandwiches while listening to the radio.

"Dad gave it to me. It's mine!"

"You wanted honey. That's my Vegemite."

Peter knocked over his orange juice during the scuffle.

It was Wednesday. The boys had soccer training this afternoon. John was waiting for the weather forecast. He would have to reschedule his afternoon if it rained.

John sighed. So often his days began with bickering, compromise and unexpected complications. He never imagined fatherhood would be like this. He wiped up the orange juice. That simple act brought Sofia to mind – again. He remonstrated with himself and turned his attention to resolving this disagreement.

He frowned at the two plates he'd placed in front of Peter.

"Sorry, Matt. Have my toast. Peter, you should have passed your brother his plate instead of scoffing both pieces."

"Aw, Da-a-ad. I'm extra hungry this morning. I thought that's why you gave me two."

"When you finish your toast, go brush your teeth. Then put your shoes on."

"Dad, what stops planes falling out of the sky?" Matt unexpectedly asked.

"What?"

"The man on the radio said there was a plane crash last night. What stops planes falling out of the sky?"

John shook his head, struggling to follow the redirection. He was still thinking about Sofia. He hadn't heard from her since yesterday morning's call.

"Are they dead," Peter piped up.

"Are who dead?" John asked.

"The people in the plane?" Peter explained.

"The people in *what* plane?"

"The people in the plane Matt said fell out of the sky last night."

"I didn't say the plane fell out of the sky, stupid. I asked why planes don't fall out of the sky."

"Don't call your brother 'stupid'."

"We should pray for the people in the plane," Peter insisted.

"That's a good idea. You can start." John continued cleaning up as the two boys prayed.

"Dear Jesus, please look after the people on the plane. If they're not dead."

"Please look after their families. It must be awful to hear on the radio about the crash and not know if they're alright. Please help the rescue people get them to hospital."

"If they're not dead. In Jesus name, amen."

"Amen."

As suddenly as they began their prayer, the two boys dismissed the plane crash from their minds. John stood in the kitchen, adding a silent prayer. When the boys started talking about the plane crash, he felt the Holy Spirit stirring. His mentor said this was his intercessor gift at work. He had learned to start praying and wait for the additional information to come to him. He must already have some connection with the people involved in the plane crash.

Two hours later, John sat in his church office working on next Sunday's sermon. His desk phone rang. His secretary knew not to interrupt him. He brushed his hand across his brow, praying for wisdom. With an effort, he forced himself to smile. One of the Bible college lecturers had insisted a smile impacted the unseen person on the other end.

"Good morning, John Edwards speaking."

"Good morning, Pastor Edwards," a quiet voice responded. The woman spoke slowly and clearly. "This is Hillary Silvania. I'm sorry to bother you, Pastor. I know you're a busy man, but Lisa-Jane insisted I should talk to you."

"Hello, Hillary. Lisa-Jane was right to put you through." As he spoke, John turned to face the pictorial directory of his congregation on the wall. The photo that matched Hillary's name depicted an older woman. She had short grey hair and wire-rimmed glasses. "I believe we talked last month at the fellowship lunch?"

"Yes, that's right. You said to let you know if there was anything you could do to assist me."

"How can I be of assistance today?" John asked, as his memory matched the conversation to the photo. He turned back towards his desk, but his eyes drifted along the wall. His chair jerked to a halt, his attention captured by the Romano couple's wedding portrait, which sat beside Hillary's photo. His foolish mind leapt to the bride's sister, Sofia. He rebuked himself, but now his heart pounded in his chest.

Straightening his posture, John seized his notepad and pen, and forced the frown from his face.

Hillary made no response. As he waited, John thought he could hear her crying. He knew not to fill the silence with words, and he used the delay to make notes of that earlier conversation. This widow attended services irregularly. Her only son had a demanding job, and when he wasn't working, he would visit her on Sundays. Her son disapproved of her Protestant conversion, even though that happened years ago. John circled the word 'Catholicism', recalling a similar conversation with Evie Romano about family disapproval. He took a deep breath – Sofia was on his mind again! He forced himself to recall what else Hillary had said about the son, sensing that he must be missing a significant connection. He heard the sound of Hillary blowing her nose, and then she spoke.

"My son Roger is a corporate pilot, and he's been flying a private jet for a local company. I don't know if you heard, but there was a plane crash last night."

"There was something on the news this morning. My sons and I were praying for the pilot and the passengers." John circled the son's name on his notepad. "Hillary, was your son on that plane?"

"Yes, Roger was the pilot. The authorities have been in touch. The impact of the crash started a bushfire. But there was no sign of my son or his influential passenger when the rescue team arrived. The rescuers think the survivors wandered further into the wilderness."

"I'm sorry to hear that. Would you like me to pray with you?"

When John had finished praying, he passed the information on to his secretary. Lisa-Jane would activate their prayer chain. He felt ineffectual, unable to offer real solace. But his faith was sustained by the certainty that God could do the impossible.

He spent time praying for the missing men, and for their families. Setting aside his sermon notes, John opened a new file on the laptop and began to research a different topic. The Holy Spirit was redirecting him. Now he wrote about the encouragement which only came from God. A familiar verse from Psalm 23 appeared on the screen as his fingers tried to keep up with his inspiration:

'Even though I walk through the valley of the shadow of death, I will fear no evil.'

ₓ✲ₑ

Wednesday afternoon soccer training was ending. John stood alone, waiting for Matt and Peter to run from the muddy field. He would purchase fish and chips for dinner tonight. Bath time would follow, then an early night for everyone. His day had been busy, and his thoughts were divided.

John had received regular updates from Hillary. Her son was still missing, and the authorities had no clues to his whereabouts. But whenever John paused in his prayers, he thought of Sofia.

He didn't notice the stranger approaching him in the gathering gloom.

"John Edwards?"

"Yes. Do I know you?"

"I saw you at the Romano wedding. I don't expect you'll remember me."

At the mention of that wedding, John froze. "You're Romano's friend?"

"Yes."

That simple answer seemed to conceal much more than John could discern. He felt increasingly uneasy in this man's presence. John checked to see where his sons were, and lowered his voice. "What do you want?"

The man passed John a black and white photograph. "This is you?"

John looked at the print. Even without the date stamp, he immediately recognised the scene. He was walking with his two sons, each holding an ice cream. John was staring directly into the camera.

"Where did you get this?"

"You need to be careful. You've come to someone's attention. The consequences could be deadly."

"Is this a threat?"

"No, a friendly warning. Romano trusts you, and I respect his judgement. I'll do what I can to protect you."

"What have I done to need this warning?"

"You hold the answer. Do you recognise this location? What happened before or after this photograph was taken?"

"Nothing; unless meeting Evie's sister Sofia counts. The boys found her crying on the pavement outside *Raphael Towers*. I walked her back to her family restaurant."

"Why was she crying?"

"I don't know. Sofia didn't want to talk about it. The boys said she came out of the building with a man."

The stranger reached into his pocket and brought out a smaller photo. "This man?"

"I didn't see him. Who is he?"

"Do you know anything about last night's plane crash in New South Wales?"

John felt the colour drain from his face. "This is the missing passenger from the crash? Sofia was with *him*?"

The stranger leaned closer. "You said you didn't see him."

"I know the mother of the missing pilot. Every time I pray for the pilot and his family, I find myself praying for Sofia too. What kind of trouble is she in?"

"I didn't say she was in trouble. If *this* man is interested in Sofia, the trouble is yours. Keep your distance. I'll look after Sofia."

"Who are you?"

"I've already told you. I'm a friend.

Friend or Foe?

ജ ✹ ൽ

Romans 6:13a
Don't allow yourself to be used
as an instrument for unrighteousness,
but offer yourself to God for righteousness,
as one who has been rescued from death.

ജ ✹ ൽ

"Wait here. If I'm not out in twenty minutes, phone me."

Piper stepped from Jenny's car. They had parked on the other side of the river. He walked across the bridge with the hurrying crowd. Night had fallen, and he hoped to remain unnoticed until he was ready to enter *Raphael Towers*. He could see no extra security. Using his phone, Piper sent his cousin Enzo a message and waited for a reply.

Come

Raymond met him in the foyer. Piper followed him into the elevator, planning an escape route should he need one. He ignored his companion's attempt at conversation. In minutes, Piper was standing on the carpet in Enzo's luxurious office. Piper dismissed Raymond. The only other person present was the family matriarch. Piper was annoyed because he hadn't known she was in Melbourne. Piper had met Doña Gabriella Marcella several times in recent years.

Their mutual dislike made Piper cautious in her presence. She seemed angry rather than grieved about her missing son.

Enzo offered no greeting. "What do you know?"

"About?" Piper wasn't going to reveal any information. He presumed the request to identify Pastor John Edwards had come from Valentino. Piper hoped the extended family had no interest in an innocent man.

"The plane crash."

"The pilot wanted a complete systems analysis, but you ordered him to take-off."

"I already know that!"

"What don't you know?"

"Your friend Romano. Could he have ordered this?"

"No."

"How can you be certain?"

"Romano has no reason, because the truce with your family is in force. Besides, he's preoccupied with his bride. Taking action against your brother would be the last thing on his mind."

"I had to ask."

"Why am I here?"

"If someone's taken my brother, I want their identity. They have influence."

"Or inside information?"

"Only the family knew where he was going."

"Trouble in your kingdom?"

"I refuse to believe any of the family is involved."

"Which leaves the many enemies you and your brother have made."

"The obvious suspects have already been questioned. No-one admits anything, and there's no evidence to point in any clear direction."

"Then it was either an accident or the hand of God." Piper was pleased to see his flippant comment reach its mark with Doña Gabriella Marcella. She bristled at the latter suggestion.

"There's one inquiry we haven't been able to follow," Enzo said. "The reason for Valentino's trip. He was sent to retrieve the woman involved in the abduction of Romano's wife. Jezebel went to Sydney but evaded the people who were waiting for her. Even though her location is known, every retrieval attempt has met with adversity."

"You want me to go?"

"You'll be well paid."

"For the return of the woman, or the return of your brother?"

"My brother is the priority. I'm insulted you presume otherwise."

"And if I can't find him?"

"Then you get the woman and find out who's been helping her."

"I'll need to use a full team. I want guarantees my people will be safe from any interference from you, or anyone related to you. Is that understood?"

"Yes."

"Transfer the first payment. When it's confirmed, I'll start my search. I won't be in contact until I've something to report." Piper turned to leave.

"Wait," Enzo insisted. "You have information on a local matter."

"Valentino made the request. When I find him, I'll give him the information." Piper had a secret advantage: his company had designed the *Raphael Towers* security system. As soon as he realised Sofia was involved, he had erased the pastor's presence from Monday's recordings. "I'll be leaving instructions, so be careful not to disrespect my decision."

"You're a suspicious man."

"Betrayal and duplicity are character building. The two of you taught me well."

This time, Piper made it to the foyer, where Raymond detained him.

"You're going to find Valentino?"

Piper despised Raymond. He knew disloyalty lurked below the surface. Enzo had only daughters, and kept them from the inner circle. Enzo's grandson had become a lawyer, but the uninitiated thirty-three-year-old wouldn't be a threat. Without Valentino, the succession battle would be between Raymond and Enzo's other three brothers-in-law.

"I'm busy," Piper said. "I have my business to manage. Why hasn't Enzo sent you to find him?"

"He knows I'm more used to following orders. I'm a humble man, unused to power and authority. Is there anything I can do to help free up your time so you can go?"

"No." The man's obsequious manner irritated Piper and he was suspicious about Raymond's persistence. "One of my lieutenants is waiting for me to walk out the front door. I've taken precautions. The counter-terrorism squad will descend on *Raphael Towers* with force. Do you want to be the one to explain their arrival to Enzo and his mother?"

"You wouldn't embarrass your family."

"Try me." Piper allowed his anger to show for a moment, answering his phone with a growl. "T minus three. Standby."

Raymond retreated.

Standing on the pavement, Piper cursed the falling rain. A taxi pulled up beside him, and the driver spoke as he opened the door: "Jenny sent me."

Piper's phone rang again. "Thanks for organising the taxi," he said.

Jenny's voice replied. "Two men are waiting to intercept you around the corner. There are probably more, but visibility's poor. There are too many civilians here."

"Someone doesn't want my mission to succeed."

"You're taking charge of the search? I'll call everyone in for the briefing."

The taxi dropped Piper near Flinders Street Station. There he disappeared among the crowd. Emerging from a side entrance, he was surprised to find Jenny waiting. His most experienced female operative had earned herself a pay rise, but he would have to change his protocol. This attractive woman's ability to predict his actions made him uncomfortable.

Jenny smirked at him, and he scowled in response. Jenny's intuition had delivered Romano's wife from captivity last month. He was sure this operative had spent too much time with Evie and caught her religion. Jenny had been teasing him by promising to pray for him. What would she say about including God on the list of perpetrators for this latest drama?

The perfect antidote for her smugness occurred to him. "I've a new mission for you. You and the pastor can pray for us while the team go to New South Wales."

"That's not fair."

"You're the one who said I needed God on my team."

The fiery conversation kept him entertained all the way to their headquarters.

The New Nanny

ॐ ☼ ॐ

James 1:17
Everything that is good and perfect
comes as a gift from the Father of lights,
who isn't like a changeable shadow.

ॐ ☼ ॐ

Who would ring his doorbell this early on a Thursday morning? John must silence them before the persistent five-thirty caller woke his boys. He threw the door open. A beautiful woman pushed past him, dragging a suitcase.

"Close the door," she insisted, and he complied. The night was warm, and his bare chest seemed to have captured her attention. His irritation overrode his embarrassment.

"Who are you, and what are you doing in my house?"

"Jenny Prescott. I'm your new nanny."

"I can't afford a nanny."

"Piper Maxwell is paying."

"Who's Piper Maxwell?"

"You met him at soccer training. He runs *Maximum Security* and specialises in protection. Romano is one of Piper's clients. Next time you talk to Evie, tell her Jenny says hello."

"How do you know Evie?"

"I'm part of her security team. It's fortunate for you Evie's on her honeymoon, so I've got time for you. I'm here to watch you and your boys. Be a dear and start the coffee machine. You'll be able to think more clearly once you've woken up."

"You can't stay here!"

"Why not? This house has three bedrooms. There's a room set aside for when your parents come to stay. Don't bother showing me. I know my way."

He tried to redirect her to the front door to make her leave, and she placed a firm hand at the centre of his chest. Her fingers were warm against his skin and he pulled back in alarm. She grinned.

"If you're worried about what people will say, you'd better get dressed. You don't want your boys to find you half-naked when they meet me."

"You can't stay here."

"Don't waste time arguing. I have my orders. If my being a woman troubles you, I know ten different ways of killing someone with my bare hands."

He took another step back, the fierce look in her eyes convincing him of her veracity.

"Get dressed and make coffee," she commanded, giving John a shove. "I'll join you in the kitchen in twenty minutes."

It was fifteen minutes when she returned.

"You didn't say how you wanted your coffee," John said.

"Strong and black, thank you. Now you're awake, I'm ready to answer some sensible questions."

"Why are you here?"

"You need to do better than that. I've checked the windows and doors. A locksmith will visit after the boys go to school. He'll install cameras and sensors at the same time."

"Is that necessary?"

She ignored him. "I've tracers for the boys to put on their backpacks. If they each had a phone, it would be easier. You'll have to make sure they understand the importance of trusting me. It wouldn't do to have them wandering off as they did on Monday, and find themselves in the wrong company."

"What kind of *wrong company*?"

Jenny ignored that question too. So much for saying she would give him answers.

"I know Sofia's family," John protested. "They wouldn't be involved in anything that would put my boys in danger. What makes Piper think we need protection?"

"Finally, a sensible question! You also know Romano. Did you hear about Evie's recent abduction? People tried to get at Romano through Evie, but Piper and Romano have made her untouchable. Perhaps his enemies have turned their attention to her sister? I've seen Monday's video. A jealous man would see you as a rival."

"You have to warn Sofia of the danger!"

"What would you have me say? 'Excuse me, Sofia, but your new boyfriend is a violent criminal, and he's using you to get to your sister's husband. Oh, and he's missing somewhere in New South Wales because his private jet fell from the sky. There's a team searching for him. Every aspect of your personal life is under surveillance.' How do you think she'd react?"

John stared at Jenny. "Why *you*? Why were *you* assigned to my family?"

Jenny laughed. "I've been teasing Piper about praying for guidance and help. Evie's rescue inspired me. Today he decided to teach me a lesson. Instead of assigning me to the outward team, he sent me here because you're a specialist in prayer. Piper said you confirmed Sofia's involvement with Valentino from your prayers. I can think of another reason you're praying for her. She's already mentioned you to her friends. But Piper dismissed your romantic interest. Be happy the assignment is mine. There are others on his team who would instruct your kids in hand-to-hand combat. Of course, I can add that to my job description if you want?"

John visualised his boys fighting each other over breakfast. "No thanks. They already do enough damage. How do I explain your presence? I won't lie, and I refuse to deceive people."

"Tell as much of the truth as you can. Say I'm a friend of a friend. I need somewhere to stay for a few days. I'm between jobs, and I've offered to help you with the boys. If anyone asks, I've escaped from a violent relationship. I'm not interested in you. That should protect your reputation."

"Is that true? Have you escaped from a violent relationship?"

"Digging for personal information? Do you want the truth? Yes, a long time ago, before I had military training. Now I can take care of myself. Don't worry about me, Pastor. I'm giving you a cover story. Don't say anything unless you have to."

"Are you a killer?"

"When I have to be, Pastor. I don't lie awake at night worrying about it." She laughed. "I've shocked you. There are plenty of stories about people killing each other in your Bible. Justice and retribution often result in death. If the situation arose where you or your boys were in danger, I'd do whatever was necessary. Your job is to pray it doesn't come to that."

"What else do you want me to do?"

"What would you normally be doing? We want to keep the boys' routines as regular as possible."

"I'd be asleep, but you fixed that. When I'm awake, I read my Bible and pray."

"Then you do that, Pastor. Go and pray for this situation. Pray for Sofia. Pray for Piper and the search team. Pray for anyone else who comes to mind, but make a list. I want to keep up with any new revelations. I'll check out your kitchen and plan breakfast. Maybe I'll pray for you? I'll wait for inspiration. What time will your sons wake?"

"In the next half hour. The boys can watch television until seven, but they have to dress and make their beds first. We leave for school at eight. Is there anything you need to know about the school?"

"No. I've already inspected the campus. Provided your boys stay where they're supposed to be, they'll be fine during the day. The risk comes at pick-up time with the extra people around. It would be easy for someone to take them and no-one would realise. You have to give me written authorisation to collect them. They go to the on-site after-school program? I'll check security there this afternoon. I know about soccer training. Are there any other occasions where someone else picks them up?"

"Only when they go on play dates. The other parent usually writes the note."

"No play dates. Tell the teacher no-one else has permission to take them. They can have friends here, where I can be sure they're safe."

"They're not going to like that."

"Trust me. I can make home more fun than someone else's place."

"What makes you think you can manage them? You don't look old enough to have children."

"I'm much older than I look. Good genetics, plus a little surgery to hide my battle scars. My brothers and sisters have lots of kids, so I'm confident your two will be easy to manage."

Dismissed, John went to his study.

He bowed his head in prayer. Then he accessed the day's online devotional readings. The familiar routine soothed his mind. How many times, since his ex-wife had left, had he cried out to God? Raising two boys alone was a monumental task. He had asked for respite, and help was delivered to his door.

Three Telephone Calls

 ॐ

Psalm 42:8
During the day God commands His love towards me
and during the night His song is with me like a prayer.

 ॐ

"Da-a-d! Breakfast's ready!"

How had he lost track of time? The boys were up, and he hadn't been there to introduce them to his houseguest. John hurried to the kitchen. The two boys were already seated at the kitchen table. The plump pancakes piled on their plates dripped with butter and syrup.

"Come on, Dad! Jenny says we can't eat until you say the blessing."

"Da-a-d, why don't you ever make us pancakes? I LOVE pancakes!"

As he sat down opposite the boys, they grinned at him.

"Thank you, Lord, for this new day, and for the provision of pancakes. Please use this food to fortify us for today's adventures. Thank you for our new friend, Jenny. You know why she's come to us. Help us to make her welcome."

"In Jesus' name, amen!" two small voices declared in unison. They began stuffing their mouths.

As John warned Peter to chew his food, his smartphone chirped. He glanced at the screen and stood hastily. "Mum, is something wrong? You never phone this early."

"Good morning, John. Everything's fine here. Your father and I are well, and we're enjoying our conference. The minibus is leaving the hotel in ten minutes, so I had to phone you now. How are the boys? Are they there?"

"It's Grandma." John set down the phone after activating the speaker.

"Good morning, Grandma. We're having pancakes for breakfast."

"That makes a nice change, darling."

"Jenny makes the best pancakes. I wish she could live here forever."

"Who's Jenny?"

"We don't know. Jenny was here when we woke up this morning."

"Was she? Darlings, Grandma loves you both very much, but she needs to talk to Daddy again. Please tell him Grandma wants to talk to him in private."

Jenny picked up the phone and passed it to John. She followed him into the next room. He turned his back.

"John, are you free to speak now?"

"Yes, Mum. Let me explain..."

"First let me tell you why I phoned. Lucinda and Fergus McLachlan are at the same conference, and we sat with them at dinner last night. Lucinda asked if we're relieved you're dating again. We're disappointed you hadn't told us."

"But I'm not dating anyone."

"If you're not dating, then who's Jenny?"

"She's, umm..."

"John, I'm your mother. You can't hide anything from me. Lucinda said she saw you outside *Raphael Towers* with a beautiful woman. The boys were with you, so there's no mistaking your identity. One of the boys was holding her hand. That's why Lucinda thought you were a couple. Are you going to deny that?"

"That wasn't Jenny." The words were out. He turned in dismay towards Jenny, who didn't conceal her amusement. "That d-didn't come out the way I wanted it to. Mum, I-I'm sorry but now isn't a good time. I have to get the boys ready for school. Bye."

He ended the call, but his mother phoned again immediately. John tried passing his phone to Jenny. "You answer it. Now my mother thinks I'm hiding two women from her."

"She's your mother," Jenny laughed. "I'll go and keep the boys on schedule while you talk yourself out of trouble. I can see why you didn't want to lie, but telling the truth is a problem too. It'd be better if you said nothing at all."

John went to his study and placed the unanswered phone on his desk. Returning to the kitchen, he discovered the boys had eaten his pancakes. Jenny set a cup of coffee on the table. She left him to look after himself while she took the boys to the bathroom.

An hour later, the boys had been dropped off at school. The locksmith was working on the new security measures. John wondered what the landlord would say. Now he was on his way to the church office. Jenny refused to let him drive. When his phone rang, John glanced at the caller ID. Instead of his mother again, it was Sofia. He fumbled to answer it.

"Sofia?"

"Hi, John, I'm sorry to bother you, but I didn't know who else to call. One of my friends is in trouble. His name's Guiseppe Amorosi, but everyone calls him Gypsy. I went to school with him."

"What makes you think Gypsy's in trouble?"

John glanced at Jenny, as she executed a daring manoeuvre at the next intersection. John grabbed for the dashboard.

"Gypsy left a message on my phone during the night, but he didn't answer when I phoned him this morning. I've been to his restaurant. He's usually there by eight, but no-one's seen him since yesterday."

"What was the message?"

"At first, he didn't say anything, and I could hear he was crying. He must have been drunk. He kept saying he was sorry. Then he said I'd been a good friend and I'd be better off without him."

"Where are you?"

"I'm outside his apartment building. Gypsy's car's here, but he's not answering his buzzer. I can't get anyone to let me in. I've phoned the police, but they weren't any help."

"Tell me the address. I know someone who can get you some answers. Drive to your restaurant and wait for me there. Don't try and find Gypsy by yourself."

"John! I phoned you because you're always calm and rational. You're supposed to pray for me, then hang up. You haven't helped me at all."

"I'm sorry, Sofia. Please go where I know you're safe."

When the call ended, John realised they were in an unfamiliar suburb.

"Where are we? I told Sofia we'd meet her at the restaurant."

"She isn't going to leave her friend's apartment."

"What makes you say that?"

"The men following her have confirmed the address she gave you. She's still standing on the footpath. We'll arrive in two minutes, and you'd better pray she's still there."

"Do you think something's happened to her friend?"

"Someone provided Valentino with personal information about Sofia. This message from Gypsy makes him the prime suspect. If Valentino kept his own counsel, applying pressure to her friends is the logical next step."

CHAPTER 16
(Friday 8th September)

Gypsy's Goodbye

ॐ☼ॐ

Joshua 21:45a
Not one of God's good promises has failed.

ॐ☼ॐ

As John stepped from the car, Sofia ran towards him. Jenny signalled, and two men approached from the other side of the road.

"Wait here!" Jenny hurried to meet the men. One of them was wearing a uniform. John attempted to keep Sofia at a safe distance.

"He's my friend." Sofia pushed past John. "If he's in trouble, I'm going to be there to help him."

John tried to keep pace with Sofia. Jenny stopped speaking, nodding to the men who walked to the security panel.

"I told you to wait." Jenny seized Sofia's arm, turning her aside.

"You're hurting me."

Jenny met her protest with a cold smile. Sofia turned her anger towards John.

"This is Jenny," John explained. "Don't argue with her. She doesn't listen. If you want to help your friend Gypsy, please do as she says."

A shrill whistle from one of the men at the apartment entrance broke the impasse.

"If you insist on coming, then promise to obey me," Jenny said, shaking Sofia so violently it must have made her teeth hurt.

Sofia nodded, and Jenny released her. Sofia rubbed her arm, where red marks had appeared on her olive skin. The trio hurried up the steps and entered the building. The door locked behind them.

"How did you get in so easily?" Sofia demanded, and one of the men pointed to the jacket he was wearing. The *Maximum Security* logo matched the badge on the door.

"You're fortunate your friend lives in one of our buildings."

Pushing forward, Sofia pressed the elevator button. "Gypsy's in Apartment 312."

Jenny lightly touched her arm. "Take the stairs."

Sofia bristled, but John drew her away.

"Your wife works in security?" Sofia said angrily.

John was horrified. "Jenny's not my wife."

Sofia glared at him, and he muttered, "I'm not married." He couldn't read the expression in Sofia's eyes.

There was an extended pause, then she smiled. "So who's Jenny?"

He sighed. "We have a mutual friend who thought we needed to spend some time together. She's supposed to help me with a delicate problem while I show her how pastoral care works."

"How's it going so far?"

"If I make it to the end of the day without her knocking me out cold, I'll be thankful."

"She needs to work on her people skills, but that doesn't explain why you're giving in to all her demands."

"If you'd been in the car when Jenny changed directions, you'd understand. I thought she was going to take a shortcut off the overpass."

Sofia took the stairs two at a time. John struggled to keep up with her, and was thankful when her energy faded. They were both breathing heavily when they arrived at the third floor. John leaned on the door to prevent her from bursting through it. He stared at her with concern. Sofia looked agitated, pressing closer.

"Sofia, take a moment to recover," he said. "While you do, please listen to me. Could you not tell anyone Jenny's a security agent? I'm having enough trouble explaining her presence without that complication. My mother thinks we're dating, which is bad enough. But if it gets out that I have a live-in bodyguard, my life will become unbearable."

"Why do you need a bodyguard, John?"

"If I tell you, Jenny will probably kill me."

She stared at him. For the second time today, he was too close to a beautiful woman. Her anger stirred his emotions, and his face turned red. He sidled away from the door.

"And if you *don't* tell me..." Sofia said, pursuing him. She had him backed up against the wall, when the door swung open.

Jenny looked from Sofia to John and growled, "John. I can't leave you alone without you getting into trouble."

"Is Gypsy at home?" Sofia demanded.

John peered over Jenny's shoulder. One of the men was emerging from Apartment 312. The expression on his face was sufficient information. John reached out to Sofia, but she rushed forward. Jenny signalled, and the security guard grabbed Sofia, but he could not prevent her from looking inside the apartment. She started to scream, and the man heaved her out of the way. Mid-cry, Sofia crumpled to the floor. John wasn't sure whether she'd fainted or hit her head against the wall.

Jenny strode over and gave Sofia a cursory inspection. "She'll be fine."

John gently placed Sofia in the coma position before he looked to see what she'd seen.

The trashed apartment told a story. From behind an upturned sofa, a pair of legs emerged. Striped trousers and soft-soled black shoes contrasted with the plush white rug. There was a dark red pool, as if someone had spilled a whole bottle of wine."Is he dead?"

Jenny nodded, as she took out her phone. She asked for silence. John listened to the one-sided conversation.

"Chief Superintendent Smythe-Jones, please. Tell him it's Jenny Prescott from *Maximum Security*. Hello, Chief Superintendent. I'm 2IC while Piper's away. I want to report a suspicious death. Guiseppe Amorosi, Apartment 312, the Bancroft Building, First Avenue, Highland Garden Estate. Yes, this is related to *Operation Phoenix*. No, there'll be no-one at the scene when your officers arrive. Consider this an anonymous tip-off. I've nothing further to report but will be in contact if I learn anything. Who will you assign to the post-mortem? Good, I'll visit him myself, so warn him to expect me."

"What happened to Gypsy? Why aren't you helping him?" Sofia demanded, pulling herself upright. "Call an ambulance!"

"It's too late for Gypsy."

"Nooo!"

"He's been dead for at least four hours."

"Did he kill himself? Is this what happened after he left that message?"

"He's been stabbed multiple times. This is murder."

John caught Sofia as her legs folded under her again. "Who are you? John said you're a friend. What kind of friend tells a chief superintendent what to do?"

"We have to leave now. Agree to come quietly, or my colleague will silence you."

One of the men stepped toward Sofia. She cried out in alarm and threw her arms around John. Jenny glared at John, and he scooped up Sofia. Hastily, he followed Jenny to the elevator, carrying Sofia in his arms.

Safely outside the building, Jenny opened the rear door of John's car. He lowered Sofia onto the seat. The reluctant passenger clung to him. Jenny pushed him in beside Sofia, then slammed the door. John began praying silently, as Jenny sped away.

"My car!" Sofia cried, leaning forward to Jenny.

"It'll be delivered to you later."

"Where are we going?"

"We'll drive around to make sure no-one's following us, and then we'll take you wherever you want to go."

"Why would anyone be following you?"

"You don't need to know why anyone's following John and me. The important thing is to make sure no-one's following you. Your friend was in trouble, and you came to rescue him."

"What kind of trouble was Gypsy in?"

"He's your friend. Did he give you any clues?"

"Last week he said he had money problems, but he solved them."

"Did he say what happened to 'solve them'?"

"No."

"When and where did he tell you?"

"Last Tuesday at *La Vita è Bella*, his restaurant in the city. My girlfriends and I were there for lunch. I went back later because I was worried – he didn't join us like he usually did, and he was drinking a lot. The girls! I have to let them know about Gypsy."

"John!" Jenny commanded. He prised the phone from Sofia's trembling fingers and placed it in the driver's hand. "You can't call them yet. No-one can know you found the body."

"I want to get out!" Sofia leapt for the door. The child-safe locks were engaged. Sofia pummelled John with her fists. "You can't keep me prisoner!"

He folded his arms around her.

"No-one's keeping you prisoner. We have to wait for the car to stop and for Jenny to open the child-safe doors. Then you can leave. Try to stay calm."

"Isn't this where you offer to pray for Sofia, Pastor John," Jenny scolded him.

"I have been!" he snapped. "I haven't stopped praying since you arrived."

"Temper, temper," Jenny laughed. She executed another sharp turn, throwing her passengers together.

An uneasy silence settled. When Sofia's crying eased, Jenny continued her interrogation. "You said Gypsy was your friend for a long time. Any other mutual friends?"

"None, apart from four other high-school friends; and the staff at his restaurant. Except..."

"Except?"

"Except he introduced me to Valentino Horatio last Tuesday. Gypsy said Valentino's brother was his landlord."

"Did Gypsy introduce you to Valentino before or after he fixed his money problems?"

"I don't like what you're implying. There can be no connection between the two. I had lunch with Valentino on Monday. I'm certain he had nothing to do with Gypsy's trouble."

"So, you know him well then?"

"Now *I* don't like what you're implying," John snapped.

Jenny laughed. "John, not everyone's as sensitive as you. Sofia, you should have seen him this morning, when I burst into his house. The look on his face was priceless. We're all adults here, John. Sofia's an attractive woman, so I'm sure she's had more than a few offers. Isn't that right, Sofia?"

John realised the two women were allied against him. He tried to put some distance between him and Sofia.

"Valentino asked, but I turned him down."

"You turned him down?" John was surprised.

"Don't look at me like that, John Edwards. I regretted it immediately, but couldn't work out how to take it back. Anyway, my saying no is your fault."

"My fault! How can it be my fault?"

"You delivered a pretty speech at Evie's wedding. You said Romano should treasure her virtue." Sofia punctuated every syllable with bitterness, "Romano would be blessed because he waited until after the wedding to jump into bed. The test for a relationship was to love the other person enough to wait for a pledge of commitment.

"You said God was an equal partner in the marriage, which made divorce unconscionable. Who would be brave enough to try and divorce God? You said lust destroyed many good relationships, and sowed seeds of suspicion and dishonesty, for a harvest of heartbreak.

"You predicted sunshine and happiness for my sister. I scoffed at your ideas, but I haven't been able to shake them. I enjoy a physical relationship and I've never said no to an appealing invitation before..."

He faced the window, fighting an impossible urge to offer her comfort.

Sofia must have read a different meaning in his silence. "I can see you're disappointed in me, John," she said. "But I'm not happy with you, either. I thought you were my friend, and you didn't tell me that your wife had died."

"What?" he exclaimed, turning to her in surprise. "Who said she was dead? My wife left me – I'm divorced."

"You hypocrite!" Sofia screamed.

Jenny braked suddenly, and leaned into the space between them to catch Sofia's hand as she tried to strike John. "If you don't behave, I'm going to tie you up."

Sofia shook herself free, and glared at John.

Jenny spoke again. "Sofia, did you hear from Valentino after you turned him down?"

"No," Sofia growled, still looking directly at John. She was answering Jenny, but he felt as if each word was an arrow directed at his heart. "I've tried to forget him. I turned him down because I was trying to be someone I'm not. I realise now I behaved like a fool. In fact, I wish John hadn't shown up to rescue me."

"I've been wondering how you came to be with John," Jenny admitted. "More than one person saw you leave with him."

John glanced forward and caught Jenny's reflection silently mocking him in the rearview mirror.

Jenny continued, "John's mother phoned this morning to ask about you. Are you sure Valentino didn't phone to ask?"

"You have my phone. You can check," Sofia snapped. "Valentino hasn't phoned or sent a message, and I haven't tried to contact him. Do you think he's responsible for Gypsy's death?"

"No, Valentino's not involved. He wasn't in Melbourne last night."

"How do you know? Where is he?"

"You don't know?"

"Don't know what? Getting a straight answer from you is impossible!"

"There was a plane crash on Tuesday evening. Valentino and the pilot are missing. My boss has been employed to find them."

"If you're looking for Valentino, why are you with John?" Sofia gasped. "Do you think John had something to do with the plane crash?"

"I'm looking for clues. John knows the pilot's mother, and he's helping. We don't know if there's a connection between Gypsy's death and Valentino's accident. It might be a coincidence."

"But you don't think so?"

Jenny turned into the *Ristorante di Fontana* car park.

"We're not being followed. For a few days, you need to be careful. If anyone comes to tell you about Gypsy or Valentino, act surprised. We'll be watching you, to make sure you're safe."

Retrieving Sofia's phone, Jenny pressed buttons before passing it back to her. Sofia accepted the phone as if it were a poisonous snake.

Jenny smiled. "Call me anytime, night or day. I won't answer, so leave a message. If you're in trouble, place the call and leave the line open." Sofia nodded, but Jenny wasn't finished. "Be careful how you use your phone from now on, because all activity will be tracked and recorded."

Sofia tried to return the phone but Jenny ignored her. "Apart from Valentino, are you dating anyone else?"

Sofia shook her head, shoving the phone in her pocket.

Jenny continued. "No? I recommend you keep it that way. Don't agree to any appointments outside your normal schedule. Until we find out what happened to Gypsy, we don't know who we can trust."

"It must be awful to be suspicious of everyone."

"If it keeps me alive and protects my people, then it's a worthwhile sacrifice. Where do your parents think you've been? Do they know you were looking for Gypsy?"

"Yes, I phoned Papa this morning. What will I say?"

"Tell them you went to the apartment building and Gypsy didn't answer. You were worried and too upset to drive, so you phoned John. All that's true. If you keep it simple, you'll be fine."

Sofia looked at John with eyes that declared she was anything but fine. She gave him a defiant smile and straightened her shoulders. Jenny opened the doors. Sofia stormed off without a backward glance.

☽ ☼ ☾

The restaurant was busier than usual when Sofia entered. Being unable to talk to anyone about Gypsy was devastating, but her anger with John helped carry her through it. Papa offered her more time to continue her search. Sofia reassured him the police would find her missing friend soon.

Two detectives visited. They only talked about Gypsy's disappearance and not his death. How was she to avoid revealing she already knew?

Papa sent them up to the private dining room, so the detectives could question her alone. The detectives were well fed while her interrogation took place. The two men were appreciative, but it didn't soften their interview technique.

Sofia was a suspect.

They asked intrusive questions. Was she or had she ever been Gypsy's lover? Did she hold any grudges against him, or have any reason to wish him harm? They already knew she'd been to *La Vita è Bella* looking for him, but not the apartment building.

The detectives noticed Sofia's reluctance. Sofia replayed the message Gypsy left her. The knowledge Jenny might also overhear increased her apprehension. When the detectives informed her they would confiscate her phone, Sofia became distraught. Her protests increased their suspicion.

One of the detectives received an incoming call. The detectives' demeanour transformed instantly. They had a whispered consultation. Then they offered an apology for causing her distress before leaving abruptly. Moments later, Jenny phoned to reassure Sofia. Then John came on the line, with another apology. Sofia silenced him before demanding that he pray for her.

ജ ✹ ൟ

It was four am. Sofia sat upright in bed, with the lights on. She picked up her phone, only to put it down again. The knowledge her call might be recorded rendered her silent.

Now, in the darkest hours, Sofia desperately needed to hear John's voice. But she feared revealing more of herself to Jenny. John said that dangerous woman was living with him. Sofia pushed aside thoughts of them alone together. What if Jenny was lying beside him, listening to every word? Sofia had thought John was a man of integrity, but now she wasn't so sure. Would he be immune to temptation?

These unexpected thoughts slapped Sofia more awake. Why did she care? Jealousy flooded her senses. Oh, God! How could Sofia imagine John would be interested in her after all she had said and done to him?

For the first time in decades, she fell to her knees beside her bed. No words came, only more tears. She longed for her childhood. Then she had knelt beside her sister, and they had prayed their simple prayers. The words of 'Our Father' dropped into her mind, and she whispered into the early morning:

"Our Father who art in heaven, hallowed be Thy name; Thy kingdom come, Thy will be done on earth as it is in heaven. Give us this day our daily bread; and forgive us our trespasses as we forgive those who trespass against us; and lead us not into temptation, but deliver us from evil."

CHAPTER 17
(Friday 8th September)

Confirmation or Confusion?

❦ ☼ ❧

Psalm 126:4
Restore our fortunes again, Lord,
like streams in the desert.

❦ ☼ ❧

The water was a deep midnight blue, warm and thick. Valentino could taste the sweetness, and it clung to him like honey. At first, the waters were still, and the deep dragged him down. He battled to regain the surface, trying to remember how he came to be in this river wild and mysterious.

Suddenly a ferocious wind roared over the river. The waters were violently astir. Fountains of spray erupted hundreds of metres into the sky. A shower of flashing rainbows brightened the night. The fury of the iridescent waves intensified. A new danger emerged – jagged rocks glowing like giant emeralds.

Monstrous breakers pummelled him. Valentino gasped, desperate to fill his tortured lungs. He surfaced again. Above the brilliant glow of the water, he saw the riverbank's rocky walls.

Frantically, he pushed in their direction. He went under again. When he resurfaced, he was further away. A final time he sank, conceding defeat.

ౠ ☼ ౫

Tiny, wake up.

Was that his name? His body was weak, and heavy with pain. Then he remembered the river and cried out.

"Valentino, you've been drugged. The antidote takes time. Breathe."

He knew that voice, but he struggled to remember a name. "Pietro?"

"No-one calls me that anymore."

Valentino felt a cool cloth pass over his face.

"Water," he croaked. Liquid poured into his mouth, and he swallowed eagerly. Then his body rebelled. Spluttering and coughing, he re-entered the dream. A strong arm held him until the spasm passed.

"Thanks for saving me from the river."

"What river?"

"I was drowning…"

The silence lengthened.

"You're safe now. I'm going to call my team. Wait here."

Valentino heard footsteps retreating, then a quiet scratching. A door opened and closed. The room's emptiness pressed upon him. Valentino fought to open his eyes. It made no difference. The room was dark. He was lying on bare ground. His fingers touched an irregular surface. Something tumbled down, rolling away into the unknown. He tried again, finding a barrier on each side. Pushing himself to his knees, he crawled until he crashed into a wall.

The rough surface tore his fingers. He had reached a dead-end. Retreating, he followed the barrier until he came to an opening. He froze. Did he hear something?

"Can you stand?"

Strong arms pulled Valentino to his feet.

"How can you see?"

"Night-vision glasses. I'll guide you."

"How did you find me?"

"Your heat signature. Your captors were clever. This junk would have concealed you in an ordinary search. Be quiet. I've dealt with one dog, but there may be others. We don't want to wake anyone. We've got about five hundred metres to go. It's open pasture. If the full moon breaks through, we'll be easy targets."

Cautiously, the two men went through the door. They followed the dilapidated building's outline. A breeze blew from behind them as they went up an incline. Towering trees stretched into the clouded sky. In the distance, a dog barked.

"Down."

Valentino fell to the ground. An owl broke the silence. A piercing cry marked the nocturnal hunter's passage. His rescuer pulled him to his feet.

Their staggered march delivered them to a barbed-wire fence. Valentino was dragged roughly over the obstacle. His legs burned, and his breathing laboured. He pitched forward into an unseen ditch. Water splashed him, returning him to the river. He screamed.

His companion swore and tossed him roughly from the ditch. Valentino collapsed onto a gravel track. He then crawled across the road, encountering another ditch. The scrubby bush that lined the verge on the other side slowed their progress. "I can't..." Valentino gasped. He fell into the prickly embrace of an unseen shrub.

His companion gave a piercing whistle. Shadowy figures emerged from the darkness and carried him away. The men were silent, careful in their retreat. He abandoned himself to the journey. The men increased their pace. The steady sound of heavy boots startled the wildlife.

Suddenly they halted. His rescuers threw Valentino into a waiting vehicle, then an engine roared.

Now they were racing uphill in the dark. An involuntary cry erupted from Valentino's throat. They continued in silence for a long time.

"We've come far enough," the familiar voice said. The vehicle stopped. There was a communal rustling, and then the headlights burst into life.

Valentino could see the outlines of four men. They ignored him.

"Where are we going?"

"There's a helicopter waiting to take you to Sydney. We have a trauma team on standby. Your brother made the arrangements."

"What happened to me?"

"You don't remember?"

"No. All I remember is the river. How did I get in that building?"

"There was no river. Your plane crashed. Someone moved you to the hut. Do you know who you are?"

"You called me Tiny. You're Pietro."

Someone stifled a laugh.

"Tiny and Pietro were friends once. Now your name is Valentino, and I answer to Piper Maxwell. Your family paid me to find you."

୫୦ ☼ ୧୩

Oliver and Nelson accompanied the victim – Piper wasn't taking any chances. He waited until the whoop-whoop of the departing helicopter faded. Turning to his remaining companion, Piper marched to their dark van.

He had hired Patrick Sims on Jenny's recommendation. Unlike the others, the young man had no military training. He didn't look like a trained killer. Patrick had been a lawyer, but was proficient in several martial arts. Jenny thought Patrick would be perfect for Evie Romano's security detail.

Patrick was equal to Piper in stature. The young man seemed comfortable in the camouflage uniform. He drove along the forest roads with confidence. Piper made a note to increase Patrick's bonus when this mission was complete.

"So far, you have only worked with Jenny. Do you have any questions about working with me?"

"Apart from the obvious – why me? Jenny said this was a test. Is she right?"

"Jenny thinks she's always right. Remind me again, how did you meet Jenny?"

"On an advanced driver course. The instructor paired us for the initial training. I was preparing for an off-road charity event. Jenny said you sent her because she drove like a maniac and you wanted a certificate to prove it. I refused to admit she was the better driver. Jenny took the challenge personally. The instructor said we were a lethal pair."

"How did you go in the rally?"

"The owner of the car insisted on driving the opening stage, and crashed before the first checkpoint. I never got to impress anyone with my new skills."

"I'm used to Jenny's driving, so as long as you get me to my destination, you'll pass. If you crash the van, you won't live to regret your failure."

Patrick's smile faded. He straightened his posture. "Where are we going?"

"Valentino was on his way to collect someone. I need to assess whether that mission had anything to do with the plane crash. I have a rural address that's a hundred kilometres north-east of here. After some preliminary enquiries, we'll return to Sydney. Valentino should be fit to interview by then."

"He was in a bad way when you found him. What do you think happened to the pilot?"

"He's buried somewhere. They need to bring in the cadaver dogs."

"What makes you so certain?"

"I'd have detected him. It's easier to hide one man. Perhaps the pilot was injured, and they couldn't keep him quiet. Or maybe they thought the family would only pay for Valentino's return."

"Do you think there's been contact with the family?"

"I would have been given different instructions if there'd been a ransom demand."

"Why didn't the original search team find Valentino? He was only a couple of kilometres from the crash site. The trail he left through the bush was easy to follow."

"A mob of kangaroos escaping the blaze would make a similar trail. The official team started at the epicentre and were disadvantaged by the fire. We began further out because we already knew what we'd find at the crash site. The original searchers followed behind the fire crews. They made an assumption the survivors would find the forestry road. They forgot it was dark and a storm was raging. We succeeded because we had different search parameters."

"So, he made it to the road. Whoever found him, took him captive. How did you know he was picked up and taken down to the old farm?"

"Training and experience. I could send you on a course if you're interested."

"No thanks. I don't have the patience, and I'm content to be the driver. Why didn't Valentino know who he was, and why did he think you were Pietro?"

"He was drugged. Our intelligence predicted the kind of drugs this outfit were cooking in their lab. I had the right antidote. Getting him out while he was raving would have been impossible."

"What was that talk about a river?"

"He was hallucinating. For whatever reason, he believed he was drowning. His body responded accordingly."

"He's lucky you found him."

"Jenny would say luck had nothing to do with it."

"Maybe she's right."

"You've both spent too much time with Evie Romano."

"Evie tells a story about a river..."

"Stop talking and let me sleep."

Piper turned his head away. His military training usually facilitated rest in extreme circumstances. But today his mind refused to set aside the reference to Evie Romano.

Early in her relationship with her husband, Evie had fractured her skull after a fall. Piper remembered the wonder on her face as she recounted her tale. While she was unconscious, she had dreamed about a 'river wild and terrifying'. Piper's imagination supplied an image. That river carried her into the presence of God.

Evie claimed that vision changed her destiny. Her certainty confounded Piper. She insisted she would not be with Romano without her encounter with God.

Piper had been sceptical. He met Evie after this event, but he had known Romano for six years.

He greatly respected that man's pragmatism. Everything about this whirlwind romance was uncharacteristic. Romano had only known her for three days when she became his fiancée.

Romano had also told him the story of Evie's accident. He continued to attest that she died and came alive again. The impact of her supposed resurrection on Romano's life was profound.

Their testimony troubled him. Piper had interviewed other witnesses. Even the cynical unbelievers affirmed the facts. The changes in her personality were significant. Piper had argued with Jenny about the implications. Long ago, he had dismissed God's existence.

His research into Evie's background changed his priorities. There were dark family secrets he held close. Only he knew the whole story. If Evie understood Piper's reasons, she would say God had a plan.

Now, his injured cousin, in a drug-induced coma, was babbling about a river. Piper didn't like coincidences. His cousin was not a religious man. If Evie's God was pursuing Valentino, there were implications for his whole family. Dismissing this as a coincidence was the safer option.

Piper's Plan

ॐ

Proverbs 8:10 WEB
Receive My instruction rather than silver,
knowledge rather than choice gold.

ॐ

"Have you heard from Piper?" John demanded.

Jenny stood beside the open front door. Her packed suitcase revealed her intent. She was sneaking off into the darkness. "You're supposed to be asleep."

"So are you. Did you leave a note?"

"I planned to call you in the morning."

"Did Piper find the missing men?"

"I can't tell you."

"Then it's not good news."

"I can't confirm anything."

"Does everything have to be a secret with you?"

"That's my mission. Yours is to talk to God. Ask Him your endless questions. Evie says He knows everything."

John inhaled deeply. He was overtired and irritable. He asked God for patience. Jenny left without another word.

She hadn't denied hearing from Piper. Something significant had happened. He glanced at the new security device beside the front door. The row of green lights told him she'd reactivated the external sensors. The danger to his family remained. Therefore, she was needed somewhere else. Silently, he prayed for her safety. He asked God to grant her success with her new assignment.

Turning the light off, he went back to his bedroom. After tossing and turning, he picked up his phone and sent Sofia a message. She wouldn't see it until the morning, but it was one way of settling his anxiety.

RUOK?

Five seconds later a message flashed back to him.

No. RU?

Not really. Trouble sleeping?

Bad dreams.

Praying.

Me too.

He re-read the message. Sofia sent another one.

I wanted to call you, but not with Jenny listening.

She's not here.

But she'll still know.

Yes.

She frightens me.

Me too.

Did Gypsy die because of me?

I don't know.

Did Gypsy set me up with Valentino? Was he paid?

No answers.

If I stayed with Valentino on Monday, would Gypsy be alive?

Stop torturing yourself. Gypsy was already in trouble.

If I stayed would I be on the plane?

Stop.
No more IFs or BUTs.
The past is unchangeable.
Now is a time to pray, trust, hope.
The future is in God's hands.

Do you think Valentino is alive?

Hope.

Thanks. UR good friend. Nite.

Sleep well. Talk tomorrow.

John stared at the heart icon she had sent.

Sofia would be waiting for his reply.

Then he remembered Jenny might be too. He chose quickly and then snapped off his phone.

ಬ ☼ ಲ

Jenny smiled in the darkness. She had been following the SMS conversation. John wasn't ready to admit he had feelings for Sofia. His smiley face icon was a slow but predictable reply. It was regrettable Sofia had turned her affection towards Valentino. It would have been entertaining to watch John try to win the world-weary Sofia.

Jenny patiently waited. Piper had assigned her to watch members of Valentino's family. Enzo had been told to keep the news to himself. The proud man was expected to disregard Piper's advice. Jenny deployed her team so they were ready to act. Jenny also informed Piper of Gypsy's death. He didn't respond to her assessment that the two cases were linked.

Half an hour before sunrise, a man hurried from the *Raphael Towers* building. He wore a hooded jacket. A taxi took him to Melbourne Airport. There he boarded the next flight to Sydney. Jenny's agent was on the same plane.

The destination was already known. However, it would be helpful to identify any collaborators. Two of Piper's operatives were already on standby at the private clinic.

ༀ ☼ ༀ

The dream about the river overwhelmed Valentino. The water launched him onto a massive boulder in the midst of the raging torrent. He was now high above the turbulence. Darkness pressed upon him. The distance between this dark rock and the light of the riverbank was impossible. Would someone come to rescue him?

A familiar voice spoke to him in the darkness.

Tiny

A name from his past. He knew that voice. Pietro, his cousin and childhood friend. No, not his friend. Their bonds of friendship tore long ago. Bitter enmity had become their currency. If that man came to save him, it would not be out of friendship.

Abruptly, he abandoned the dream. He was alone. Medical equipment tethered him to the bed. Impatient for answers, he tore the leads from his chest. Silence fled. A crowd rushed in.

"Mr Horatio! Stop!"

He ignored them, ripping out the intravenous drip. "Where's Piper?" Valentino threw off the sheets to reveal a hospital gown. The room spun. He focused on the cold floor beneath his feet. "Bring me some clothes."

A man in camouflage gear spoke from the doorway. "My orders are for you to stay."

"Where's Piper?"

"He's on his way. Do you know who you are?"

"Of course!"

"Get back into bed. Let these people do their job. Don't make Piper rescue you a second time."

Valentino took a stubborn step, and his legs collapsed. Firm hands returned him to the bed. He felt the prick of a hypodermic needle, and the room faded.

When he opened his eyes again, Piper was seated beside him.

"How long did I sleep?"

"Long enough."

"I can't stay here. I have business to finish."

"Already dealt with, but not as you intended."

"What do you mean?"

"You can't fight the hand of God."

"You make no sense."

"Evie Romano intervened. Your uncle Augustus received payment to stop pursuing the woman who abducted Evie."

"What!"

"Evie had a dream and contacted me. The target comes under God's protection. There's no other explanation – how else could Evie know my plans? What makes no sense is God telling Evie to protect her enemy. Augustus took this as a powerful omen. Your uncle has now washed his hands of the matter. I suggested his actions had brought a curse upon his family. He repented – but not before accepting Romano's money."

"What curse?"

"What other explanation could there be for your plane falling from the sky?"

"I can think of several."

"Agreed. You have many enemies. The greatest danger comes from within your family."

"I can take care of myself."

Piper's cold stare challenged the lie.

"I have to get out of here."

Piper put out his hand. "Stay. Let your enemies come to you."

"Why are you here?"

"I've already told you."

"Why do you care what happens to me?"

"Perhaps your enemies are my enemies. Before you boarded the plane, you sent me a message. Even if your brother hadn't asked, I would have come looking for you. What do you want with Sofia Fontana?"

Valentino kept his silence.

"How much did you pay Giuseppe Amorosi?"

Valentino held his gaze steady, but Piper's anger awakened an uneasy fear.

"Amorosi's dead," Piper added.

"Not by my hand."

"No, but he realised his betrayal had endangered Sofia."

"Is she safe?"

"Yes. Evie would say God is protecting her sister. Sofia escaped the trap you set for her, then fell into the arms of one of Evie's friends."

"Why do you keep referring to Evie and her God?"

"I'm a realist. There are too many coincidences. Each time someone turns their hand against Evie, something unexpected happens. She claims God is protecting her, and the evidence is growing."

"What evidence?"

Piper smiled. "Enough questions. Tell me about the river?"

The change of topic caught Valentino by surprise. The sweat beading on his forehead gave away his growing panic.

"What river?"

"You said I saved you from drowning, then you talked in your sleep. If I hadn't heard about Evie's river, I'd have dismissed your ramblings. Her vision marked a choice between death and life. I'll wait to see what your outcome is. What did the voice say to you?"

"I heard no voice but yours. You called me 'Tiny'."

Piper laughed. "God isn't impressed with your power. You'd better take care. Evie sent you a message." He handed Valentino his phone.

> But if God is behind it, you cannot stop it anyway,
> unless you want to fight against God (Acts 5:39)

Valentino's hand trembled, but he looked up in defiance. Piper was playing games.

Secrets and Suspicions

ಬಿ ☼ ೞ

Ephesians 5:8 WEB
For you were once darkness, but are now light in the Lord.
Walk as children of light.

ಬಿ ☼ ೞ

Five restless nights had passed since Sofia found Gypsy's body. She struggled to maintain her calm facade. A small newspaper article announced her friend's unexpected death. Whispered speculation in her broader circle of friends mentioned suicide. But the police had not returned.

Neither had she heard anything from Valentino. Sofia learned through John about the recovery of the pilot's body, and the mother's overwhelming grief. Roger Silvania had been found in a shallow bush grave many kilometres from the crash site. The authorities were puzzled, and the investigation was ongoing. The media had now dropped that story, and Valentino's name was never publicly released.

Last evening, Sofia had an unexpected encounter with the pilot's mother. Hillary Silvania, reserved and quiet but holding herself erect, was among the guests from John's church who came for a meal at *Ristorante di Fontana*. John had not been present. Sofia had mumbled something to

Hillary about being sorry for her loss, and then busied herself serving other patrons. She later overheard her father telling Hillary that his daughter was also grieving, and then heard Hillary's gentle promise to remember Sofia in her prayers. Sofia dropped something so she could bob down and wipe away her sudden tears.

There had been no further contact from Jenny. The dark car parked outside her house still followed her to work every morning. Whatever the danger, it still hovered. Through her, it threatened her family.

It was Tuesday again. Sofia must pretend nothing was bothering her. She sat at the table with her friends, sipping white wine. Their lunch venue today was a cosy little restaurant in Fitzroy. They had the dining room to themselves. Sofia should feel relaxed. At ease with her companions and anticipating a few hours of fun.

Instead, she was frowning at the extra seat. Which of her friends had suggested Sofia invite her sister Evie? Since her encounter with Jenny, Sofia was suspicious of everyone.

Evie and her husband had returned from their honeymoon on Sunday. They had dinner with the family on Monday. Sofia's dire predictions were disproven. Her slender sister's adoration towards her imposing husband was unabated. Indeed, she seemed more affectionate and devoted. Evie's dark beauty had intensified with her deepening love.

Sofia must have mentioned this to Natalie, who passed it on. Each of her friends had phoned. In the past, she wouldn't have hesitated to give her opinion. Since Gypsy's demise, she held back, unsure which of her friends was trustworthy. Only John knew her emotional turmoil. Her deepening dependence on that man was another closely guarded secret.

Two strangers entered the dining room, taking a window table. The blonde woman seemed familiar. The attractive young man was tall and wore a tailored grey suit. Sofia felt a stab of regret over losing Valentino. A few seconds later, her focus shifted.

"Sofia, your sister is here!"

"Evie! Over here!"

Sofia was surprised by her friends' enthusiastic welcome. She hurried to embrace her sister. Over Evie's shoulder, Sofia noticed the blonde woman watching them. Suddenly she recognised her – Jenny! What was she doing here? Was this a coincidence, or was Jenny following her sister? Evie must have heard her gasp. After glancing in the couple's direction, Evie smiled.

It had been decades since Evie last met Sofia's friends. Evie had lived in Sydney for twenty years. Sofia compared her sister's modest beauty with the studied perfection of her friends. Her heart quaked. Compared to these friends, Evie appeared innocent and untouched by the world. Only Evie seemed to notice Sofia's smile wavering, and squeezed her sister's hand. In response, Sofia blinked back a tear and picked up her wineglass.

During the meal, Evie cheerfully endured questions about her relationship with Romano. The thoughtful young woman had brought photographs from her honeymoon. She kept Sofia's friends entertained with little stories.

Romano had taken her to Tasmania, where they toured the island state in his Maserati sports car. The couple had spent a fortnight enjoying the sights. Wherever they went, Romano's giant stature and colourful tattoos had attracted attention. Their accommodation had included expensive resorts and intimate little bed and breakfast establishments. None of the Tuesday Girls had been to Tasmania.

"It sounds like the perfect destination for our next Tuesday Girl adventure," Lauren said. "Evie could be our tour guide."

"I don't think Romano would let her come," Sofia said too quickly.

"Would he be scandalised by our behaviour?"

"It wouldn't be anything like our last trip. Evie, we went to Bali last time."

"Of course, we don't take our husbands or children on our trips. In Bali, we spent most of our days on the beach."

"Our nights were dedicated to drinking and dancing. Even a little holiday romance to spice things up, when the right opportunity came our way."

"We thought Sofia had found herself a new man."

"Do you remember François, Sofia?"

"Of course she does."

"If she doesn't remember, the rest of us do. François turned up everywhere."

"What he lacked in age and height, he made up for in persistence."

"And stamina. Sofia held off his advances until our last evening."

"Evie's heard enough," Sofia protested.

"Sofia lost her handbag over the side of the tour boat. François leapt over the side to retrieve it. He'd earned his reward, and only then did she discover what she'd been missing. Her report the following morning revealed his exceptional prowess in bed."

"You do remember, Sofia. You're blushing," Lauren remarked. "Your sister's a married woman now. Talking about our conquests is one of our pleasures."

"Did you ever hear from François?" Kylie asked.

"Of course not. We both knew it was a casual holiday fling. While you remember the adventure with such delight, I had a few hours of pleasure and then I discovered my ruined passport. I remember the trouble at the airport, and afterwards I had to organise a replacement."

"We don't need a passport for Tasmania," Natalie quipped.

৪ ☼ ৫

At the nearby table, Jenny spoke quietly with Patrick Sims. He was the perfect companion for this assignment. His polished good looks concealed his role as bodyguard. One of the advantages of shadowing Evie Romano today would be a leisurely lunch. Romano was paying, and they both ordered the largest steaks. Patrick was the designated driver, so Jenny allowed herself an indulgent glass of wine. She planned to interrogate Patrick about the rescue mission. Piper Maxwell had been reticent with the details – until today, even keeping Jenny away from the other operatives.

For some reason, Piper saw Evie's protection as the higher priority. Piper had always been loyal to Romano. Was it professional pride? Or Piper's determination to face off against his estranged family? Both Romano and Piper were intelligent, strong and fiercely determined. Separately, they were formidable, but together they seemed invincible.

Piper had changed since Evie's thwarted kidnapping three weeks before her wedding. These thoughts drew Jenny's attention back to Evie. Again, she pondered the influence this woman had on her giant protector. Romano's patience with Evie had been unexpected. He could have taken her by force, but instead chose to win her heart.

"The two sisters are strikingly dissimilar," Patrick remarked.

"You think so?"

"Sofia looks like she's on the prowl for her next sexual conquest. Evie's more like an innocent child."

"Which sister is your type?"

Her companion laughed. "Neither. I prefer women with a little mystery, but with guaranteed rewards. Are you more like Sofia or Evie?"

"I'm the kind who'll kill you while you're sleeping, for your impertinence."

"Piper said you're more bark than bite."

"Did he?" Silently she promised to make Piper eat his words.

"He said you'd want information about the recent mission. I'm permitted to tell you certain things, but only if you ask the right questions."

Their food arrived. Jenny efficiently sliced into the rare steak with her knife. Glaring at him, she stabbed the severed morsel and ate from the blade.

"Start talking," she growled. Her steak was delicious, made even tastier by the discomfort of her companion. Half an hour later, her curiosity was satisfied. Jenny reviewed the main points while eating her dessert.

"Let's summarise your information. Piper made a cursory inspection of the crash site. He found a trail leading to the same road where you were parked. After detecting Valentino's hiding place, Piper executed the retrieval alone. He had the right antidote in his first-aid kit and saved the victim's life. The doctors said it was a miracle Valentino survived. They used those exact words?"

"Yes."

"After sending Valentino to Sydney by helicopter, Piper went to rural New South Wales. There he identified his next target. Everything was in place for the retrieval. But he answered his phone, climbed back into the van, and told you the plans had changed. You drove to Sydney where Piper had a meeting. Piper then went to the private clinic to meet Valentino."

"Right."

"Who made the call?"

Patrick hesitated. His unconscious glance toward Evie was sufficient.

"Something happened between Piper and Valentino? Valentino thanked Piper for saving him from drowning. During your long drive, Piper muttered about 'that river'. Afterwards, he swore everyone to secrecy. He said I'd made too much of Evie's 'miraculous' rescue. He didn't want anyone encouraging me."

"Hmmm."

"Piper will interrogate you when we get back, so tell him this. Piper shouldn't have sent me to stay with Pastor John. If he thought Evie's miraculous rescue was memorable, there's a lot he doesn't know. More than one person has seen '*that river*'."

Jenny smiled sweetly, and Patrick squirmed.

"Don't worry," Jenny assured him. "I'll be praying for your safety."

Jenny glanced across to the Tuesday Girls. She decided there would be time for another glass of wine, followed by coffee.

"Tell me about the assassination attempt again."

"Thomas followed the assassin from Melbourne. When they were within sight of the clinic, Piper pulled everyone out. In preparation, he'd told the hospital staff Valentino was still asleep. No-one was allowed in to disprove that. It was night, and the room was dark. Piper followed the assassin in but was too late to stop Valentino. The attacker's poison was used against him."

"The assassin – it wasn't one of the family, but a minion? With his death, whoever sent him remains unknown. It's not like Piper to leave a loose end."

A Hopeful Heart

❧ ☼ ☙

Psalm 127:1
Unless God builds the house the labourers work in vain.
Unless God watches over the city,
the watchman guard it in vain.

❧ ☼ ☙

It was Saturday evening, five weeks since Gypsy died, and the restaurant was full. All the waitresses were busy. A customer approached the bar, wanting to change their meal order. Sofia left her deputy Danielle in charge, while she carried the customer's request to the kitchen.

Minutes later, Danielle came looking for her. "There's someone here to see you, Sofia."

Sofia checked her hair and make-up in the mirror beside the swinging doors. Standing at the bar was a familiar figure she thought she would never see again. Valentino smiled and enveloped her in his firm embrace. She forgot where she was and kissed him.

"Sofia," she heard Papa behind her. She blushed and tried to pull away. Valentino kept one arm around her waist.

"Papa, this is Valentino Horatio. Valentino, this is my father, Benito Fontana."

"It's a pleasure to meet you." Valentino shook her father's hand. "I hope we have many opportunities to become better acquainted. I only need a few moments of your daughter's time."

Papa nodded and continued his circuit of the dining room.

"What time do you finish?" Valentino asked, his desire for her evident.

Sofia's mind scrambled for a plan. "After eleven, but I have two of my children with me. Marco's in the kitchen, and Matilda's waitressing. If you come back at ten, I'll reserve you a table, and we can talk then." Sofia was breathless with anticipation. All thoughts of the promise she had made to herself about waiting for a commitment flew from her mind. He smiled in agreement, kissed her again, and then he was gone.

"Sofia?"

"Yes, Papa?"

"Someone special?"

Sofia smiled at her father's hopeful expression.

"My Prince Charming, and I don't intend to lose him again."

ᘒ ☼ ᘓ

(Sunday 15th October)

Staring at the dim ceiling on Sunday morning, Sofia thought about the promises she had broken. Sleep eluded her. There was still one promise she intended to keep. Last night, Danielle had driven Marco and Matilda home, and Sofia's youngest son had asked if she would be there to make breakfast. She had promised him she would be. No matter how complicated her relationships, she was always home before dawn. She had not foreseen how difficult it would be to slip away.

Sofia remembered the knowing look her sixteen-year-old daughter had given her, which had made Sofia hesitate – but Valentino was insistent. When they arrived at his apartment, his intentions were clear. She had been a willing participant. Afterwards, he wanted to talk about their future, but she silenced him with another kiss. "No promises," she whispered. "My life is full of broken ones, and I don't want to ruin this moment."

Later, he had taken her on a tour of his luxurious apartment. There was a full-sized grand piano in the white living room. Remembering their first date, Sofia asked him to play. His music helped silence her doubts. Afterwards, he programmed his sound system to continue the music. They drank wine. Valentino talked about his favourite composers. Then he asked if she had travelled overseas. Retelling her adventures with the Tuesday Girls to Bali and New Zealand amused him. He talked about the exotic places he had visited, and she was fascinated.

"I'll show you the world if you promise to stay with me."

His smile had captivated her. Now he slept restlessly beside her.

"Sofia!" When Valentino called out in his sleep, his arms reached for her. "Sofia, don't leave me! Promise me you'll never leave me!"

She wrapped her arms around him, whispering to calm him. How many nights had Sofia's children slept beside her, needing her comfort? Memories came unbidden. At first, there had only been Leonardo. A scandalous divorce left her to raise her son by herself. His wicked father Nicholas was banished from her life before her son was born. To her shame, her choices had torn her comfortable family asunder.

Her jealousy had led to her sister's exile. Nicholas had lusted after Evie, and Sofia had lied, blaming her sister, to have her sent away to Sydney.

Sofia's dignity, pride and self-respect were damaged. She had promised her firstborn she would make up for her foolish mistakes. The debt was high.

A few years later, falling in love with Sven had been unexpected. The European tourist had walked into the restaurant one evening. His enthusiasm for life had enchanted her. She expected nothing more than a few nights of passion, but Sven moved into her home. He was a remedy for her loneliness. Her second pregnancy destroyed any hope Sven would be a father for her children. Sven confessed a wife and child at home, and abandoned her.

Determined not to make the same mistake again, Sofia had been more cautious. Leonardo was six and Matilda three when she married Theo. Everything about him seemed perfect. During their brief courtship, Theo showered her and the children with lavish gifts. Her family was eager to see them married.

One day, an angry woman turned up at the restaurant, in search of Sofia's new husband. The woman showed photos proving her earlier marriage to Theo. The other wife gave a heartbreaking account of an emptied bank account, and loans Theo had committed her to. After financially ruining her family business, he had disappeared. In her search for him, she had uncovered another two women who shared a similar fate.

Horrified to discover her new husband was both a bigamist and a fraud, Sofia handed him over to the authorities for prosecution. She only learned she was pregnant again after his excision from her life.

Three times, Sofia bore a child without the support of the father. She had promised she would never make that mistake again, and had taken the appropriate action. There would be no heirs for Valentino.

Her tears dampened the pillow where he lay. She gently traced the outline of his face in the dimness.

Sofia watched the awakening dawn through a chink in his bedroom curtains. Classical music still quietly played in the background, but it no longer soothed her. Valentino seemed much thinner and more solemn now. The easy laughter was gone.

She had accepted his apology for the lack of contact. The destruction of his phone during the plane crash explained why she hadn't heard from him. His long recovery in a Sydney hospital explained his troubled sleep.

It soothed her soul to have someone who needed her. Sofia dozed.

When Dreamers Dream

ॐ

Matthew 6:21 WEB
For where your treasure is, there your heart will be also.

ॐ

The familiar roar of crashing waves warned Sofia she was dreaming. But there had been a subtle change. The humidity was oppressive. Tropical jungle overhung the riverbanks. Immediately ahead was a series of rapids. Jagged, green-tinged rocks stabbed upwards out of the rainbow spray. The violent torrent surged below her – she was clinging to a branch.

"Sofia!"

Someone clung to a boulder in the midst of the river. What was this man doing in her dream? A huge wave swamped the rock, sweeping him from view. He re-emerged, driven towards the rapids.

"Sofia! Help me!" he cried, submerging again. She recognised his voice.

What was she to do? She was safe here, but Valentino needed her. Did she care enough to try and save him? Sofia let go of the branch. The waves rose over her.

With a gasp, Sofia awoke. Her heart raced. Her first thought was to call John Edwards. He would accept her frantic call with patience. John always prayed with her until the panic subsided. The usual confusion made her desperate. She tried to sit up, but a heavy weight lay across her. In horror, she remembered where she was. How could she think of calling John when she was in bed with Valentino?

In the semi-darkness, the nightmare pursued her. Memories of her passionate reunion with Valentino flashed through her mind. Remorse underlined her weakness. It was late, and Marco would be awake.

"You're not leaving me already?"

Valentino's arms dragged her back under the covers. She pushed against him.

"I have to go. I promised Marco I'd make him breakfast."

"He's a big boy. He can make himself breakfast."

"I promised!" Sofia insisted, and he studied her intently. Temptation almost overpowered her. "I'm supposed to be home before dawn."

"Phone him and say you're taking him out to breakfast. You promised your son a special breakfast, and I can make it happen."

"There are my other children to consider. Breakfast will not be enough to bribe Leonardo and Matilda. What am I to say to them?"

"Tell them I've asked you to marry me, and I wouldn't let you go."

"What?"

Valentino reached under his pillow and produced a spectacular diamond ring. "Marry me, then no-one will question why you're in my bed after dawn."

Her tears flowed as Valentino slipped the ring onto her left hand. It fitted perfectly.

"Am I still dreaming?" she whispered. Valentino brushed away her tears and kissed her.

"If this is your dream, I don't want you to wake up."

₧ ☼ ₨

Sofia phoned home. Matilda answered with a snarl.

"Where are you? I've convinced Marco you're still asleep, but he's getting impatient. You'd better buy something on the way, so you can pretend you went out to get breakfast before he woke up."

"Valentino's providing breakfast at his apartment. Tell your brothers to get dressed. A car will collect you in half an hour. I've some important news to tell you."

"This had better be good," Matilda muttered, and hung up.

Had Sofia made the right decision? She turned towards Valentino, who was talking on his phone. He reached for her as he ended the call.

Half an hour later, Sofia was standing in his lavish bathroom, preparing to dress after her shower. She watched Valentino shave. There were cosmetics and women's toiletries in his bathroom cupboards. She was jealous of the other women who had shared his life. He had already surprised her by giving her a complete change of clothes. She admired her new dress in the mirror. Sofia pushed aside the question of how he knew her exact requirements.

"You were sure I'd stay."

"If not last night, then soon. I wanted to be ready."

He sounded genuine, and she dampened her suspicion. Sofia remembered her harsh judgement when Evie had accepted Romano's gifts. Romano had transformed Evie's appearance from old-fashioned to spectacular. His choices revealed her petite figure and accentuated her delicate beauty. Sofia had expected Romano to take advantage of her sister's naivety. How wrong she had been. Another regret.

Sofia inhaled sharply. She had forgotten it was Sunday!

"What's wrong?" he asked. Valentino set aside his razor to hold her.

"I can't stay with you all day. I can apologise for missing Mass with Mama. But Papa never accepts any excuse. The children and I have to be at the restaurant by one o'clock. My sister and her husband will be there."

"Surely your Papa will accept your fiancé at lunch? I know we aren't married yet, but I believe the family invitation would extend to me too?"

Sofia blinked in surprise. "Of course you'll be welcome. Are you sure you're ready for this?"

"It's time your family learned about our plans. If I survive your parents' scrutiny, I'll introduce you to my mother this afternoon."

"You have to survive breakfast with my children first," Sofia reminded him. "They'll be here soon, and I won't have them finding us undressed."

A Timely Test

ಐ ☼ ಚ

Micah 6:8

The Lord has shown you what is good.
What does He require of you, but to act justly,
to love mercy, and to walk humbly with your God?

ಐ ☼ ಚ

As he drove them to *Ristorante di Fontana* for lunch, Valentino was confident in his welcome as a future son-in-law. His only uncertainty was how Romano would respond. He regretted this complication. Valentino had not foreseen that their inevitable meeting would be today. Too late, he realised he should have asked Piper to deliver a message. Nothing must interfere with Valentino's relationship with Sofia.

Sofia's children had behaved as expected. Her eldest son, Leonardo, seemed more mature than his nineteen years. His quietness spoke volumes. He had feigned disinterest in the luxurious apartment, then ordered sparingly from the menu. It would be easy to persuade Leonardo to get a separate apartment.

The middle child had gazed at him with speculation. Sixteen-year-old Matilda alone was fair-haired. It seemed inevitable the girl would follow after her mother in affairs of the heart. As she assessed his value, Matilda paraded herself before him. He knew she was ready to leave home. Once, he might have been tempted, but he was wary of capricious girls. Now Valentino sought a mature woman. Someone who would be satisfied with the security he had to offer.

A whirlwind of curiosity and chatter, the youngest son was impressionable. The grand piano in the living room had instantly drawn him. After Marco had bashed out a few bars of Chopsticks, he was exploring again. Valentino would have to be careful with this teenager. He asked too many questions. Marco was tall for thirteen. His innocence was reminiscent of Valentino's cousin Piper at a younger age.

Valentino's future was set by thirteen, his heart already poisoned by his family's evil influence. He had ridiculed Piper's focus on justice and mercy. When Piper had asked permission to join the army, the family believed they would benefit, but Valentino saw it as a betrayal. He knew his cousin was running away.

Valentino's attention returned to Sofia's youngest son. Would this youth also run? How would that impact on his relationship with Sofia? Sofia's love for her youngest child was strong, but he could not risk his family gaining control of the boy. It would be prudent to separate them soon.

He smiled at the secret knowledge Sofia could have no more children. When would she broach the subject with him? That would reveal how secure she felt with their relationship. Valentino was undecided whether he would make a similar confession. His first rebellion had been to ensure his family would be deprived of another heir.

His two daughters were with their mother. He had cultivated his ex-wife's resentment into hatred to keep the girls safe.

These thoughts preoccupied him as he drove Sofia and her offspring to the restaurant. The three children disappeared through the private entrance. Sofia was flustered. Valentino held her, offering the security of his presence.

Romano's red Maserati roared into the car park. Sofia looked up, and Valentino held her firmly in place. Let them come to him.

"My sister Evie's here."

Romano stepped out, towering over the sports car. The slender woman who joined him emphasised Romano's bulk. Valentino had only seen Evie from a distance. He marvelled at the difference between the two sisters. Cosmetic artifice and her excellent sense of style enhanced Sofia's beauty. Her sensual allure was undeniable.

Despite their age difference being only three years, the younger sister seemed child-like. Her unbound hair and modest dress emphasised her simplicity of style. It was immediately apparent she only had eyes for her husband.

"Evie's changed so much since she met Romano. But today she's glowing. I wonder if she's already pregnant?"

Prudently, Valentino held his tongue. There was no easy way to explain how he knew the Romano couple were expecting twins. His family had been accidental witnesses when Evie made the announcement to her husband on Friday evening, at his brother's nightclub, *Renaissance*. Valentino had only paid attention because his cousin Piper had been there as part of Evie's security detail. His brother Enzo was more interested in Romano, a man he had tried unsuccessfully to influence. Then unexpectedly, their mother confessed prior patronage for Evie. Doña Gabriella Marcella proclaimed a covenant of protection to Evie and her husband, in exchange for a blessing. Enzo did not seem pleased that the matriarch had declared the Romano couple untouchable. It would not be long before Enzo's aborted plan to control Evie through her sister reawakened.

How many more lives would this family destroy? Immediately, Valentino brought forward his own plan to break free from them. Recent events confirmed he should take Sofia with him.

Romano's stony glare fixed on Valentino as the sisters embraced. A silent warning passed between them. Neither of them wanted the women to know the details of their previous association.

"Evie, I want to introduce you to Valentino Horatio." Sofia was oblivious to the tension. "He's asked me to marry him."

"Hello, Evie. Congratulations on your recent marriage."

Was it his imagination? Did Evie take a step backwards? Her eyes narrowed, and her smile faltered. He was sure they'd never met. He hadn't known of her existence until Piper had called him to deal with her kidnappers. Was it possible she had seen him then? If so, it added another complication.

Marco rushed back into the car park. "Hurry up!"

Should Valentino offer up a prayer of thanks for such a providential intervention? Perhaps there was something to his mother's claim that Evie brought a blessing to anyone who was on her side. His plans to rescue Sofia from his family must win him favour with God.

Sofia led the way to the dining room. Valentino strained his ears to hear the whispered conversation behind them.

"Keep your thoughts to yourself, little Evie. Piper and I will take care of him..."

A Dangerous Decision

ଓ ☼ ଓ

Ephesians 6:10 WEB
Finally, be strong in the Lord,
and in the strength of His might.

ଓ ☼ ଓ

The message came mid-afternoon, only minutes after their return to his apartment. Without looking at his phone, Valentino knew Piper was on his way.

Matilda and Leonardo had left them to meet with friends. Her parents had been persuaded to look after Marco so Sofia could prepare to meet his mother.

The meal had been pleasant. Benito and Rosa had been cautious about the engagement. Sofia had seemed oblivious to the tension between the Romano couple and Valentino. As there had been no opportunity for Romano to speak with Valentino alone, this visit was inevitable.

"I apologise, Sofia. We have company, and I have some documents to prepare."

"Is everything okay?"

"My cousin Piper is unpredictable, but he's one of the few people I trust. We've not been on good terms recently, but I can assure you he's reliable in times of trouble. He was responsible for my rescue."

Before she could reply, there came a firm knock at the door.

"You let Piper in, while I get the documents."

Sofia was at the door when he returned from his study. Valentino was wrong. Piper was not alone. An unknown woman accompanied him.

"Hello, Sofia," the woman said. "May I introduce my employer, Piper Maxwell. Valentino is expecting us."

"He was expecting Piper, but he didn't say anything about you."

The woman grinned at Piper. "I told you he wouldn't read your message."

"Piper," Valentino demanded. "Why does Sofia know your companion?"

"This is Jenny Prescott, my Second-in-Command. She's here to support Sofia."

Jenny walked around the room with an electronic gadget in her hand. After completing a circuit she nodded, and Piper continued. Had she scanned his apartment for listening devices?

"Your plane crash coincided with a request to identify John Edwards. He was already known to us. Once we recognised his link with Sofia, and realised she'd been with you, we began watching Sofia."

"You should have told me," Valentino growled.

"You didn't ask," Piper said.

"I'm asking now. Who is John Edwards?"

"Sofia will tell you."

"He's a professional counsellor," Sofia said. "I've talked to him on the phone every day since I found Gypsy's body.

Jenny has my calls recorded if you want to confirm he's only a friend."

"Jealousy is unbecoming, cousin," Piper interjected. "Time is limited. Romano wants to know why you're marrying Sofia."

"That's none of his business," Sofia spluttered.

Piper said, "How much does she know?"

"Know about what?" Sofia demanded.

Valentino glared at Piper. "I wanted to shield her."

"Shield me from what?"

Valentino took Sofia in his arms and led her to a sofa. He would have to tell Sofia enough of the truth to satisfy his cousin. Piper and Jenny remained standing.

"The plane crash was no accident. Someone tried to kill me, not once but twice. Piper believes someone in my family is responsible. That's why I didn't return straight away. I needed to be strong in case they tried again."

"Have they tried?"

"Not yet, but as soon as I learned your friend Gypsy was dead, I became concerned for you. I knew Gypsy was in debt to my brother Enzo. It was my brother who sent me to visit Gypsy the day we met. Gypsy was already talking about you before you arrived. I was a fool and fell into their trap. Enzo was furious when I came back from our date without arranging to see you again."

"Why would your brother be interested in me?"

"You're Evie's sister. My brother wants leverage over Romano. He tried to get to him through Evie. When that failed, he looked for another angle."

"I don't understand!" Sofia sprang to her feet. "Why did you ask me to marry you?"

"I want to protect you from him. If you're married to me, Enzo won't touch you. My mother wouldn't allow it."

"What's your mother got to do with this?"

"My mother knew Evie in Sydney. She's offered Evie a covenant of protection. Enzo knows better than to break our mother's promise."

"You tell a colourful tale, cousin," Piper interjected. "If you don't tell Sofia you love her, she'll walk out that door."

"Words are cheap." Valentino picked up the documents and began to spread them out. "Many men have declared their love for Sofia, but she's alone. I have another way of showing her how much she means to me. I'm making Sofia my legal heir. Piper, as soon as you witness my signature, I'll transfer the first instalment into her bank. Over the coming weeks, we'll go through my assets and decide what she wants to keep, and what I will sell."

Sofia opened her mouth to protest, but Valentino shook his head as he drew her closer.

"Are you sure you want to do this?" Piper asked after he and Jenny examined the documents. Valentino knew Piper understood this would draw out his hidden opponent. Piper studied him before speaking again. "Who knows about this?"

"Only the lawyer, and now you. I went to a law firm without family connections. I wanted to secure Sofia's future, in case anything happened to me before the wedding."

"What about your previous wife and your daughters?" Piper asked.

"I've already made a generous settlement. My ex-wife has a wealthy husband who has adopted the girls. They're moving to Europe. My father set up a trust fund for them. Their finances are secure."

Piper seemed thoughtful. "You've been planning this for a while?"

"I knew the break from my family was coming."

"What if Sofia doesn't want to marry you now?"

"She keeps the money, and if anything happens to me, she'll inherit my estate. I'll have to trust you and Romano to keep her safe."

The room fell silent.

"If you'd told me this yesterday, I'd have walked away, but I've already given you my promise." Sofia studied her new engagement ring. "You cried out for me in your sleep, and I know you care for me. With or without your money, I want to marry you."

Valentino felt unexpectedly relieved. He leaned towards her and kissed her briefly, before returning his attention to his cousin.

Piper and Jenny witnessed his signature on the documents. Valentino gave one copy to Piper for safekeeping and presented another to Sofia. The final copy lay on the coffee table.

Valentino turned to Piper. "My mother will arrive in thirty minutes. Are you staying?"

Piper declined. His pen remained on the coffee table. Valentino pocketed it. There had been no listening devices before Piper arrived, but Valentino was sure there was one now.

"What are you going to tell Romano?" Sofia asked Piper.

"The truth – you're making an informed choice to marry Valentino."

"Thank you."

"I'll ask your sister to pray for you. There's trouble ahead. You'll need a miracle to come through this unscathed."

The tall security agent left without another word. Jenny followed him, pausing in the doorway. "The usual security measures remain in place. If you need help, Sofia, you know who to call."

An awkward silence followed their departure. Before Sofia could find her voice, there came an insistent rap-tap-tap at the door.

"My mother's early," Valentino muttered.

Sofia ran to the bathroom, and he suddenly realised she was in tears.

He swore. He hadn't counted on Piper's visit upsetting Sofia, and he felt a small regret. Valentino expected his mother's visit to end unpleasantly, once he drew the battle lines.

The rapping sounded again. Patience was not one of his mother's virtues. He straightened his jacket and opened the door. He encountered another surprise. His mother was not alone. Without waiting for an invitation, Doña Gabriella Marcella swept into the room, her extended entourage following in her wake.

"You're early, and I didn't invite anyone else."

"I'll bring whomever I choose." His aged mother took a regal position on one of the sofas. She gestured with her hand, and the other women arranged themselves around the room. "I've ordered refreshments. What was so important you insisted I visit you here in your apartment? Something you didn't want your brother to hear?"

When Sofia emerged from the bathroom, Valentino hurried to her.

"I'm sorry," he whispered. "I didn't know my mother would bring everyone."

Sofia took a deep breath and smiled. His admiration for her increased. He led her by the hand towards his mother. "I would like to introduce you to my fiancée, Sofia Fontana. Sofia, this is my mother, Doña Gabriella Marcella Horatio."

The contrast between the two women was dramatic. Sofia stood at ease in her colourful attire, sensuously dark. Where had she found this new strength? She faced his unsmiling ninety-two-year-old mother without hesitation.

The ancient woman was pale, her white hair pulled severely into a bun and topped with a lace veil. Her elegant floor-length black dress emphasised the thinness of her frame. His mother held herself upright with pride. Her only adornment was a gold crucifix paired with a long string of pearls around her neck. She grasped an ivory-handled walking stick, which she now rapped on the floor in annoyance.

Sofia murmured a greeting and waited for him to introduce the others. He began by seniority.

"My sisters, Theresa, Beatrice, Cecilia and Diana." The four women nodded their heads in turn. Each one was elegantly dressed and adept at concealing their ages. They had been born two years apart. Diana was the youngest at fifty-four, eleven years older than Valentino.

"My sister-in-law Sabrina. She's recently celebrated her sixtieth birthday." Sabrina attempted a gracious smile. She was the opposite of his sisters, who were thin like their mother. Sabrina's hair was dyed blonde, while his sisters were dark.

"The younger generations can introduce themselves."

One by one, the younger women gave their names. Collectively, they were all beautifully presented.

There was a knock at the door, and Sofia answered it. She played hostess for his extended family as if it were an ordinary occurrence. Three waiters wheeled in draped tables bearing assorted delicacies. There were hot beverages in shiny silver pots. Sofia served each woman in turn. She began with his mother, then his sisters and sister-in-law. She continued until she had served everyone, before bringing

Valentino his coffee. Her smile remained welcoming. Only her trembling hand on his arm revealed her emotions.

"You're nothing like your sister," his mother declared. "She would not bring dishonour to her family by playing the harlot with my son."

"You're right," replied Sofia firmly. "I'm nothing like my sister. I'm a twice-divorced mother to three teenagers, and I know how to take care of myself. I've had many lovers, and I'm determined to make your son happy."

One of the younger women giggled, and someone silenced her.

"You have three children? Sons or daughters?"

"I have two sons and a daughter."

"Will you give my son an heir?"

"No."

His mother's countenance darkened. He had better follow through with his plan before she stormed from the scene.

"I invited you here to give you this," Valentino said, handing his mother the legal documents. "Following the wedding, I'll be leaving to start a new life with Sofia. I've served the family well, but you and my brother have declared me useless, so I'm making myself redundant."

"You ungrateful boy!"

"I've already discussed this with my uncle in Sydney, and he understands my situation. Augustus has offered me his support."

Doña Gabriella Marcella straightened to her full height, her white knuckles clutching her cane. Valentino moderated his expression. The family arose en masse and followed his mother from his apartment. A few made an awkward attempt at saying farewell. One of the younger women turned back from the door. She rushed over and hugged Sofia, before making her escape.

This sensitive gesture proved too much for Sofia. As the door closed behind them, she dissolved into tears. "You said your mother would approve of me!"

"That was before she met your sister. Now everyone must measure up to Evie's standards. I could apologise, but I predicted her reaction."

"You could have warned me!"

"I hadn't counted on Piper's interruption or my mother's early arrival. I'm sorry, Sofia. Dry your eyes. You stood up to her. I'm very proud."

She sniffed. "I don't like being compared to Evie. I've tried to be like her and failed miserably. I've only myself to blame for this mess."

"Is that why you were so distant on our first date?"

Taking the handkerchief he offered, she nodded. He smiled as another puzzle piece slipped into place. Guiding her back to the sofa, he sought out her phone.

"Now would be a good time to call your counsellor."

Sofia gasped, her eyes wide.

He continued, "You're distressed, and I understand your need." To his immense satisfaction, she attempted a smile.

"I fccl much better already. I have you, and you're all I need."

CHAPTER 24
(Monday 16th October)

Stressful Surprises

❦ ✵ ❧

Psalm 119:165 WEB
Those who love Your law have great peace.
Nothing causes them to stumble.

❦ ✵ ❧

Sofia paced the room. Why was she hesitating? She had chatted with Evie during lunch yesterday without any awkwardness.

The phone in her hand buzzed with an incoming call. Sofia glanced at the caller ID. It was her sister.

"Hello, Evie."

"Hi, Sofia, are you free to talk?"

Sofia caught her breath and dropped onto her bed. "Is everything alright?"

Evie laughed. "Hmmm, I think so. I'm still getting used to being married. Sebastian wants me to stop working, but what will I do all day? He asked me if I was joining you for lunch again this week. That's one of the reasons I'm calling."

"The Tuesday Girls would love you to join them, Evie, and so would I. Your presence will deflect some of the attention from me. I still haven't told them about my engagement."

161

"They'll be excited for you, Sofia. Are you feeling uncertain?"

Sofia bit her lip. "You said there was more than one reason you phoned?"

"Sofia, I don't know if I can say this over the phone."

"Why not?"

"I'm better face to face. I need to see how you're responding."

"Speak freely. I'm your sister. I won't hold back if I've something to say."

"Okay – right – well, I was praying for you this morning..."

"You were praying for me!"

"To be honest, I pray for you every morning, so that's not unusual. But while I was praying, I believe God told me to call you. He said you had something to ask me. Am I making any sense?"

"Yes, Evie, you're making perfect sense. I've been thinking about calling you for the past two hours, and wasn't sure how to begin."

Evie sighed. Sofia sensed the silence between them was not empty.

"I wish I had your faith, Evie. You're able to stop and pray in the middle of a crisis, then pick up again as if nothing happened. John's the only other person I know who does that."

"John Edwards? I didn't know the two of you were friends. He asked after you yesterday. With all the excitement, I forgot to pass on his greeting."

"I'm glad you forgot. My friendship with John makes things difficult. Valentino says he understands why I needed a counsellor, especially after I found Gypsy dead..."

"You found Gypsy? Sofia, I didn't know!'

"No-one's supposed to know. Jenny made us promise."

"Sofia, are you crying?"

"I've been crying a lot lately. John said God's softening my heart so I can learn to accept His forgiveness."

"There's truth in that, Sofia. Thanks for letting me into your confidence. I'll talk to Jenny. I felt sure you recognised her last Tuesday. You were right to warn me to take care with Sebastian, but not for the reasons you thought. He's an honourable man, and other people have tried to take advantage of his situation. That's why I have bodyguards whenever I go out alone. Jenny, and Patrick Sims, the man who was with her, are my favourites."

"I met Piper Maxwell yesterday," Sofia continued. "Piper wanted Valentino to explain his recent troubles. I remembered the things I said about your relationship with Romano, and I felt ashamed. I'm sorry for not listening to you."

"You met Piper? You had an eventful afternoon. How did you fair with your future mother-in-law?"

"It was a disaster. Valentino's mother took an immediate dislike, and I didn't help myself."

"Oh, Sofia, I'm sorry."

"Evie, she said she knew you. I'm sure you'd remember her – Doña Gabriella Marcella. She was dressed in black from head to toe. She was disappointed because I'm not like you. I got angry, and I was rude to her."

"What did Valentino say?"

"He apologised for not warning me."

"It sounds as if there's lots for me to pray about, Sofia. Don't hesitate to contact me. I'm here for you."

Her sister prayed aloud. Sofia experienced the same serenity that came when John prayed for her. After the conversation ended, Sofia sat with her eyes closed. But the peace didn't last.

This time it was Valentino phoning. Sofia's heart skipped a beat.

"Sofia, I've been trying to contact you for the past half hour."

"I'm sorry. I was talking to Evie."

"What did she say to our request?"

"I forgot to ask her."

"Sofia! We agreed that asking Evie to host your children was important. Romano's place is like a fortress."

"I still don't understand why they're in danger. You said your mother offered Evie's family a covenant of protection. Doesn't that apply to my children?"

"My mother disapproves of you. My enemies may decide your children are outside the covenant. They could try to come between us through them."

"It doesn't feel right to ask Evie to take in three teenagers."

"It's only temporary. I'm sure my enemies will act soon, and then we'll be free to make other provisions."

"I'm seeing Evie tomorrow. Romano wants her to come to lunch with the Tuesday Girls. I'll ask her then."

"You need to phone her now. Circumstances have changed. I'm going overseas again, and I won't go without you. Do you know where your passport is? I need to arrange visas for you. Our flight leaves on Friday morning."

"I can't drop everything and leave the country."

"You promised you'd help to secure our future. Have you changed your mind?"

"No, but—"

"Talk to your sister, and make the arrangements. We'll only be away for a week. Tell your family I'm nervous about flying, or tell them I'm not well enough to travel alone. I'll call by the restaurant in an hour."

Sofia held her head in her hands. What was she to do? Everything he said made perfect sense, yet her mind screamed resistance. She fell to her knees but was unable to find the words. Would God listen? Her phone rang again.

"Sofia, this is Jenny. Phone your sister. Piper says you should go on this trip with Valentino. Leave your children with Evie. Someone will secretly travel with you. There's no need to mention my call to Valentino. Piper will tell him what he needs to know."

Jenny didn't wait for a reply. Sofia sighed. She had tried praying, and this answer came. She picked up her phone and made the call.

"Sofia? Is something wrong?"

"I'm sorry, Evie. Valentino has to go overseas. He's still recovering from the plane crash and wants me to go with him. I said I have the children to think of..."

"Sebastian and I will have them."

"Are you sure?"

"There's plenty of room, provided Leonardo and Marco are still happy to share. Sebastian said I should offer to have them when you go on your honeymoon. I'm sure he won't mind if it happens a little sooner. When do you have to leave?"

"Friday morning."

"Do you know where you're going?"

"I forgot to ask. Valentino insists this will be the last time he has to travel for his brother. He's making big changes before the wedding, so we have a better chance of making this relationship work."

"I'm praying for your future happiness."

Evie's words haunted Sofia.

ঙ ☼ ଓ

"I don't believe this!" Leonardo was furious. "How could you ask Evie? You selfish—"

"Think what you like. It was Romano's idea to invite you." Sofia was glad she had gone out to the restaurant car park to meet Leonardo. "I've tried to do my best for the three of you. Matilda and Marco are okay with this. Valentino needs me, and I'm going. Just remember it's not my fault if you get into trouble while I'm away."

He drove away without waiting for Marco to come out. Matilda was already at home. Sofia waited for the tears to stop. Screeching tyres announced Leonardo's unexpected return.

"I've talked to the Boss. He put me straight about some details you neglected to tell me."

"Did he?" Sofia bristled.

"Yes. You should have said the Boss is worried about Evie's health. Did you know she's pregnant? No, I didn't think so. She hasn't told anyone yet. The doctor said she has to take extra care. Looking after us will be a welcome distraction."

CHAPTER 25
(Friday 20th October)

Seeds of Suspicion

ಜ ☼ ಜ

Jeremiah 30:21b
"I will draw him near, and he will approach Me;
because he had boldness to approach Me," says the Lord.

ಜ ☼ ಜ

"What are you doing here?" Valentino leapt to his feet. An elegant older woman wearing high heels and heavy makeup stopped at their table.

"It's nice to see you too, little brother. Hello, Sofia. You remember me, Theresa, his eldest sister? I'm looking forward to this little holiday. Thailand is one of my favourite destinations. You haven't met my husband yet, Raymond Serpios."

Raymond stepped forward, and Sofia shook his hand. The rotund little man with the receding hairline smirked at her. He avoided Valentino's glare. Valentino laid hold of Sofia's arm, and Raymond released her.

"What are you doing here?" Valentino repeated.

Theresa laughed. "You didn't think Enzo would send you to Thailand alone? You told Enzo this would be your final overseas trip for the family. Enzo has to ensure you don't sabotage any future deals."

167

"That explains Raymond's presence. But you've always refused any business involvement."

Theresa stared back at him. Only the family knew his sister's real age. The seventy-two-year-old spent thousands of dollars maintaining her youthful appearance. He felt sorry for Raymond, ten years younger but ancient in comparison.

"Enzo told me you were bringing Sofia. What do you think she'll do while you're attending your meetings? We can take her sightseeing. Now she won't languish in the hotel *alone*."

Valentino marked Theresa's choice of words, not liking her suggestive intonation.

"You said 'we'. Who else is coming?"

"Your other sisters refused to miss out. I've left them in the bookshop. Their husbands are checking in our luggage. We all flew to Sydney last night to avoid having an early start. I don't know why you didn't book one of the direct flights from Melbourne. That would have been much more convenient. It would be easy to think you wanted to make it difficult for anyone to accompany you. Look at the results of your selfishness. Poor Sofia's already drooping."

Valentino frowned, shrugged his shoulders and sat down. Sofia dropped into her seat and looked from him to Theresa. His sister didn't wait for an invitation to sit with them. Raymond hurried towards the coffee machine. The First Class Lounge was almost empty.

Valentino's eyes narrowed. He had considered and rejected the possibility his enemy would travel on the same plane. He viewed Raymond as impotent. The small man always annoyed him with his subservient manner. Was Raymond the pawn of one of the others, or had Valentino been wrong in his assessment?

Was Theresa the mastermind? His failure to consider his sister's influence hit him hard. He remembered Theresa's ruthless ambition when she was younger. Breaking eye contact, Theresa turned her attention to Sofia. Valentino felt a twinge of guilt.

"Sofia, is this your first trip to Thailand?"

"Yes."

"I can't imagine you've had many opportunities to travel. I'm surprised Valentino was able to get your passport and visas organised at short notice. Some of the countries on our itinerary can be problematic."

"I've been overseas several times with my girlfriends, so I'm not a novice. Valentino went to Canberra for the visas."

"Here comes Raymond with my coffee, just the way I like it, without needing to be told. He's such a considerate husband. I feel sorry for you. My brother thinks only of himself. He'll forget about you as soon as you satisfy his immediate needs. But perhaps that suits you? His meetings will leave you free to seek other entertainment."

Valentino placed his hand over Sofia's. "I trust Sofia to make the right decisions," he assured Theresa. His sister smiled, sipped her coffee, and made no further comment. The group sat in uncomfortable silence until the lounge attendant approached. She informed them their flight was ready to board.

₧ ✲ ∓

Standing in the shorter queue, where Business and First Class passengers were brought together, Sofia felt anxious. She leaned closer to Valentino, savouring the scent of his aftershave. He wore his customary dark suit, white shirt and tie. Sofia had teamed a simple linen dress with her flat sandals.

Without her heels, she felt small beside him. Her fiancé smiled at her, before looking over her head. Sofia followed his gaze. His family were joining the line.

"You have an admirer," Valentino said. Sofia glanced towards the economy passengers. An attractive young man was staring at her.

Mindful of Theresa's suggestive comments, Sofia put her arms around Valentino's waist. She silently vowed not to look at the other man.

"I've many admirers. But I'm promised to you. When I commit to a relationship, I don't look elsewhere. I take your comment as a warning, though. Your sister would enjoy accusing me."

"You only have to put up with her for the week. After that, it won't matter what she thinks. I'll be free." He kissed her as if affirming his pledge.

Valentino planned to walk away from his family. What if he expected her to make a similar sacrifice? She had not expected her lifestyle to change. Why was she travelling overseas? She should be helping her parents with the Friday preparations.

When it was their turn to board the plane, Sofia followed Valentino. Upstairs, she was in awe of the spacious seats and the additional legroom. Valentino dealt with her hand luggage. He sat down, and invited her to face him on the bench seat that would become his footrest later in the flight. Sofia smiled as he held her hand. Later, she would occupy the seat beside him, with only a small divider between them. There would be plenty of room for her to fully recline when she needed to catch up on her rest. The extra comfort would make the nine-and-a-half-hour trip easier.

One by one, his sisters and their husbands were seated nearby. Each one of his relatives paused to acknowledge their presence. There were only forty seats on this level. Sofia thought about Jenny's promise that she wouldn't travel unprotected. How would they follow her in Thailand? She glanced down at the silver bangle Evie had asked her to wear. Did it conceal a tracking device? To diminish its presence, Sofia had added three similar ornaments.

The wrap-around booths hid the nearby passengers. Sofia would pretend his family weren't here. One of the flight attendants came to welcome them. Champagne would be served immediately after takeoff. Two meals were scheduled. They could choose from the menu, between traditional Thai cuisine or Australian fare. Sofia began to feel more comfortable. She sent a message to Evie to say the flight was departing.

Take-off was as thrilling as always. Unfortunately, the added luxury did nothing to compensate for the family's interference. At irregular intervals, someone found a reason to intrude. The men came seeking clarification about the future business meetings. Valentino dismissed them rudely. These men were bold with their stares. Sofia had dressed to please her fiancé. Now she longed for something more concealing. She wouldn't trust herself alone with any of them. For the past five years, Sofia had denounced Romano for his criminal past, but she had never felt threatened by him. What did this say about these men?

His sisters asked impertinent questions.

"How long do you think you can keep Valentino interested?"

"Do you know he prefers young girls?"

"Have you agreed to an open relationship?"

"Do you feel any shame in accepting his money?"

Valentino left her to fend for herself.

Later, Valentino dismissed her to her own seat, and turned off the overhead light. There was a four-hour time difference between Sydney and Bangkok. It would still be afternoon when they arrived. Rest was essential because dinner with his family was the next ordeal. She lay still. He was facing her and she didn't want to disturb his sleep with her own restlessness.

And she didn't want to risk the return of her river nightmare.

An Anticipated Arrival

ॐ ☼ ॐ

Isaiah 26:4
Trust in the Lord forever,
for the Lord God is an eternal Rock.

ॐ ☼ ॐ

"Is that all the luggage you brought?"

Sofia spun from the baggage carousel. Theresa stood behind her. Raymond was loading a trolley with expensive matching luggage. The other couples also had loaded carts. Sofia looked at her battered suitcase.

Valentino had left Sofia to collect their luggage while he made travel arrangements. They still had to pass through customs, but he assured her this would be easy. He returned as she was retrieving his black suitcase from the conveyer belt.

The line through customs was long. A uniformed man rushed forward when she and Valentino approached.

"Mr Horatio. It is a pleasure to see you again. Please come this way. We have been expecting you and your guest. The remainder of your family are on their way?"

"Hello, Mr Wattana. Thank you for meeting us. My fiancée is looking forward to her first visit to Bangkok.

Where else would I choose to stay but your fine establishment."

"Your family have always honoured us by staying at the *Maena Sakhay*. I remember your mother attended the grand opening twenty years ago. She's not accompanying you on this trip?"

"Mother prefers the dry season."

"Understandable. The monsoons are still upon us. The weather will be changeable. I have arranged priority service for you through customs. Please accompany me."

The small man bowed graciously. He left them with the customs official. Sofia now understood Valentino's request to pack sparingly. It took only a few minutes for both of them to undergo the mandatory inspection. She glanced back. Raymond was beginning a more extensive process with that mountain of luggage.

Valentino swept her towards the exit. Outside the air-conditioned building, the humidity hit Sofia. A light rain was falling. They moved along a covered walkway towards a second building. The building's tinted windows bore an image of a life-sized helicopter. Once inside, air-conditioning chilled them.

Another uniformed man bowed. "Your helicopter is ready, Mr Horatio. Please come this way. I will bring the remainder of your party when they arrive."

Sofia hurried to keep up. Again, they were outside. The uniformed man held a large red umbrella over their heads. The helicopter rotor blades were already turning. Another uniformed man took their luggage. There were two empty seats, but Valentino didn't wait. Valentino gave the helmeted pilot a signal. As the door slammed shut, the pilot increased the engine's power.

Sofia had never flown by helicopter, and hurried to put on the headphones. She grinned at Valentino but he was studying the pilot.

"It takes ten minutes to get to the hotel," Valentino informed her. "But the helipad on the roof only accommodates one landing at a time. I've chartered a larger helicopter for Theresa and the others. They'll have to wait until this one has cleared the landing area. We'll have time to shower and change before we see them again."

His kisses said more.

Sofia thought of his family. "What about their luggage?"

"Their luggage will go by car and get there in half an hour if the traffic is good. That should delay them further. I'm sure Theresa will want to change before dinner."

"Are you okay? You're watching the pilot."

He laughed and relaxed into his seat. "I've been back into the flight simulator and am cleared to fly again. Some of my meetings will be outside Bangkok. I'll pilot a chartered helicopter to and from those locations. I want to make sure I'm back with you in the evenings." He kissed her again. "I originally planned to take a Robinson three-seater. But with the others tagging along, I've booked an Airbus. The Airbus requires two crew, so I need another pilot. Raymond complains about my unnecessary risks."

"Do you take unnecessary risks?"

"Only to frighten Raymond. Nothing I haven't already perfected in the simulator. At first, I thought I could discourage him from accompanying me, but he's proven persistent. But I didn't expect to see him or Theresa at Sydney airport. I'd hoped we'd have Bangkok to ourselves."

Rat-a-tat-tat. Rat-a-tat-tat.

Valentino smiled at Sofia, still in her separate dressing room, as he passed the open doors on his way up the long hallway towards the apartment entrance. Valentino walked along a wood panelled gallery decorated with gold framed paintings and antique statues. He wore loose black pants. An open-necked blue shirt revealed the gold cross on his muscular chest, a legacy of his association with the deceased pilot Silvania. Valentino's feet were bare, and his hair damp.

"Theresa, what a surprise. You're on your own?"

Theresa went into the formal living room. She chose one of the armchairs, then served herself from the champagne in ice buckets on the coffee table.

"The others will be along later," Theresa said. "Dinner will be delivered here because your dining table seats ten. We need to get some of the finer details finalised tonight. We don't want any public unpleasantness."

"I was surprised to find Mother's favourite suite allocated to me," Valentino replied. "I expected you to claim it for yourself, since you usually share with her."

"I felt like a change. Besides, if I stayed here, one of the other girls would want to join me, and for once I wanted a suite to myself. Raymond and I are in Enzo's usual suite."

"So where are the others staying?" Valentino asked.

"We're all on the thirty-sixth floor. I thought you'd be happier to have two floors between us."

Sofia came into the room, and Valentino poured her a drink. He slipped his arm around her waist.

"You look lovely," he whispered, and Sofia sighed. A tentative smile formed on her lips. She was wearing a long sleeveless cotton dress that fitted perfectly. The set of bangles and his ring were her only accessories. He approved her decision to go for a more casual look.

Sofia's attire contrasted with his sister's elaborate silk outfit and her ostentatious jewels. Theresa favoured heavy rings and gold bracelets. She also wore a double-stranded pearl rosary and a gold crucifix. That had been a seventieth-birthday present from their mother.

"Theresa says we're dining here."

Sofia nodded and took another sip.

"I trust Sofia's happy with the suite?" Theresa asked with an unpleasant smile.

Sofia finally spoke. "More than happy. Do I have you to thank?"

"Yes. I thought the second bedroom would be appreciated. It will give you both privacy for entertaining."

Sofia stiffened at the insult. "Valentino won't be 'entertaining' other women."

"I was thinking more of you, Sofia," Theresa explained. "My brother will be away during the day. A beautiful woman like you will attract attention. I wanted to save you the problem of bringing someone back to my brother's bed."

"Your presence will be a helpful reminder I'm saving myself for Valentino," Sofia replied. Then she turned to Valentino. "There aren't enough chairs. Should I go and fetch two more?"

"If you hadn't sent the butler away, you could have summoned him," Theresa retorted. "But I've taken care of that too. When I phoned to arrange for dinner, they informed me of your rash decision. Your butler will return soon. He can move the furniture and extend the table. That knock at the door will be the others. Sofia, go and let them in."

CHAPTER 27
(Friday 20th October)

Change Is Coming

ഇ ✡ ഌ

Ephesians 1:4
God chose us before the beginning of the world
to be holy and without fault before Him.

ഇ ✡ ഌ

When Sofia answered the door, she discovered Theresa was wrong. Mr Wattana, the man from the airport, had come to reinstate the butler.

"Please accept my apology for using the main entrance. I wanted to ensure Mr Horatio approved the counter-instructions for the evening."

"The apology should be ours, Mr Wattana, for inconveniencing you. Are you telling me there's another entrance? Could you show me?"

Sofia moved towards the hallway, and the two men followed. Mr Wattana led her to another door.

"There are four entrances to your apartment. The main entrance, a private entrance to each of the guest wings, and this one. It opens into the pantry. Your butler Chaisai will come and go by this entrance. That allows him to perform his duties without being intrusive. He sleeps here, making himself available to serve you at any time. The dining room is through there. Usually, Chaisai would have explained this when he welcomed you. I understand Mr Horatio was eager to refresh after the long flight and sent Chaisai away."

"Again, I apologise for that error. Mr Wattana, I appreciate the gracious way you have come yourself to explain our mistake."

Mr Wattana stood taller, his smile widened. Determined to build on this small beginning, Sofia continued into the dining room.

"I'd like to observe the preparations. At home, my family has a modest restaurant, and I'm responsible for training our staff. I'm always curious to see how other people do things."

"I will leave you with Chaisai," Mr Wattana said with a bow. "May you enjoy a pleasant dinner, and I hope your stay with us is joyous, Miss Fontana."

Helping Chaisai extend the dining table helped settle her nerves. They brought in extra chairs. Chaisai left her standing in the alcove looking out at the city. Twilight had fallen and the city lights called to her from the darkness. It was six-thirty here, ten-thirty at home.

Thoughts of home reminded her about her secret phone call. While Valentino was greeting Theresa, Sofia had phoned home. Evie was at the restaurant. Marco was busy and had only a few words to say, and her mother and father were equally distracted. Matilda had declined to talk to her at all. Sofia's heart ached to be with her family. She brushed away tears.

If Evie were here now, Sofia would ask her to pray. It had been hard to confess to her sister how she felt at his family's treatment.

"It's only shameful, Sofia," Evie had said, "because they're looking at your past. God loves you. He paid the price for your past sins."

"I've tried to change, Evie. But even though I know it's wrong, I can't resist temptation. I want to show God I'm worthy of His forgiveness, but then I do something that disproves it."

"None of us is worthy, Sofia. Forgiveness and salvation are gifts. It's impossible to earn them, no matter how hard we try. That's why Jesus came and died. His sacrifice paid for everything. God gives His forgiveness to anyone who asks, despite their unworthiness. God starts changing people from the inside after they receive His gifts."

Now as she stood in the alcove, Sofia searched for reassurance.

God, I need Your help.

"Sofia. Everyone is here." Startled, she turned as Valentino took her arm. Their guests were seated, the men on one side of the table, each opposite his wife. The two seats at either end were still empty. Sofia heard a whisper. Was God talking to her?

Start as you intend to proceed.

Those words came with power and assurance. Sofia took a small step, and then another. She claimed the nearer seat and smiled at Valentino. While he walked to the far end of the table, she glanced at their guests. During the flight, Valentino had coached her. Here they were arranged by seniority.

At seventy-two, Theresa was fourteen years older than the next sister. Opposite Theresa sat Raymond Serpios. Beatrice was opposite Luigi Paulini. Cecilia sat facing Orazio Ferro. Diana, the youngest at fifty-four was closest to Sofia. Diana's husband Fabio Abatangelo was staring at Sofia. He responded to her glance with a wicked grin. His hand disappeared beneath the table, and she felt him touch her knee. Sofia hastily moved further away.

Looking along the table, Sofia watched Valentino sit down. Chaisai and a uniformed waiter were standing at attention beside him. No-one said anything. Sofia looked to Valentino for guidance, but he remained obtuse.

Theresa glared at her brother.

"Theresa, who says the blessing before a meal in your family?" Sofia asked.

"Mother usually presides over the table, or Enzo in her absence. Tonight, Valentino's the host, but you can see how inept he is. As his consort, you'll have to take charge."

Start as you intend to proceed.

Sofia nodded, bowed her head and began to pray. The prayer she uttered was unfamiliar, the words seeming to bubble out of her.

"Holy Father, Creator and Sustainer of life, please listen to Your humble servant and grant this petition. May Your forgiveness, grace and mercy wash over us and make us worthy of Your generosity. We are imperfect and in need of Your sustenance. Bless the food placed before us. We are thankful for this provision.

"Bless Your servants who prepared this meal and grant them rest from their labours. Bless those who serve us. May they find joy in the work of their hands. Watch over each of us as we sit here in Your presence. May we be better people for the fellowship we share this evening. Take care of our loved ones – those who are not with us this evening – and keep them safe.

"These things we ask in the name of Jesus Christ, Saviour, Redeemer and Lord of All. Amen."

Opening her eyes, Sofia raised her hand and smiled at Chaisai. The uniformed butler and his companion stepped forward. They began delivering heaped plates to the table. Next, they served individual plates of rice, starting with Valentino. She was unable to read her fiancé's expression. Everyone was staring at her. The silence grew. Valentino pushed back his chair and stood, reaching for his champagne glass.

"I'd like to propose a toast," he declared. Each of his family took up their glass. Sofia was pleased to find her glass full.

"To Sofia, for showing exceptional patience with my family."

The others mumbled their reply, and he sat down.

"One more thing," he continued. "I've listened to the way you've insulted my fiancée. I'll tolerate it no more. And you men, I've been watching you. I'll kill the next man who touches her."

Without waiting for a response, Valentino reached for one of the central bowls. He served himself, before picking up his fork and beginning to eat.

Sofia stared at him. Fabio went pale and fumbled with his cutlery. Diana frowned at her husband and shook her head. Now, none of the men would meet Sofia's eye, and only Theresa was eating as if nothing untoward had happened.

"Take no notice of his melodramatics," Theresa advised. "He's made threats before, but never over such a trivial matter. We all know he's capable of violence. You've made your point, little brother. Now let's enjoy the meal and put this misunderstanding behind us. We only wanted to test how steadfast Sofia would be. More than one of your little playmates has run away when faced with your family."

"Sofia won't run away." Valentino looked down the table as he drained his glass. "She's promised to marry me."

Sofia looked into his stony countenance, raising her glass to take a small sip. She forced herself to keep smiling. "It takes two to make a marriage. You've made promises of your own, and God will hold you accountable on my behalf."

Nervous laughter rippled around the table.

Sofia's fiancé leaned back in his chair and laughed heartily. He reverted to the charming man who had captivated her heart. She was impressed by his chameleon qualities. He inspired both terror and admiration in her.

Conversation flowed around Sofia. Occasionally, someone thought to include her. But afterwards, she remembered nothing except his constant scrutiny. The food was delicious, but her appetite small. She had been careful how much champagne she drank. Valentino rose to his feet as the waiters removed the last plates. The warrior look was back.

"Sofia, take my sisters into the living room. The men and I will withdraw. I've tomorrow's meeting details to finalise, and will come to you as soon as I can. Chaisai, bring coffee to the study and then take care of the ladies. While we're meeting, I don't want to be disturbed."

Valentino exercised absolute authority now.

A few minutes later, the women were seated in the living room. Sofia wondered how the conversation would proceed. Would they continue to talk about the intimate details of their affluent lives? Or would they reveal more of their brother's secrets?

"You're quiet, Sofia," Theresa began. "During dinner you hardly said anything."

"I hoped no-one would notice," Sofia confessed. "I don't understand your family. You seem to be playing some cruel game. I don't know if I like any of you, or whether I should treat you as my enemies."

"We are equally unsure about you," Theresa replied. "You're not like Valentino's young women. He picks them up and discards them without a second thought. They're nothing but a harmless distraction to balance his professional life."

"Valentino's jealous outburst tonight was a surprise," Diana added. "He usually doesn't mind if the other men engage in some harmless flirtation."

"Suddenly, our brother is talking about leaving. About abandoning his role, one he created for himself. Enzo has given our little brother power and influence. That allows him to pursue his ambitions. With your arrival, Valentino has changed direction."

Cecilia and Beatrice added their thoughts too.

"You're the first girlfriend to accompany him on a business trip."

"That makes us wonder what power you have over him. Why would Valentino throw his whole life away for you?"

Sofia was determined to be honest.

"I didn't ask him to make any changes. I'm struggling to understand any of this. If I had the choice, I'd rather be at home with my family."

"Shall we declare a truce?" Theresa suggested. "No more talk of our mutual suspicions. Tomorrow we can have breakfast together. Then we'll visit the *Chatuchak Weekend Market*.

CHAPTER 28
(Saturday 21st October)

Morning Messages

ঝ ☼ ঙ

2 Corinthians 4:18
Don't focus on what is seen, but on what is unseen.
The things that are seen are temporary
but the unseen things are eternal.

ঝ ☼ ঙ

It was still dark outside when Sofia was woken by a demanding kiss.

"It's almost time for me to leave," Valentino said. "I want you to understand how important you are to me."

When he left the bed, Sofia sat up, drawing the silk sheet around her.

"What time is it?"

"Five am. The helicopter takes off at five-thirty. I sent Chaisai downstairs to collect a briefcase I left here on my last visit. It's been locked away in the main safe. I've time for a quick shower." He walked towards the bathroom. "Come and talk with me."

She followed him, the silk fabric flowing behind her.

"I'm reluctant to leave you, Sofia. You must be careful today. Bangkok can be a dangerous place. Keep your bag close, and watch out for pickpockets when you go to the market. And be careful of strangers. We don't know who can be trusted. Don't let anyone come into the apartment while I'm gone, not even my sisters. Only Chaisai is to be here with you. Mr Wattana has vouched for him – he comes from a local family indebted to me."

"You're more involved with your brother's enterprise than you told me?"

"Does that change things between us?"

"How many people have you killed?"

"What have my sisters been saying?"

"I saw the way your family responded to your threat last night.

"I've gained a reputation. If people believe the rumours and tremble in fear, then I don't need violence to get what I want."

"What kind of business negotiations are you working on?"

"I told you my brother is building an international empire. I've helped him achieve that. We'll have to discuss this later, Sofia. I have to go. Here's Chaisai with my briefcase."

Sofia clutched the drooping sheet to her. The butler stood in the open doorway. Valentino laughed as he kissed her. "Your modesty's endearing, Sofia. You give yourself freely to me, yet you're careful around other men."

Valentino was still laughing as he left the apartment. Chaisai silently followed him from the room. Sofia put on one of the plush robes and went to the bathroom window. She wondered if she would be able to see his helicopter departing. She had forgotten to ask him where he was going so how would she know where to look?

Chaisai spoke quietly, and she jumped.

"Mr Horatio said for you to go to the living room window and he will fly past. I was only to tell you if you searched for him. He said this would confirm you are worthy of his trust."

She trembled at these words. What would have been the outcome if she had gone back to bed? She obediently walked to the living room. Chaisai had opened the curtains and turned on the lights. The helicopter flew past the window before rising into the air and disappearing.

"Is there anything Miss Sofia requires?" Chaisai asked. She smiled at the use of her name. He stood at the furthest side of the room.

"What time is sunrise, Chaisai? I'm restless – I don't usually wake this early. If it weren't dark, I'd go down to the pool for a swim. Would it be too cold?"

"The sun rises in forty minutes. There is a light rain falling. The overnight temperature dropped to twenty-four degrees. You would consider that warm. There would be time for Miss Sofia to enjoy a bath and some fruit. An attendant will take you to the pool when it opens at six o'clock. Perhaps the gods will favour you, and the sun will break through the clouds? Then you can enjoy the sunrise."

"I serve only one God." The words pricked her conscience. "I haven't done anything to deserve His favour. But I'll go and see for myself. I don't need an attendant. I'm sure I can find my way."

"Mr Horatio said you go nowhere alone."

"And if I refuse?"

"I would have to let Mr Horatio know of your decision. He would not be happy with my failure."

"Are you afraid of him?"

"Only a fool would not be afraid of a man with great wealth and power. If I may be bold, Miss Sofia, you must show him respect. He rewards obedience."

"And if I fail to obey?"

"You say You serve one God, the Christian God. I have heard many times the Christian wedding vows. Your God asks you to honour and obey your husband?"

"He's not my husband."

"Your God sees you living with Mr Horatio as if he were your husband."

"My sister uses a similar argument, Chaisai. You can leave me now. Come and tell me when this attendant arrives."

Sofia returned to the bedroom and picked up her phone to send a message.

> Evie, please tell my children I miss them.
> 5:40 am here. I am alone.
> Planning a sunrise swim in the pool.
> Then I meet his family for breakfast on the terrace.
> Today we are going to Chatuchak Market.
> Wish you were here.

Sofia checked the screen to confirm there was nothing Valentino might question. She pressed send, while praying Jenny still monitored her phone. Sofia waited for the marble bath to fill, turning on the small television embedded into the wall. The lively music did nothing to alleviate her emptiness.

At six o'clock, Sofia walked from the bedroom, wearing a short sarong over her pink bikini. This revealing outfit had seemed perfect in Bali. There, she had stepped from her room directly onto the sand without any concern about who might see her.

A young Thai girl waited nervously. She glanced at Sofia from beneath her long black fringe, a trembling smile of welcome on her pretty face. The uniform hung loosely on her tiny frame. The red hat perched above a long plait marked her as a *Maena Sakhay* employee.

Chaisai said, "Miss Sofia, here is your attendant, my sister Prija. Her name means intelligent and smart. Mr Wattana is proud to offer her for your service. She will carry your bag and look after your possessions while you are in the pool. Do not be afraid that she is small. She has been trained to deal with many dangers, and her loyalty to Mr Horatio is without question. He rescued her from slavery and our family will be eternally grateful."

Sofia looked at the pair with fresh eyes. "Hello Prija, thank you for being my companion. Having you with me will bring great comfort. I pray a blessing on you and your family."

The girl bowed and reached for Sofia's burden. Chaisai pressed a bowl of chopped mango pieces into Sofia's hand. He insisted she ate from it before he allowed her to leave. Sofia smiled at his stern countenance. After she had taken a few pieces, he stepped back with a smile.

It must be too early for other guests – Sofia and Prija were alone in the elevator. Prija glided ahead, choosing a shelter beside the three-tiered pool. Sofia took off her wrap, passing her bangles and phone to the girl. The sky was heavy with dark clouds as Sofia slipped into the water. She had the pool to herself as she focused on her stroke.

"You have a message," Prija informed her when Sofia dragged herself out of the water. The girl passed her the phone, and there was Evie's reply.

God is with you. He takes care of His own.
Sebastian said not to worry.
Help is close at hand to those under his protection.

Sofia lifted her eyes heavenward in silent thanks. Then the sun burst through the clouds. The rays sparkled on the clear blue water.

"Good news, Miss Sofia?"

"A small blessing from my sister, Prija. God has answered my prayer. The sun is shining. We've time for a walk before I meet Valentino's sisters for breakfast. Take me around the hotel grounds."

Prija set off with Sofia walking beside her. The girl became more talkative as time passed. Returning to the pool, they found other guests enjoying the early morning sunshine. Sofia glanced around as she drew herself from the water. On the opposite side, two men were preparing for their swim. One of them turned as he removed his shirt, and she recognised him from the airport. He waved then dove into the pool, swimming away to the furthest end.

"Is that someone you know?" Prija asked.

"I think he was on our flight. I remember standing near him at the airport. What a coincidence he's staying at the same hotel."

Fifteen minutes later, an anxious Chaisai greeted Sofia's return.

"There you are, Miss Sofia. Mrs Serpios came looking for you half an hour ago. She was angry when I wouldn't open the door."

"But I'm not supposed to meet them until nine. What explanation did you give?"

"I said Mr Horatio left orders you were not to be disturbed. Mrs Serpios insisted she must come in and wait for you to awaken, but I refused. Eventually, she went away but has phoned four times. You are to join them at the terrace cafe."

"I'd better hurry. I'm sorry, Chaisai. I shouldn't have stayed away so long."

She left Prija and Chaisai whispering together. Sofia selected a loose-fitting cotton dress. The tension in her shoulders was back, and she sensed the beginning of a headache. Grabbing a bottle of chilled water, she drained it. After that, Sofia stowed two more bottles in her shoulder bag. They nestled beside her purse. She hadn't seen any bottled water on the terrace, when Prija showed her where the buffet breakfast would be served.

Prija escorted Sofia down to the terrace cafe before bidding her farewell. Breakfast was a bountiful buffet.

"Good morning, ladies," Sofia apologised, as she sat down in the empty seat at the sisters' table. "Theresa, I'm sorry I wasn't there when you called to collect me. I forgot you said you were coming, and the morning was lovely down at the pool."

"You were at the pool? The butler said you weren't to be disturbed. I presumed you were asleep."

"Valentino woke me before he left. Our butler has strict instructions. No-one is permitted in the suite while Valentino is away. He seems to have included his family in that restriction."

"Valentino doesn't trust you," Theresa said smugly.

"After your comments yesterday, his suspicion is understandable. He knows you'll watch for any reason to accuse me. He's taken precautions. Can you see the tiny girl standing over there? Prija has accompanied me all morning."

"Get yourself some breakfast," Theresa said impatiently. "The hotel limousine is waiting to take us to the market. It's only a ten-minute drive, but we need to hurry if we're to get there before it becomes crowded. Have you exchanged your money yet? No, I thought not. I've taken care of that for you. I hope fifty thousand bhat will be sufficient?"

Sofia accepted the bundle of unfamiliar notes. She frowned.

"Thank you, Theresa. How much is this in Australian dollars?"

"Approximately two thousand."

The colour drained from Sofia's face. She remembered Valentino's warning about pickpockets. Thrusting the money into her bag, she knew she needed a bigger purse.

"Don't worry," Cecilia advised her. "You'll soon get used to the local currency. It's always entertaining to bargain for what you want. If you run out of cash, I can lend you some. I always take too much with me."

"I'm going to check out the buffet," Sofia said, hurrying towards the laden tables. She avoided looking at the two men who approached the buffet at the same time. Prija stepped from her position to stand with Sofia.

"Prija, I've been given fifty thousand bhat for my trip to the *Chatuchak Market*. It's far more than I thought I needed. I know nothing about your customs. Is it acceptable to barter here or is that impolite? Should I pay the asking price?"

"The stallholders will look at the women you are with and treat you as an American tourist. When you request the price, it will be more than double what they should accept. Make a low offer. If you decide someone has been polite and courteous, then offer more. Don't reward a greedy stallholder. You can be generous, but you must be careful. The stallholders pass messages between them."

"Could you come with me?"

"I'm sorry, Miss Sofia. I am not permitted to leave the *Maena Sakhay*. A private guide will escort your group at the market."

CHAPTER 29
(Saturday 21st October)

Bitterness and Betrayal

ಏ ☼ ಓ

Matthew 15:8 WEB
These people draw near to Me with their mouth,
and honor Me with their lips;
but their heart is far from Me.

ಏ ☼ ಓ

Hurrying over breakfast, Sofia struggled to drink the coffee Cecilia gave her. She took a few sips and set the cup aside. Bitterness lingered as Theresa hustled her out to the waiting car.

When the limousine arrived at the market, clouds vanquished the sun. The crowds seemed undeterred. Stalls with colourful umbrellas suspended overhead stretched as far as she could see. This market was huge.

Theresa marched directly towards a tiny woman waiting beside the gate. A smile spread across the guide's face.

"Mrs Serpios. A pleasure to serve you again."

"Kirikait, thank you for waiting. We've brought the newest addition to our family with us."

"Here is an itinerary for your approval."

"You'll love *Phuhying Swy*," Cecilia informed Sofia, looking up from the list. "Our brother likes his women to

195

dress well. The extra cost to have dresses made to measure is minimal."

"We should leave that visit until later," suggested Diana. "Air-conditioning will be a welcome change by then."

"We want to visit the potion shop we discovered last time," Beatrice added.

The guide wrote in her notebook. "Are we ready to begin?"

The covered market had narrow walkways. As Sofia stepped under the canopy, a wave of sound assaulted her ears. The occasional English phrase rose above the cacophony of foreign tongues.

The shops were jumbled together in no logical order. It would be easy to get lost in this rainbow-coloured maze. The first store on Kirikait's itinerary sold jewellery from a wooden shop front. The other women selected hand-crafted gifts for daughters and grand-daughters. Sofia found a pair of silver bangles. She watched the other women haggle over the prices. Pleased when her smaller offer was accepted, Sofia placed one on her arm. The second bangle was a gift for her sister. Her companions moved on too soon. That happened frequently. If Sofia paused to bargain over a purchase, Valentino's sisters would disappear. She would have to hurry to find them again.

Two hours passed. Beads of sweat dripped from Sofia's brow. She drank both bottles of water. The other women seemed unaffected by the heat. Kirikait led them to an air-conditioned building. They were treated to a fragrant foot massage while they drank herbal tea. This shop sold body lotions and oils, and Sofia selected gifts for her friends.

There was no sign of Valentino's sisters when Sofia returned to the walkway. Tears pricked her eyes.

God, what am I to do?

Someone tugged at her bag. Thankful for the sturdy strap, Sofia wrestled the bag close to her body. Her unknown protagonist was quick. A thin blade slashed towards Sofia. Someone shoved Sofia out of the way. Sofia shouted, and the attacker ran off into the crowd empty-handed.

"Are you okay?" a deep voice asked. Sofia gazed into blue eyes. The young man from the airport had his arms around her, forming a shield between Sofia and the crowd.

"Sofia!" Theresa's raised voice rang out. "Who is this man?"

Sofia pushed herself free. The rescuer turned to face Theresa.

"I'm Patrick. I've saved Sofia from being mugged. Do you want me to find a policeman?"

"We'll make a report when we get back to the hotel," Theresa insisted.

"Will you be okay with these ladies, Sofia?" Patrick asked, studying her reaction.

"Yes. Thank you for helping me."

"You're staying at the *Maena Sakhay*, aren't you? Meet me later, and we can talk about what happened over a drink?"

"That's impossible. My fiancé would kill you. He's a jealous man."

"Sofia!" Beatrice dragged Sofia away. "Sofia! Be more careful."

"And keep up. You're going to lose yourself." Diana grabbed her other arm. Sofia glanced back over her shoulder. Patrick was still standing there. Another man joined him. Both looked in her direction, and neither of them was smiling.

Her companions hurried her away.

"Where are we going?" Sofia asked.

"There's a tea room near here. You could return to the hotel if this recent adventure has been too much," Diana suggested.

The thought of returning to the hotel was tempting, but Sofia knew this might be her only excursion. Valentino's restrictions would intensify when he found out.

"I'll be fine. There's so much to see, and I've more gifts to buy."

"Of course she'll be fine," Theresa snapped.

They finished their iced tea and savoury pastries. Now Kirikait led them deeper into the market. Here the walkways narrowed. There were few Western tourists, and pungent odours made the atmosphere oppressive. The stalls sold incense sticks, amulets and idols. Sofia fought the urge to flee. She could not explain her aversion. But she refused to enter the darkened fortune teller booth.

"Why are you standing here?" Kirikait asked. "The wise woman will tell your fortune. You could buy a special charm or a powerful potion, even ask her for a curse to use against your enemies."

With a shudder, Sofia moved further away. She purchased a bottle of fruit juice while watching for the others. When they emerged from the darkness, her juice was almost gone.

"You wouldn't come in, Sofia, so the fortune teller chose for you," Beatrice said. "This concoction increases wisdom and discernment. When you need inspiration, place three drops on your tongue."

Sofia examined the small brown bottle. Cecilia took her juice to free Sofia's hands. Sofia opened the potion and sniffed. She screwed up her nose while Beatrice mocked her.

"Are you worried we're trying to poison you? Here, let me take some."

Before Sofia could respond, Beatrice consumed a few drops of the foul-smelling liquid.

"Urgh. The fortune teller was right about the bitter taste. Diana, give me one of your mints."

"I don't have any mints," Diana protested, but she searched anyway. Her hand brought out a partially consumed packet of mints. "I didn't know I had these."

"See, Sofia, the potion's worked already." Laughter followed this remark. "Now it's your turn. Cecilia, give me Sofia's juice. That will dilute the taste."

Sofia wanted to avoid a public scene. She gagged on the concoction and had to cover her mouth. Diana passed her a mint.

The bitter aftertaste lingered. Sofia felt dizzy and uncoordinated. She perspired excessively, and the women urged her to consume more drinks. Everything tasted foul. Sofia's sensible dress clung to her. Diana purchased a more revealing one and helped Sofia change. Stumbling into the walkway, she caught sight of her reflection in a mirror.

God, what's happening to me?

A wafting breeze fluttered her short skirt. Sofia felt the heaviness lift. At the next stall, she found a loose beach wrap. Cecilia scolded her when she declared her intention.

"You're not thinking clearly, Sofia. You should use your generous curves to your advantage. Feed our brother's jealousy to keep him interested."

"No-oo," Sofia argued. "God duzn' wan' me to dress l-like a-a whore. I don' wanna make him zhe-lush."

She brushed Cecilia's restraining hand away, paying the full price. The stallholder grinned. Sofia thrust the wrap over her head and pulled the translucent layers over her body.

Turning, Sofia caught Beatrice and Theresa whispering.

"You're over-heated and ill-tempered, Sofia. Beatrice is getting you another drink. We'll have to shorten our visit to the market. Kirikait will take us directly to *Phuhying Swy* from here."

Beatrice returned with a sickly-sweet drink for Sofia. Her throat was parched, and she drank it greedily. Then they twisted and turned from one walkway to another. Kirikait delivered them to *Phuhying Swy*. The air-conditioned coolness was welcome. Sofia smiled at the colourful fabrics. She looked at the price tags but couldn't focus. She held a lovely floor-length silk dress before her in the mirror.

"You have to try that on," Diana advised her. "They'll make one to your measurements and deliver it to the *Maena Sakhay*. It'll be ready tomorrow."

"You should get one of these dresses too. This design would be perfect for you," Cecilia added, draping a shorter dress over Sofia's arm.

"And this one," Beatrice added.

An enthusiastic seamstress took Sofia behind a brocade curtain. Sofia was fitted and measured for five dresses. When the saleswoman finished writing up her order, Sofia fumbled with the payment. The woman helped her count out the notes. Her doubts about the transaction increased when she found her companions had disappeared.

An Isolating Incident

❦ ✺ ❧

Romans 8:26 WEB
In the same way, the Spirit also helps our weaknesses,
for we don't know how to pray as we ought.
But the Spirit himself makes intercession for us
with groanings which can't be uttered.

❦ ✺ ❧

Sofia was tired of these childish games. If she could find her way to the street, she would hire a taxi and return to the hotel. Was it lighter at the end of this row? As she hurried, the promised afternoon storm began.

Sofia struggled through the crowd. An umbrella seller blocked the walkway, swamped with customers. Sofia turned down a twisting side lane, unable to find her way back to familiar territory. The smell of incense intensified.

Panic seized her. She imagined hands pulling at her clothes. Then she felt a familiar tug on her bag. Dragged backwards, Sofia's response was slow. A group of men encircled her. They pushed her towards a curtained entrance. The closest man waved his knife.

With a shout, Patrick appeared from nowhere, a whirl of arms and legs. Three men fell to the ground. Their companions fled. The man with the knife lunged. Sofia twisted away, screaming as the blade sliced her arm.

Patrick shoved her out of the way. "Run!" Her attacker slashed at Patrick.

Her arm was stinging. Sofia held her other hand over the wound as she fled. She was gasping for breath when she burst into the open. No-one pursued her. But where was Patrick? Sofia stood in the driving rain. What should she do? The mobile phone in her bag was useless. What good would it do to call home? She didn't know where she was in this sprawling precinct. How would anyone find her?

But these attackers had found her twice. What was to prevent them from attacking again? Her feet stumbled forward. Swept along by the crowd, her weariness grew, as did her thirst. Someone bumped her, and she fell to her knees. A moment of clarity reminded her to pray.

Lord, help me.

Looking up, she saw a coffee seller. Sofia was shaking and had no voice. She pointed to make the woman understand. The vendor told her the price. When Sofia fumbled with the money, the woman asked a different question.

"Do you need help? Go to the emergency phone. Look for the big sign."

Sofia slurped the iced coffee as the river of people moved her on. Everyone was hurrying to get out of the rain. The crowd ebbed and flowed. At every intersection, Sofia fought against the changing tide. She would not enter that maze again.

After Sofia disposed of the empty cup, the phone in her bag began to ring. Sofia wrestled it from concealment.

"'lo?"

"Sofia. Stay where you are. We're coming to get you."

"Uh?"

"This is Thomas, Patrick's friend. He's hurt. Sorry it's taken me so long to contact you. No-one told us you run like a gazelle. I couldn't keep up. I had to go back and get Patrick – he had the tracker. We know where you are, so stay put. We'll see you in five minutes."

Two men under a red umbrella pushed through the crowd. Thomas had his arm around Patrick. Sofia stared at the bloody shirt.

"Sofia! You're drenched. Why didn't you get an umbrella or seek shelter in one of the restaurants?"

"Y-yoo... shh-edd... shh-t-a-ay!"

"We have to get you some dry clothes and check out that arm."

Thomas had done all the talking, and Sofia peered at Patrick.

"Don't worry about him. He's tough. It looks worse than it is. Come on. Standing out here makes you an easy target."

Scandal and Sorcery

ಹ ☼ ಛ

Ephesians 4:26 WEB
Be angry, and don't sin.
Don't let the sun go down on your wrath.

ಹ ☼ ಛ

The long hike from the helicopter to the remote regional base had exposed Valentino's physical weakness, his loss of stamina and endurance since the plane crash. Then his relatives had interfered in the negotiations. He had consoled himself with the promise of a pleasurable evening with Sofia.

His exhausted companions would cause no more trouble today. He had been on the *Maena Sakhay* helipad long enough to get rid of them, when Theresa and Beatrice arrived. Theresa took delight in delivering the news of Sofia's absence. Sofia had become bored and gone looking for trouble. There had been a street fight. Sofia was last seen leaving the *Chatuchak Market* in the arms of two young men.

Their news was a devastating blow. After enduring their account, he phoned Sofia.

"Where are you?" Valentino snarled.

He didn't recognise the male voice. "Bumrungrad International Hospital, Emergency Department."

He swore and hung up, his face red. "When I get back from dealing with Sofia we're going to talk."

"You can't blame us for Sofia's behaviour," Theresa said triumphantly.

Valentino stormed back onto the helipad. The other pilot was waiting in the aircraft.

"Bumrungrad International Hospital," Valentino spat from the co-pilot's seat. "Radio ahead. I want my fiancée waiting when we arrive."

The brief flight passed in a blur. Too soon, the pilot called the hospital radio operator. The rotor blades were still whirling rapidly when Valentino thrust the door open.

A group of men waited for him. Two of them were security guards, small in build and unarmed. A third man was probably the hospital administrator. As Valentino advanced, a worried man in a white coat stepped forward.

"Where's Sofia?" Valentino demanded.

"Miss Fontana is in a critical condition. I am Dr Pin Baelmuntrisuma. I assure you our hospital is providing the best possible care."

"Critical?"

The doctor's words were like an icy slap. An unknown fear gripped Valentino.

"Mr Horatio, Miss Fontana has been poisoned. We await the toxicology results. While she was incapacitated, someone attacked her with a knife. Another patient was wounded defending her. He is in surgery now."

Valentino felt torn. He needed to verify the doctor's report but wanted to interrogate his family.

"I'll talk to my pilot. Then take me to her."

Valentino dismissed the pilot then strode back across the roof. He followed the four men. Another security guard stood to attention outside Sofia's private room.

"We will leave you here," the doctor said. "If you have any further questions, please ask the nurse in charge. It will be another hour before we get the toxicology results."

All three security guards remained outside the room. Valentino glared at them. He was much taller, and they seemed intimidated by his bulk. Reluctantly, they moved aside but stood watching from the doorway. Sofia lay with an intravenous drip attached to her left arm. Above her right elbow was a white bandage. Her dark hair was untidy, her face pale.

"Sofia!" Valentino roared and she turned frightened eyes towards him.

An unknown man leapt to his feet, taking up an offensive pose. Valentino fought the temptation to snap this man's neck.

"Think where you are, man," the stranger said. "Calm down. Sofia's suffered enough already."

"Who are you?" Valentino growled.

"Thomas Demistrani, from *Maximum Security*. Piper Maxwell assigned me to Sofia. And he told me not to trust you."

Valentino softened his countenance, "I didn't mean to frighten Sofia. You work for Piper? I don't need his interference."

"Sofia wouldn't be alive without Piper's interference."

"What happened?"

"Your family betrayed her," Thomas answered.

"C-co-inch-a-dnce," Sofia stammered. "Lo-ssh-t."

Thomas swore. "Sofia's still unwilling to believe your sisters are responsible."

Sofia sighed. "Tho-mus, go to Pat-rich. Safe with V-val-en-tee-nno."

Thomas shook his head. "I'll be right back. Don't try to move her."

"I can see she needs help," Valentino protested. "I had nothing to do with this. But I'll find whoever's responsible..."

Thomas left, and Valentino slammed the door ignoring the security guards' protests. Now he was alone with Sofia. He crossed the room, and gently took her chin in his hand, tipping her face to look at him.

Valentino looked into her eyes, noting her unevenly dilated pupils. Her skin was a sickly grey. Sofia struggled to stay awake. A foul odour hung over her. She reached out, and he softened into her embrace.

"M-m-m sh-o-or-ry," she whispered.

He held her for a few moments and then released her.

"My sisters said nothing about this attack, and I wouldn't have given you time to explain," he confessed. "I intended to kill you. Only your illness has saved you. I'm releasing you from your promise to marry me. When we return to the hotel, I'll sleep in the other wing."

"N-no-oo-oo," Sofia's eyes fluttered open. "L-ll-uv ooo."

"I'm not who you think I am. I've been using you. You mean nothing to me – you're only in Thailand as bait. I picked you because of your strength and resilience. That money is supposed to be your compensation."

He watched comprehension dawn in her. Sofia turned away. When Valentino was sure she was asleep, he kissed her cheek. "I miscalculated, Sofia. This wasn't in my plan. My evil led to this, and I'll never forgive myself."

CHAPTER 32
(Sunday 22nd October)

Disrupted Dreams

⁎

Psalm 16:8
I look towards the Lord.
Because He is right beside me, I will not be moved.

⁎

Jenny Prescott stood beside John Edwards' bed. "Wake up."

"What?"

Jenny tore off the bed covers and dragged him upright. She threw an armful of clothes at him. He caught them in confusion.

"Get dressed," Jenny told him.

"What are you doing here? It's Sunday morning. In a few hours I'll be delivering the weekly sermon. I'm not going anywhere."

"Get dressed. Or do you want me to help you?"

"Tell me why you're here."

"I'll tell you while you dress. See, Jenny's turning her back, so she doesn't look."

"Your sarcasm's worse than your anger." She hurled his hiking shoes at him.

"Okay, I'm getting dressed. Why am I putting on these clothes? It's too cold to go anywhere in these."

"When you get to Thailand, you'll be complaining about the heat."

"Thailand? I'm not going to Thailand – I don't have a visa, and who's going to look after my boys? Wait – did you say Thailand? Is that where Sofia went? Has something happened to Sofia?"

John dropped onto the bed, his head in his hands. He prayed for the wisdom to be obedient if this was God's direction.

"I took your passport and applied for the visas, in case they were needed. I forged your signature on the forms. A team is leaving Melbourne for Bangkok on the next flight. Piper wants you with them. You have to make Sofia come home.

"In answer to your other question, while you're overseas, I'll stay with your boys. Your mother should arrive this afternoon, or Monday at the latest. Once again, I'm left behind to take care of the domestic scene while everyone goes off on the assignment.

"I need you to bring everyone home in one piece. Keep saying those prayers, Pastor. Evie and I will be praying here. I heard you say three people praying increased the chance God would listen. Piper needs all the help he can get."

"I didn't say it would increase the chance, but it does help build our faith in God's ability to listen. The collective faith releases a powerful answer. You said Evie's praying. What about Romano? He should be praying too. That makes a team of four."

"Romano's going to Thailand. That's his car in your driveway now. Take this backpack. I've included everything you need. Here's your passport."

"This isn't a joke? You're sending me to Thailand?"

A horn sounded.

"Would Romano be waking the neighbourhood if this were a joke?"

ഇറ ☼ ോ

The taxi delivered Valentino and Sofia to the *Maena Sakhay Hotel* after dawn. The antidote for the poison coursed through her system. The toxin was a concentrated form of a common herbal medicine. In its benign form, it was traditionally used to subdue wilful children and reluctant brides. Valentino recognised the name. He had used it many times. In small doses it had no lasting effect. It rendered the victim compliant and open to persuasion. Sofia's dose was extreme – potentially lethal. The doctors were surprised she remained conscious.

When questioned, Sofia remembered the bitter coffee at breakfast. And then the potion Beatrice had bought. Everything she ate and drank afterwards sustained the bitterness. Until then, she had made no connection to her growing distress and confusion. The revelation turned her thoughts inward. Her new silence made Valentino uncomfortable.

Chaisai was waiting for them when Valentino unlocked the apartment. Sofia went immediately to the master bedroom and closed the door.

"I've moved your belongings as you requested, Mr Horatio. Is everything well with Miss Sofia?"

"No, Chaisai. Things are not well. I need some sleep. Sofia's not to leave the apartment. Wake me if she tries. Don't wake me for anything else. I'm expecting a visitor – Piper Maxwell. When he arrives, let him in. He may have others with him. No-one is to know I'm expecting Piper. Understood?"

Valentino took a long shower, then carefully dressed in a fresh linen shirt and loose pants. He wanted to be ready. He lay down and stared at the ceiling. He hoped Sofia slept. He wore her engagement ring on the chain around his neck. It served to remind him of his vow.

Sleep came, but brought Valentino no peace. The dream had returned, but now the river wild and dangerous brought recognition. It was the riverbank where he had walked yesterday. He revisited the tropical warmth as the heavy scent of the jungle awakened after rain. The scene reflected the darkness of his soul. His doom awaited him in Asia. He knew he would answer to God for his sins.

As he struggled against the torrent, the faces of his many victims floated beside him in the waves. And there were the others killed in his service. Roger Silvania was the last of these. Valentino had fought to keep Silvania alive, but his unknown enemies had prevailed. The dead men's eyes were unseeing, their mouths silent.

Then he heard a scream. What was Sofia doing in his dream? He saw her clinging in desperation to a moss-covered branch. The shock brought him awake in a sweat. Was he too late to save her?

Her scream pierced the air again, distant but real. Valentino jumped from the bed and rushed along the hallway. There he encountered Chaisai, carrying a metal pan.

"Hurry." Chaisai ran towards the study.

Sofia stood on a padded chair. Dumped on the floor was a pile of white cardboard boxes, their contents spilled onto the polished teak floor. As he watched, a swathe of expensive silk wriggled. A creature wrestled its way free and scuttled across the floor. There were more creatures, some as big as his hand. Chaisai stalked the room with his pan. How had jungle scorpions come into the apartment?

He knew their sting was painful but rarely fatal. But Sofia's immunity was compromised. One of the creatures began climbing the leg of her chair. Valentino pulled the switchblade from his belt and threw it. The scorpion writhed. Sofia stared as Valentino approached and dispatched the animal with a flick of his wrist. He seized Sofia, threw her into the bedroom, and slammed the door.

It took fifteen minutes for Chaisai and Valentino to kill the intruders.

"How did these scorpions get in, Chaisai?"

"They were in the dress boxes delivered for Miss Sofia. I thought this would cheer her up. I left the boxes here while I prepared breakfast. The heat from the lamp must have woken them. Miss Sofia came in and picked up the first box. 'There's something alive in here,' she said. I leapt across. Unfortunately, I knocked the others onto the floor. That was when she screamed."

"Go and tell Sofia it's safe. I'll dispose of the evidence later. I'll also apologise to Mr Wattana for damaging this chair and pay to have the floor repaired. Ask Sofia to get dressed. Take her breakfast through to the dining room so she doesn't have to look at this mess."

With great care, Valentino shook out the silk dresses and folded them over the chair. He scraped up the hard-shelled bodies and placed them in the boxes. There were two different species, and he divided them accordingly. Valentino carried the boxes to the pantry.

"There are thirteen black, and seven green ones." He watched closely to determine if these numbers were significant. He knew Chaisai was superstitious. Chaisai frowned.

"A powerful curse has been placed on Miss Sofia."

"I was already cursed," Sofia said from the doorway. "Falling in love with Valentino was supposed to break it, but now my situation is even worse. But I've talked to my sister Evie on the phone. She told me curses have no power over me because I've surrendered my life to God. If that's true, then death means nothing to me. Your enemies can't hurt my immortal soul. I'm going to the pool for a swim. Valentino, come with me, please?"

Valentino blinked in surprise. His restrictions had failed to keep Sofia safe. Perhaps he should follow her example and surrender?

Waiting and Watching

ಐ ✸ ಚ

1 Corinthians 13:8a WEB
Love never fails.

ಐ ✸ ಚ

Beside the pool, Valentino watched as Sofia dove into the sparkling water. He hadn't seen her wearing that pink bikini, and he was tempted to join her. But he was supposed to be her protector.

Sofia swam for half an hour and was smiling as she came from the water. Valentino passed her a towel. She asked for her silver bangles as soon as she was dry. He looked at them and pondered their significance.

Sofia lay in the sun until she was too hot. He marvelled at her peace of mind. The waterproof patch on her arm was the only evidence of her recent adventure.

Her companionable silence comforted him as they rode the elevator. If only things were different between them.

"Chaisai, we're back," she called out as they entered the suite. "Chaisai!" she called again heading towards the dining room. "Where is he?"

"You change, and I'll find him," Valentino turned towards the pantry. Sofia cried out. He ran to the living room and halted on the threshold. Four Asian men were advancing towards Sofia, armed with knives.

"How did you get in here?" he shouted, reaching for his hidden switchblade. Valentino threw his knife with a sharp twist. The closest man clutched at his throat and dropped to the floor in front of Sofia.

"Then there were three. Who will die next?"

"You don't have another knife."

"I know more than one way to kill you."

"And what about Sofia?" His real enemy stepped into the room. Raymond had a handgun pointed at Sofia. "While you're busy fighting, who will protect her?"

"What do you want?"

"I'm going to take your place. Soon I'll control these Asian negotiations. Enzo revealed your secret Thai-Myanmar project while you were missing. He was furious because crucial information would die with you. It was easy to persuade him he needed insurance. That's why we're all here. The family's fortunate you survived."

"Let Sofia go, and I'll tell you everything."

"Sofia's part of the deal. She's a beautiful woman. Think carefully about that. I won't hesitate to kill you, and then who will stop me from selling her."

"Sofia means nothing to me."

Raymond laughed. "Don't waste my time with your lies. Sofia, hurry into the next room and get changed. I've chosen a dress for you. Valentino needs reminding what's at stake. If you take too long, I'll send these men to help you. Your lover has killed their leader, and they want their revenge."

Sofia hastened to obey.

"What happens now?" Valentino feigned disinterest.

"I have a helicopter waiting. The meeting you scheduled for this afternoon is still going to happen, but it will only be the three of us. The others believe you cancelled it. I intend to cut Enzo out of the deal. He'll never know what went wrong."

"Does my sister know?"

"She's helped by distracting you."

"You speak as if Theresa was dispensable, but without her you have nothing."

"Is that what you think? Your family has a shortage of male heirs. I've had many sons to other women, and my sons have positions of influence in your family. One day, they'll claim your family business as their inheritance. Getting rid of you is the first step."

Sofia returned wearing a short silk dress that fitted her perfectly. Her silver bangles jingled as she moved, and she was carrying her phone. Raymond reached out and took it from her.

"Valentino, slide your phone across the floor to Sofia," Raymond commanded.

"I need my phone for the coordinates," Valentino protested.

Raymond laughed. "I have that information. That's why I encouraged our brothers-in-law to complain yesterday about the long walk, and then request a meeting place that was less remote."

Valentino obeyed, and as the phone came to a stop at her feet, Sofia bobbed down to retrieve it. Raymond took her arm and held the gun to her side. "The only thing you need is your briefcase. You changed the combination for the room safe. Your butler died denying he could open it."

Sofia choked back a cry. Raymond shoved her into a chair, and signalled with his gun for the knife-wielding men to stand guard.

Valentino walked to the safe to retrieve the briefcase. While his body concealed his movement, he slipped several useful items into secret pockets in his trousers. Raymond would presume he was unarmed.

Raymond was standing in the doorway drinking whisky from a glass when Valentino returned with the briefcase.

"Stop there," Raymond warned him, and one of the men pressed a knife to Sofia's throat. A trickle of blood began to flow. Sofia sat rigid and tense with her eyes closed. Valentino froze. Raymond disappeared into the study, returning without the phones or the glass. "It's time. These men will accompany us to the helicopter."

Raymond hid the gun in his pocket and took Sofia's arm, forcing her to walk in front of him. Valentino followed, while the armed men stayed close. From the elevator they all went through the helicopter lounge without anyone questioning them. Then the three Australians crossed the helipad alone.

"Mr Horatio will take over," Raymond informed the pilot. "We'll drop you back at the heliport. Sofia, get in the back, and I'll sit beside you."

After dispensing with the pilot, Valentino turned the helicopter away from the city. Raymond was cheerful. Valentino glanced at Sofia, who stared out the window. She was twisting those silver bangles.

Valentino had questioned Piper after Sofia's sister was abducted, about how he had located the girl in record time. Piper had suggested Evie had worn a tracking device. Valentino's suspicions about how Piper's men found Sofia at the market strengthened.

After they'd been in the air an hour, Raymond gave him the new GPS coordinates. Valentino already knew where he was going. Yesterday's extended trip had been a distraction.

Enzo was building an eco-lodge as a cover story. Valentino hoped it went ahead. The locals would need other employment when the drug cartel fell to the authorities. He glanced at the fuel gauge. After illegally crossing into Myanmar, they were nearing the extent of their limited range.

"The clearing should be on our right," he informed Raymond. "Tang said to follow the river and look for a signal fire. They will lower the camouflage netting when they hear us."

"There's the river!" Sofia cried. He turned the helicopter, dropping below the canopy. He hovered over the roaring torrent. Spray flew hundreds of metres into the air, rainbows forming around them.

"I've been dreaming about this river," she said.

Sofia's confession shocked Valentino, causing the helicopter to dip. Raymond swore.

"Take us higher. There's the signal fire," Raymond shouted.

"Tell me about your river," Valentino said after regaining control.

"Evie said my recurring dream is a message from God. She talked about a similar river that once carried her into God's presence. I've been dreaming about this river since I met you."

"Are you sure it's the same river? How can you dream about somewhere you've never been?"

"It's a God thing. God knows everything, God sees everything, and God's everywhere. I needn't be afraid. If God made the river, then I can let the torrent take me where I need to go."

"And if that leads to your death?" Valentino asked.

"What if death isn't the end? What if it's a new beginning?" Sofia replied.

Raymond laughed. "I thought Christians didn't believe in reincarnation."

"Not reincarnation, but new life. God takes us to live with Him forever," Sofia said.

"You're talking about heaven?" Raymond sneered. "What about hell? Do you believe in that too?"

"Yes, and I don't want to go there."

"You're keeping the wrong company. Your lover's taking you straight to hell."

"Only God knows a man's heart," Sofia insisted.

"What about your first husband? Do you think he went to heaven or hell?" Raymond asked.

Valentino gripped the controls and gritted his teeth. He could not afford to lose his temper now.

"You know Nicholas?" Sofia asked in surprise. "I haven't heard anything since his involvement in Evie's abduction. I don't know if he's alive or dead."

"Oh, he's unquestionably dead. I was there," Raymond gloated. "Nicholas squealed like a pig. When Valentino tired of his whining, he killed him. Then your lover chopped him up and fed him to the sharks."

Valentino lost control, as he dropped the helicopter into the clearing. The machine bobbed back into the air and spun around, tipping dangerously to one side. As he fought to regain control, one of the rotor blades sliced into the foliage. Debris showered them.

"You fool! Are you trying to kill us?" Raymond screamed, wrestling his gun from a pocket.

"I'd willingly take you to hell, but Sofia deserves to live," Valentino snapped, as the craft finally settled on the ground.

"I misjudged the landing. You should be careful not to distract me."

Raymond held Sofia back. "Get out," he said to Valentino. "Remember, I have Sofia."

As Valentino stepped into the clearing, a group of men emerged from the jungle.

"What's going on?" Tang asked. The man wore combat fatigues, and his companions had automatic rifles. As the commander of a small army, he was always suspicious. It had taken months to earn his trust.

"Renegotiating who's in charge," Valentino conceded.

Tang looked scornfully towards Raymond. "You're letting this man control you?"

"I do as he says, or he kills Sofia."

"My men could take him down. Just give the word."

The militia leader raised his hand, but Valentino restrained him.

"I'll do this my way, but thanks for the offer. I need to get Sofia away from him first."

Tang turned to examine her more closely. "This Sofia is special?"

They watched Raymond push Sofia ahead of him. Valentino wished she was wearing something less revealing.

"Sofia's one of God's chosen ones," Valentino tried to sound convincing. "God will protect her. Yesterday she was attacked by armed men. God sent two warriors to protect her – two strangers who risked their lives. Even this jungle won't keep God's warriors from rescuing her."

"But you haven't suffered because you desire her?" Tang argued.

"I've made a vow to her God to protect her, and whether I live or die is in His hands," Valentino insisted.

"Whether you live or die is in my hands," Raymond hissed as he joined them, and he shook Sofia.

"We've wasted enough time," Tang said. "There are rumours the army is near here. Let's go."

Jungle Jeopardy

ಏ ☼ ಚ

Psalm 28:7a
The Lord is my strength and shield.
My heart trusts in Him and He helps me.

ಏ ☼ ಚ

A misty rain fell. The hidden river gurgled nearby. Sofia stumbled on the uneven path that led up into the forest. Raymond cursed her clumsiness. The first time she fell, Valentino turned back to help her, and Raymond slapped her as a reminder to keep his distance.

They arrived at a camp deep in the jungle. Tang warned Valentino and Raymond that if they expected to live, they would put aside their feud. To underline his authority, Tang removed Sofia to the edge of the large clearing. An armed guard had orders to shoot her if there was trouble.

Sofia sat on a log beside a sulky fire, enduring her ordeal without weeping or complaint. The rain had stopped, and insects buzzed around her. The smoke was an inefficient deterrent.

Tang sat between Valentino and Raymond when they joined the circle of men around a nobler fire. Small animals roasted on spits over the glowing coals. The men ate with their fingers, slicing off pieces of meat with their knives. No-one offered her anything. Her guard leaned against a tree, smoking a putrid cigarette. From out of the jungle, other men came and went from the fire, their weapons held in readiness. As the humidity increased, Sofia fought to stay awake.

Hello, God. I'm in trouble. I can hear Your river calling me. I'm terrified. Please take me in Your hands and keep me safe...

ဆ ✿ ɞ

Piper stood at the desk, impatient for information. "Valentino Horatio's expecting me."

"I'm sorry, sir, but there's no answer from the suite," the female receptionist said.

"Can I speak to someone with higher authority?"

"Of course, sir. Mr Wattana will be with you directly," she said.

As Piper stepped from the counter, John and Romano approached.

"Sophia isn't answering her phone, but the tracking app says she's in this hotel," John said.

"Her phone may be here, but we're too late." Piper frowned. "They're in the Penthouse Suite. It's a serious offence for the butler not to answer the room phone."

An older man wearing the *Maena Sakhay* uniform approached them.

"I'm Mr Wattana. You have some concerns about one of our guests?"

Piper's eyes narrowed in recognition. "Mr Wattana, you may remember me under a different name. I used to be called Pietro Gallo. My grandfather is Augustus Gallo."

The old man's eyes widened in recognition. Piper continued, "My cousin, Valentino Horatio, summoned me. I've arrived to find him missing."

"Mr Horatio has important business and is often away," Mr Wattana said politely.

"His fiancée is also missing, and the butler isn't answering the phone," Piper snapped.

"Excuse me, Mr Wattana," the receptionist called across the room. "These gentlemen are also looking for Mr Horatio."

Piper glanced towards the new arrivals. Three men who weren't in uniform but held themselves with the confidence of law enforcement officers turned. They marched across the foyer towards them.

"It appears you have a bigger problem, Mr Wattana," Piper said. "Valentino knew when I would arrive. He's invited these officers to join us. There will be trouble when they report his disappearance to their superiors. Take us to his suite, and I'll do what I can."

Mr Wattana nodded. The three officers stepped inside as the elevator doors were closing. They each had their identification wallets open, and Piper dismissed them with a wave of his hand.

"No time for introductions," Piper insisted. "You already know who I am, and I know who you represent. Secrecy remains a priority. This operation has become personal, and I'll tolerate no interference."

No-one spoke in the crowded space.

The elevator arrived on the thirty-fourth floor. The 'Do Not Disturb' notification was active on the main entrance to the suite. Mr Wattana led the way along the hallway. He took out a single key on a brass chain. Piper had been correct in his assumption. This older man wore a servant's uniform to conceal his authority.

On the counter inside the door were two cardboard boxes which oozed a foul liquid. Piper read the top label. He flipped up the lids to reveal the mutilated scorpions. The muck on a battered frying pan told a gruesome tale. "Someone sent Sofia a nasty gift."

A peeled mango lay spoiling on a cutting board, and more fruit was lying on the floor.

"Is this the butler's room?" Piper asked. He found a body slumped over the bed. The handle of a kitchen knife protruded from his uniform. Mr Wattana cried out, but Piper held him back. Piper looked to the three officers and shook his head. "Wait until we know more. Keep quiet while I search. I work best without distraction.

"Romano, you search the rooms to the right. This hallway leads to the guest wing. There are a few rooms to check. John, you go with him and keep trying Sofia's phone. She may be hiding somewhere. Everyone else with me – Mr Wattana, you can wait here."

Mr Wattana shook his head, indicating that he didn't want to be left behind.

Piper moved through the apartment with the confidence of one used to being obeyed.

"The dining room's clear, now the living room — here's one of the attackers." He hurried forward and examined a body on the floor. The other men stood a short distance away, as Piper carried out his investigation. "Looks like a local ruffian; fits the description of the market attackers. Died instantly, still has his knife. Valentino killed him." Piper pointed at the weapon. "That's his blade. My cousin rarely misses."

The three officers exchanged glances at this revelation, and Mr Wattana looked away. Piper ignored them, continuing his monologue as he moved around the room.

"From the body's position, the attackers were hiding in the next room and took Valentino by surprise. He would have been over there near the dining room to throw his blade with such force. There are no signs of a struggle. They must have caught Sofia before he could do anything else."

Romano and John rejoined them.

"The rooms were empty, but your cousin's clothes were there. We found damp towels in the bathroom, and someone slept on one of the beds with their boots on," Romano said.

"There was nothing of Sofia's in those rooms," John added, turning his attention away from the body to try phoning Sofia again. Music began to play. "Her phone's in there!"

John rushed into the smaller living room. The others followed. Two mobile phones sat side by side on a table. An opened bottle of whisky and a single glass sat beside them. Chairs had been dragged over to a separate table and bottles of local beer were scattered on the floor.

"Four locals and one mastermind," Piper surmised. He turned towards the study. All the furniture was upended. Tossed on the floor was a bowl of fruit. Piper bent down and looked closely at the damaged teak floor. "That is from the earlier scorpion episode."

"How can you be sure?" one of the officers asked.

"That mark was made by the butler's saucepan. And this is where Valentino skewered one of the scorpions. There's no gore on the blade in the other room, so he had time to clean it. The only things harmed in this room were the scorpions and the antique furniture. Now, let's check the master bedroom. Sofia's clothes are in the dressing room.

She went down to the pool this morning, but afterwards, she changed in a hurry."

Piper turned abruptly and spoke severely to Mr Wattana. "How does Valentino travel to his meetings? By car, or helicopter?"

"Helicopter."

"Quickly, find out when the helicopter left. And how many passengers were collected."

As soon as the older man left, Piper turned to the three officers. "Have you been fully briefed for *Operation Phoenix*? Good. I'll leave you to take over here. I'm going after the hostages. I need a contact number so I can keep in touch. Be discreet. Otherwise, the operation will fail. Avoid telling the family what's happened, to buy me more time."

Piper pocketed both phones and beckoned to John and Romano. They left quickly, meeting Mr Wattana in the hallway.

"They left in a helicopter six hours ago. Mr Horatio was the pilot. There were two passengers, another man and a woman. Is there anything more I can do?"

"Keep what you know to yourself. I've asked the officers to be discreet. There's no need to panic your guests. Forget you've seen me. If any of the family should ask after Valentino, you don't know anything. Do you understand? Someone will call for Sofia's belongings in the morning, so make them secure. Here's my card."

"What now?" Romano asked as they left the hotel.

"The others are meeting us across the Chao Phraya River. Thomas is bringing the tracker."

"Why didn't you get the tracker first?" John asked.

"I had to make sure the bangle wasn't there. Pastor, you'd better pray she's still wearing it, and we pick up the signal when we get near. Finding Valentino's phone was an unexpected bonus. He's left us coordinates to follow, but finding her in the jungle will require another of Evie's miracles."

"Who are you phoning now?"

"I need a little distraction. Those men we met at the hotel can provide it. We have to go into armed militia territory. A squadron of jets will send the rebels into hiding. I want to be able to slip in and out without anyone getting in our way."

⁎

Sofia awoke. She lay on the damp mulch beside her log. The fire had died, and insects crawled over her. She scrambled up, brushing them away. A strong wind blew, and it started to rain. Within minutes, the jungle floor was awash. Sheets of rain smashed against her, bruising her skin. Her dress clung to her body. She crawled to the nearest tree seeking shelter. The armed guard had vanished. The other fire still smouldered, but she was alone.

The storm was brief. The late afternoon sun returned, and the jungle grew steamy. Sofia was miserable. She walked around the clearing, listening for clues. Then she returned to her log. A puddle had collected in a hollow. Sofia slurped the liquid greedily and looked for more. While she searched, a sudden roar erupted overhead. Somewhere high above, jets were flying past. Afterwards, the jungle fell strangely quiet, and only the voice of the river reached her ears.

The sound of approaching gunfire from across the clearing broke the silence. Valentino burst into the open.

"Sofia, run!" he shouted.

She turned and fled. Valentino's pounding feet drove her onward along an unfamiliar trail. The sound of the river intensified. The path in front of her suddenly disappeared, and she slid to a halt. Sofia retreated from the crumbling bank. She stared in fascination as the water devoured the soft earth. There was no time to warn him. Valentino grabbed her as his momentum propelled him out over the torrent. Her head went under the churning water. Sofia clung to him in desperation, but the water was too powerful. Torn from his arms, she plunged into her dream.

Rescue of Recovery?

ঙ ☼ ଷ

Deuteronomy 30:11
For this commandment which I command you today
is not too hard for you or too distant.

ঙ ☼ ଷ

"We move as soon as it's light." Piper's small team huddled around the lamp. They had already dismantled their makeshift camp.

Piper unfolded the large contour map on the ground. As he spoke, he pointed to different locations.

"We're here. It should take an hour to reach the river. We're aiming for this section, near the third series of rapids where the river widens. The flood crest from yesterday's storm should have passed in the night.

"If we fail to find anything at the river, we'll hike back to their helicopter. This area is where that transponder was picked up. The reports I received overnight indicate there's a rebel base camp to the northwest. Somewhere here, an easy hike from the helicopter. The task force is searching for the rebels in this area, upriver from the base camp. We're focusing downriver."

"What else did you learn? Was Sofia seen?" Romano asked.

"Preliminary reports confirm three Australians, including a woman, were at the camp. All three supposedly died as the government troops closed in."

"So, this is a recovery mission?" This question came from Nelson Felmingham, a brilliant strategist with jungle training. "If they died at the camp, why are we down here? Why focus on the river?"

Nelson, and Oliver Johnston, the final member of Piper's team, came with them from Melbourne. Piper was not ready to admit he was following a hunch. John and Romano were alert. He attempted a convincing bluff. "My cousin would take the quickest route out. The river's an obvious choice."

"Even in full flood?" Nelson asked.

"The rebels were heavily armed. Given a choice between a bullet or a fast-moving river, my cousin would have backed himself and chosen the river."

Nelson shook his head. "How would he convince Sofia to jump in the river?"

"Sofia has a connection with rivers," John conceded with a frown. "Perhaps she saw this as her destiny."

"Thomas said she swims like a mermaid," Oliver reminded them. "Have you had an update from him? He wasn't happy remaining in Bangkok."

"Someone had to stay in case Sofia returned. Thomas reported nothing useful. The family are in hiding. We still don't know which of them accompanied Valentino and Sofia. Patrick's impatient to be released, and the doctors may discharge him tomorrow."

Piper refolded the map to define the search area.

"We'll break into two teams. Oliver, take the helicopter and search the river. Start near the base camp, but be careful."

Oliver leaned closer and Piper continued. "Use the heat-seeking radar to alert you to ground activity. We're on the wrong side of the border. Both the government forces and the rebels will shoot you down. Even though we refuelled before crossing the border, we have limited flight time. One of your priorities is to identify safe landing sites."

Piper looked at John, who was listening carefully. "John, I'm sending you as his spotter. You'd only slow us down on foot. Oliver will tell you how to use the equipment. The heat-seeking radar has an audible alarm, so you should focus on trying to pick up the tracker signal. The receiver's range is fifty kilometres with accuracy to one hundred metres. But that's in an urban setting. We don't know what impact the jungle will have on the signal. There are too many unknowns." Piper turned back to Oliver. "Make a couple of passes rather than waste fuel in a more focused search. Stay with the river, and pray for a miracle. Keep radio contact to a minimum. If you don't find anything, we'll regroup here." Piper pointed to the rendezvous point.

Oliver wrote down the map coordinates in his notebook, then stood, shouldering his pack. He nodded to John and the pair moved off towards the helicopter. Piper put the map back in the waterproof case, took out his hand-held GPS tracker, and stood. Romano and Nelson rose to their feet in readiness.

"If there are no more questions, let's go," Piper told them.

ஐ ✺ ❀

Sofia lay still, waiting for the dream to end. The roar of the water was fading, but it was taking too long. Then she remembered the preceding day's adventures. Was that horror part of the dream? She longed to open her eyes and find herself in the hotel bedroom.

But what if it wasn't a dream? Memories of being pummelled by a raging river flooded her mind. Her whole body ached, and she moaned. There was something sharp digging into her back. Her arms and legs were cramped. She must be lying on ground strewn with branches. Sofia tried to open her eyes again. A heavy blanket was smothering her. She wrestled to free her arms, desperate to claw away this suffocating mass, but she was bound.

Without her sight, her imagination populated this strange bed with a thousand creatures. The heavy smell of rotting vegetation filled her nostrils. Sofia choked in disgust. She renewed her attempt to sit up, flexing her knees and rocking her torso. Weird cracking and groaning sounds erupted around her. The world lurched sideways and shuddered. That added to her confusion. Where was she?

A voice called to her from far away.

"Sofia, you have to wake up. Sofia. O God, help me. Sofia, I can't reach you."

Sofia. Awake.

Sofia came fully alert. She remembered everything clearly – the jungle, the armed men, and the storm. Valentino's shout for her to run and the terrible leap. She had expected to die, but she was alive.

Her arms were immobile, but she could move her head and upper body. With all her strength, Sofia bucked and jerked. She ignored the crick-cracking sounds that greeted her movement. A raft of muck slid down her face. She spat, gasping for breath. Then her eyes flew open.

Morning sunshine forced her to filter the terrifying scene through narrow slits. She was high above the water. The river stretched before her. It surged through a narrow rock-lined gorge, before dividing into two tributaries.

The torrent on her left was still raging over the rapids as the rainbow spray rose into the air. The river must be furious to have lost her. The waves seemed so far away.

"Sofia?"

Valentino lay on a debris-strewn outcrop of rock, covered in mud and looking up at her. Sofia hung like a twisted scarecrow, tangled in the branches of an ancient tree. The roots remained buried in a narrow cleft in the rock. The weathered tree had survived the flood. It had collected a tangle of broken branches, vines and jungle litter as the water receded. These had woven together like an untidy tapestry, holding her fast.

Sofia looked from the rocky outcrop to the second tributary. Even in the short time since she opened her eyes, the mud revealed the receding water level. The river had found a crack between two boulders, creating a waterfall. The escaping water forged a new path as it pushed against the softening earth. Sofia watched great swathes of dark mud slither downward, exposing massive tree roots.

With a mighty crash, a giant tree fell into the river. It tore out nearby trees and delivered them to their watery grave. The water exploded with the power of their fall. Mud splattered Sofia. Giant boulders dislodged, tumbling down to add to the growing mound. What had been a new river was fast becoming a dam. Water piled up on one side and a muddy shallow formed on the other side

"Sofia," Valentino called again, bringing her back to her predicament. "You have to free yourself. I can't climb up to help you. If you can get down, we have a chance. But if there's been another storm further inland, the water will rise again. You might not have much time."

Sofia focused her energy on freeing her right side. The skin tore on her forearm. Blood flowed, and she bit her lip. Stubbornly she pushed back the pain until her arm broke free. Sofia sobbed with relief. Then she heard a new sound. The whoop-whoop of a helicopter carried to her over the water, growing steadily louder.

"I can hear a helicopter," she shouted. Valentino was already looking in the same direction. He crawled towards her tree seeking a place of concealment.

"Sofia," he cried. "Keep still."

Sofia watched as the small dot in the distance grew. As the machine approached, the air around her began to stir. Strong gusts of wind whipped up by the rotor blades picked up small sticks and dollops of sun-dried mud. Sofia cried out in alarm and tried to protect her face.

She peeked through her fingers. The machine was close enough to make out two figures in the cockpit. Now larger branches were swaying and shifting as the whole aerie shuddered. The delicate balance broke. A sickening crack echoed through the ravine. With a scream, Sofia pitched forward. Her woody cocoon plummeted towards the ground.

The boulder rose to meet her at an alarming speed, but then it passed by. With an eruption of mud, Sofia landed face down in the shallows. The swirling water enveloped her face as the mud consumed her. In wordless desperation, her heart cried out to God. Darkness fell and the river's distant song faded.

Eager to Escape

℘ ☼ ℘

Romans 12:12 WEB
Rejoicing in hope; enduring in troubles;
continuing steadfastly in prayer.

℘ ☼ ℘

"Sofia!" A voice was calling through the fog. She could feel an arm around her, holding her upright – keeping her head clear of the slurry. "Sofia," Valentino cried again. "I don't have the strength to hold you above the water. I'm going to drag you higher up the bank. I can't break you free. Some of the larger branches have smashed but the vines are still holding everything tight. Can you use your free arm to claw your way forward?"

"I can try. Valentino, what happened to the helicopter?"

"After the tree broke, it hovered overhead. I couldn't leave you to drown, so I crawled out. The pilot waited long enough to confirm I'd reached you, and then flew away to land somewhere. You have to get free before someone gets here."

"Who were they?"

"I don't know. The markings were from Bangkok. They could be looking for us. I'm hoping it was Piper."

Sofia was puzzled. "Why would Piper be here?"

"I asked him to come."

"And if it isn't Piper?"

He didn't answer. Sofia heard him groaning as he seized hold of a branch. He lurched forward, before collapsing in the mud. Valentino tried again and again. Each time, they made a little progress. More than once Sofia went under the water. Sofia had to push with all her might to raise her head above the muck, and then he would hold her. When her panting ceased, he would rearrange his grip and try again.

Little by little, he dragged her until he reached a waist-high obelisk. This rock had been uncovered by the receding water. He pulled himself upright and heaved. Sofia wrapped her arm around the spire and wrenched herself onto her knees. With a mighty grunt, Valentino pushed, and the mud released her. Clinging to the rock and panting, the weight of the tangled carapace pulled her backwards. Valentino held her fast.

"This is going to take time," he warned her, as he attacked the vines and branches that confined her. He had a thin blade in his left hand, and he slashed and gouged with this feeble weapon. His other arm hung useless at his side.

When he had severed a length of vine, he looped it around the rock to anchor her. This extra support enabled Sofia to assist. She concentrated on liberating her other arm. Then she tore at the remainder of the bindings. Her fingernails ripped, but she ignored the pain.

With a mighty crash, a massive load fell from her as a large section of vine-entangled jungle debris broke away. The momentum pulled her backward into the mud, but Sofia frantically clung to her rock. She wrestled herself free from the remaining constraints. Breathless and exhausted, she leaned against the rock with her eyes closed.

Valentino fell silent.

Raising her head, she looked for him. Valentino lay on his back, collapsed in the mud. His breathing was irregular. Sofia crawled towards him, sobbing and calling his name.

Sofia's tears fell on his unresponsive face as she knelt beside him. She wriggled her hands under his body and tried to drag him from the mud. She couldn't move him. Sofia lay beside him weeping and wordlessly pleading with God for mercy. Wrapping her arms around him, she held him close and rocked. She sang a tuneless lullaby until weariness overcame her.

"Sofia," Valentino's voice was loud in her ear. She awoke with a start. How long had she been asleep? The thick mud clinging to her had baked in the sun.

"Sofia, you have to go. I want you to live."

"I'm not leaving you," she protested. "I refuse to give up hope."

"Sofia, there's no hope for me. I've lost too much blood. The river's calling me."

"We're safe from the river here." She renewed her rescue efforts.

"Sofia, save your strength. If you won't leave, sit and talk with me until I go."

"You have to stay with me until Piper gets here. He'll know what to do."

"I was already dead when I hit the water. More than one bullet found its mark. I fought to stay alive until you were free."

"You were shot? What happened?"

"A squadron of jets flew overhead. Raymond told them I was a government informer, but Tang said he could no longer trust either of us. He and I were bound together and dragged off into the jungle. They were discussing plans for our execution, but I managed to escape."

"What happened to Raymond?"

"I've had my revenge. Sofia, when I'm dead, take back your ring. Make a new life. Don't let my family rob you. Sofia – so dark. Hear the river..."

"Turn away from the darkness, Valentino. Look for the light. God offers everyone a chance for salvation. Call out to Jesus and be saved. Death is a new beginning for those who belong to Him."

"I'm evil."

"No. Your deeds were evil, but even at our worst, God wants to make each of us pure and clean. Call out to Jesus and be saved."

"Too late," he coughed, and blood trickled from his mouth.

"It's never too late. Please, Valentino. You can't leave me here knowing you died without hope."

"Sofia?" He opened his eyes and focused on her face. "Thank you – for refusing – to – give up – hope." His voice was barely a whisper. "Loving you – best thing..."

❧ ☼ ☙

Piper's rescue team stood high on the bank above the new tributary. Two bodies lay stranded above the muddy waterline. There was no sign of movement, no response to their calls.

When the news reached Piper that the missing pair had been found, a brief celebration had given them new energy. Oliver found a small clearing not too far from the river. The ground team turned aside to use their machetes to prepare the landing site. It had taken valuable time, but it was essential. The helicopter circled overhead until Oliver determined it was sufficient for their needs. The radar revealed they had the jungle to themselves.

"Nelson, secure these ropes to that stand of trees," Piper commanded. "Oliver, have you finished making those stretchers? John, help him carry them over. Romano, bring me the first aid kit and those life jackets."

"Why do you need lifejackets?" John asked as Nelson and Piper wrestled into them. Romano tied another pair of floatation devices and a heavy waterproof bag to a rope.

"There's been another storm further north, and it's blowing this way," Piper replied. "The next flood crest may be here before we're ready. We have one chance to get them out. Nelson and I will remain tethered. We might have trouble escaping the mud.

"Wait until Nelson and I are on the ground before lowering everything else. Don't let go until I give the signal. Romano, we may have to rely on your strength to get us back up the cliff."

It took ten minutes to satisfy Piper's stringent requirements. Then a further twenty minutes for the two men to carefully lower themselves down. The newly exposed cliff face was prone to slippage.

"Lower the other ropes," Piper shouted as he and Nelson stood beside the deeper mud. Their boots were slowly sinking, and cool dampness oozed between Piper's toes. His military training kicked in, and he shut out the distraction. "I'll wait for the gear. You go and find out if we're too late."

Nelson squelched his way across the gap towards the prone figures.

"Sofia's still alive," Nelson shouted. "Her pulse is faint. Bring over the saline, and I'll set up the IV. It's too late for Horatio. He's been dead at least an hour."

Piper swore, then focused on preparing the emergency supplies. He would find it hard to forgive himself. But he had work to do. Piper carefully passed Nelson the saline and some bottled water to wash away the mud.

While Nelson took care of Sofia, Piper picked up one of the stretchers. He unfolded a body bag over it, before carrying it across to his cousin. Piper rolled the lifeless body into the bag. His training sustained him through the morbid task. Nelson reached over to prevent the slurry from flooding the bag. Piper could not resist confirming his cousin was dead. Then he closed the zipper, sealing Valentino's fate.

"Carry Sofia to the cliff and tie her to the stretcher there. Send up the equipment. Then come back and help me with the body."

Nelson nodded, lifting Sofia onto his shoulder. He took care with the intravenous line. Piper watched him take giant steps through the mire. Piper said his silent goodbyes to his cousin as he knelt in the mud. He had questions that remained unanswered. Memories of their shared childhood flashed through his mind. Piper thought bitterly of their separation. He vowed to make this family pay for their corruption and betrayal. And he promised Valentino he would keep Sofia free to rebuild her life.

Piper examined the chain he had removed from the dead man and placed it around his neck. The small cross would remind him of his promise. Then Piper examined the ring. He would have to wait for Sofia's recovery to satisfy his curiosity. As he delayed, the call of the river grew louder. Piper shuddered.

"Do you hear that?" Nelson asked as he waded through the sludge. "The river has found its voice. We have to get out of here."

The pair grabbed the poles and raised the stretcher above the mud. Reaching the cliff, they tied their burden securely and watched as it made its way up. They grabbed separate ropes and expertly began to climb. They were only halfway up the cliff when the first waves surged over the temporary dam wall. The torrent roared at them as the water rose higher and higher.

"Get us up!" Piper shouted, and Romano's giant figure appeared above them. He hauled on both ropes with all his strength. The two climbers flew upwards. As soon as their feet were on the firmer ground, Oliver and John slashed their tethers with machetes. Everyone fled from the crumbling edge. Above the roar of the water, the closest trees groaned and screeched. Then they toppled into the flood.

"Romano, your time in the gym was well-spent," Piper remarked. Nelson and Oliver picked up the lighter stretcher. John walked beside Sofia, carrying the saline bag. They headed into the jungle. The path they had slashed through the undergrowth was narrow. Piper waited until they were out of sight before he turned towards the second stretcher.

"Death isn't the end," Romano said quietly, as he took up his position at the rear. "God waits to greet His children as they come home."

Piper laughed bitterly. "Valentino was no saint. If there's an afterlife, he's gone straight to hell."

"You said he was different when you talked to him. God's been pursuing both your cousin and Sofia. He was with them in this crisis. God always accepts a repentant sinner, even when that decision comes at the last minute. Valentino died protecting Sofia, and God will take that into account. God considers there to be no greater sacrifice than when a man lays down his life for someone he loves."

"There'll be time to talk about this later. Move."

Heavy droplets of rain fell as the helicopter prepared to take off. Piper frowned as he stepped aside to take an incoming call.

"We brought the Australian's body out to the helicopter," the voice informed him. "My forces are leaving the area. You have a limited window to retrieve the helicopter. Manage this, and no-one will ask any questions. My men have lowered the camouflage nets, but the next reconnaissance flight will pass by in an hour."

"Is there room to land a second helicopter?" Piper asked.

"No. Is that a problem?"

"No."

"Consider my debt repaid."

The line went dead.

Piper hurried to the waiting helicopter.

"There's been a change of plans," Piper said, signalling Oliver to take off. "Pass me some ropes. I need to drop down to retrieve the second helicopter. They have lowered the camouflage netting. Activate the receiver and follow the ping. We have to be quick. There'll be a reconnaissance flight soon, and they'll shoot us down if we're still this side of the border."

"Why not leave the helicopter?" Nelson asked.

"There's another body to retrieve. I won't go home without answers. There's also a reward to collect. It's only fair my family pay."

Hearts and Hands

❀

Psalm 51:12 WEB
Restore to me the joy of Your salvation.
Uphold me with a willing spirit.

❀

John watched as Piper shouted at the bathroom door. "Sofia, you have to come out. We're due at the airport."

There was no answer.

Piper turned to Romano and John. "One of you will have to go in there."

"Don't look at me," Romano said. "She already hates me for marrying her sister. Isn't this why we brought John?"

"She threw her breakfast at me at the hospital," John protested. "Piper, you're the trained commando."

"Romano doesn't pay me enough," Piper answered. "I agree with him. This is your assignment, John."

"I'm the last person who should go in. The shower's still running. What if she hasn't any clothes on?"

Piper grinned at John's hesitation. "That's her third shower since she left the hospital. She should be clean by now. Turn off the water, throw her a towel and tell her to get dressed. If that fails, throw her a bathrobe and Romano will carry her onto the plane wearing that. We have the release letter from the hospital explaining her medical condition. That should get us through security in a hurry. I'm sure you'll think of something."

John felt like a condemned man. He said a quick prayer. Then he gripped the doorknob, but it didn't turn. John sighed with relief. "It's locked."

"Sofia, open the door or Romano will break it down," Piper shouted.

Instantly there was a click, and the door opened inward. Sofia reached out and grabbed John by the shirtfront. She dragged him into the bathroom, slamming the door again.

"What are you doing here?" she hissed.

He had his eyes closed, and he wasn't expecting her to shove him. "John, open your eyes."

He cautiously obeyed. Sofia was standing before him, fully dressed. His eyes focused on her injuries. Her face was battered and bruised, and one of her eyes was swollen shut. Her lips were cracked, and her face was peeling. Sofia had concealed the rest of her injuries. What was she wearing? Over a long floral dress, Sofia wore a man's silk shirt. It was too large for her small frame. She held the flapping sleeves crossed over her chest.

"Why are you angry at me?" he asked.

"John, where were you when Valentino was dying? Why didn't Piper find us sooner? Why did God let me live? I have a thousand questions, John, and you won't answer any of them, so I'll settle for the answer to a single question. Why are you here?"

"If I promise to answer, will you come with us to the airport?"

Sofia wrenched the door open. She stormed past Piper and Romano, through the apartment and into the hallway. "I thought we were in a hurry?"

The three men followed her out to the forecourt, where the taxi was waiting. Romano carried Sofia's bag. She climbed in beside the driver, and her companions took the rear seat. This hotel was close to the airport. The driver attempted polite conversation, which was met by Sofia's prickly silence.

When they arrived at the airport, John hastened to open Sofia's door. She glared at him. He followed her inside, noting her movement had slowed. She favoured one leg and walked as if each step was torture. All the bravado had deserted her.

Piper produced the tickets and her passport, before leading the way to the check-in desk. At the security checkpoint, the uniformed men looked at Sofia's injuries with suspicion. Piper handed them the hospital documents for inspection. A guard waved Sofia on. Piper and Romano also passed by quickly. Then the officer selected John for a more meticulous examination.

John rejoined them in a small cafe near their departure lounge. Sofia was sitting in the corner. She had a bottle of water clasped between her sleeve-covered hands. Romano and Piper had ordered coffee and left John the seat beside Sofia. John sat down and waited. A waitress delivered their drinks. John accepted his cup. Sofia raised her sad eyes and glanced around the table, her gaze settling on John.

"I came to the airport, John. Now you owe me an answer. What are you doing here?"

"Jenny came and dragged me out of my bed," John told her. "Your fiancé asked Piper to bring me. I was supposed to persuade you to come home."

"Why would Valentino want John here?" Sofia directed that question at Piper.

"He knew you trusted John."

"What made him think that?" Sofia asked.

"He saw the tapes."

"What tapes?" John interjected.

"The tapes from the security cameras outside the *Raphael Towers* building," Piper told him. "Remember I showed you a photo, John. The tapes showed you holding Sofia. Valentino was jealous."

"If he was jealous, why would he ask for John?"

"Valentino was planning for the future," Piper said. "He didn't expect to survive. John's his replacement to keep you safe from his predatory family."

"Whoa," John said. "No way. I'm not his replacement."

"So, you don't want me?" Sofia asked.

"I didn't say that."

"So, you do want me?"

"I didn't say that either," John glanced sideways to the other men. They were trying to conceal their amusement. "The timing's all wrong. Your heart's broken."

"How long would you wait, John? A month, two months, a year? Would you let me fall for another villain and do nothing to save me? What kind of man are you to say you care for me and do nothing to protect me?"

"I never said I cared..."

Sofia laughed bitterly and pulled up her sleeve. She fought to remove her engagement ring from her swollen finger. John looked at her torn nails and winced at her pain. She placed the ring on the table between them.

"Valentino said he didn't care for me either. He said he was sorry he'd involved me in his troubles. I gave him back his ring, and I hated him for hurting me. He sent for you because he thought I'd be desperate after he rejected me. I was a fool to think he loved me, but he was the greater fool to think a man like you would want me. You know all my secrets, and you would never make that mistake."

"If you gave him back this ring, why do you have it now?" John asked.

"Piper gave it to me at the hospital. Valentino said I should keep it after he was dead. I put it back on because I didn't want to lose it, but now I don't feel right wearing it. You can have it, John. Find your boys a nice mother and live a happy life."

John looked at the ring, before sliding it back towards her. "Sofia, you're hurt and angry now, but these feelings will pass. Keep the ring. If you decide you don't want it later, you can sell it. When you first wore it, you were happy, and someday in the future, you'll be happy again."

"Is that supposed to make me feel better, John? Another promise for me to hang on to until reality hits me? Do you know what hurts the most, John? I was so desperate to be married.

"I had doubts, but I stomped on them. I promised I would make this relationship work, even if I had to break all my other promises. I would do whatever was necessary to make Valentino want me. That's how pathetic I am, John.

"I don't want your pity. I was willing to give up everything that mattered to me for an impossible happy-ever-after. Instead, I got what I deserved. The ring no longer belongs to me. You can sell it, or give it away."

John picked up the ring. His heart was racing. Did he have the courage to speak the revelation God had given him? "You said I could do whatever I want with this ring? Then I'll claim it as my possession. I'm going to give it to you to take care of for me. Give me your hand, Sofia."

Slowly Sofia held out her hand, and John pushed up the silk sleeve to reveal her wounded fingers.

"The man who gave you this ring paid with his life to prove his love for you. It wasn't the happy-ever-after kind of love, which was imperfect and would fade over time. Instead, it was a love that acknowledged he'd harmed you and broken your heart. He had nothing more to give you but the chance for you to live and love again.

"You said you hated him, but you stayed by his side long after he died. Both the love Valentino offered you as he was dying, and the love you showed him in return, is the sacrificial love that comes from God. God gave each of you an opportunity to make an offering. I believe God has received both sacrifices and will bless your obedience. He will continue to call you and lead you. God promises to take care of you forever.

"You no longer need a husband to achieve happiness. Only when you understand that will God reveal the future he has for you. God has made provision for both a husband and other children. God's love never fails and lasts forever, and He never breaks a promise."

Sofia was weeping, and her hand trembled. Carefully, John twisted the ring to restore it to its former home.

"With this ring," he said softly, "God makes you a promise. He will make sure you don't fall in love with another villain. He will be the true friend who listens to you in the watches of the night. God will warn you when you are about to stray. He will give you the wisdom and discernment to make a better life for yourself and your children. These men are God's witnesses. I deliver this promise in the name of God, Father, Son and Holy Spirit. Amen."

CHAPTER 38
(Wednesday 25th October)

Trials and Temptations

℘ ☼ ℘

℘ ☼ ℘

Their flight was behind schedule. It arrived at Sydney airport at three o'clock on Wednesday morning. Piper sent Romano and the others to find Sofia and John. He had negotiated with the airline to transfer her dead fiancé's ticket to John so she would not travel in First Class alone. Piper, Romano and the rest of his team had been seated in the lower section.

Piper hadn't slept during the flight, and his mood was grim. Repatriating two coffins was a complicated process. One coffin was destined for Melbourne. But a Sydney funeral director was collecting Valentino's body. Impatient to rejoin the others, Piper scanned the main hall. Romano was easy to find, standing tall above the crowd. Sofia and John were with him, at the foot of the escalator. Piper strode over to them.

"I thought the authorities had deported you," Romano said.

"The paperwork had to be checked and confirmed. The supervisor wasn't happy to be hauled out of bed so early. Did Patrick and the others make their Melbourne flight?"

"Yes. Thomas sent a message ten minutes ago to say they were boarding their plane," Romano replied.

"Why aren't we on the same flight?" Sofia asked, her exhaustion evident.

"Unfinished business. Let's get a taxi and find a hotel."

Piper rubbed his forehead to ease the dull ache, then shouldered his bag. He turned to find his way blocked by a middle-aged man. Piper swore.

"I'm sorry you're not happy to see me, Piper," the Italian-Australian said, with a smile that said otherwise. "Your grandfather sent me to collect you. Augustus received your news with great sorrow. He has made the appropriate arrangements."

The attractive man turned towards Sofia and bowed graciously to her. "Miss Fontana, my name's Ricardo Barononi. We're sorry for your loss. This has been a great shock to everyone. If there is anything you require, you have only to ask. Consider me your humble servant.

"I'm to take you and your companions to Valentino's Sydney apartment, where you may rest. I will collect you at noon and take you to the cathedral to confirm arrangements before the funeral. His mother Doña Gabriella Marcella has decided not to wait for his sisters to return from Thailand. The service is at two."

Ricardo offered Sofia his arm, but she chose instead to walk beside him.

"I don't like him," John muttered, as he picked up his bag and prepared to follow her.

Piper turned to John. "Augustus is wasting no time in planning for her future. Hurry and catch up with them. You don't want him alone with her." John looked at Piper and then towards Sofia. Piper watched John's reaction and was satisfied when the pastor hurried away. He turned to Romano, who was frowning.

"Why the interest in Sofia now Valentino's dead?" Romano asked.

"Sofia inherits Valentino's estate. The family, both here in Sydney and in Melbourne, will want to regain control of his assets. Once the transfer's settled, Sofia will be extremely wealthy. I don't think she understands that yet."

₧☉ℚ

The Sydney apartment had a view of the harbour. The sky was lightening when Sofia and her group arrived. Sofia puzzled over the rude way Piper dismissed Ricardo, closing the door in his face. Standing in the middle of the spacious living room, she was not surprised to see a grand piano. It was white like all the larger furnishings. Sofia walked to the piano and lifted the lid, striking one of the keys. The note rang out, adding to her melancholy.

Sofia walked around the room. She ran her hand across the polished surfaces and examined the colourful artwork. She could imagine Valentino filling this room with his presence. Sofia half expected him to appear at any moment. She stood looking out the window and could see by their reflections the others were watching her.

"Is there anything we can get you?" Piper asked from across the room. "I know where most things are."

"I could do with a drink, but the doctor said I should stick to water for the next few days. Show me where I can lie down. If I have a funeral to go to, then I need some sleep."

"The master bedroom's through here," Piper said.

Sofia followed Piper through an archway. He left her after opening the bedroom door. Sofia sighed. She went to the built-in wardrobe and opened the doors. The closet was full of his clothes. Sofia changed into one of Valentino's crisp white shirts.

She walked to the adjoining bathroom. As in Valentino's Melbourne apartment, women's toiletries sat beside his requirements. Sofia sprayed his familiar aftershave into the air. What comfort was there in knowing she was the last woman he had loved when there had been so many? Sofia threw herself across the king-sized bed and cried herself to sleep.

🙂 ☼ ᘯ

A few hours later, Sofia's screams brought John instantly to his feet. He had been resting on one of the sofas. John had been dreading the return of her nightmare, and hurried to her bedroom. Sofia's eyes were closed, and she was wrestling an invisible enemy. Her heart-wrenching terror ripped at his composure. That was the first time he had been present to hear her screams. He began to pray aloud as he sat beside her on the bed. Sofia turned towards his voice and threw her arms around him. He embraced her until the sobbing subsided.

"Everything under control?" Piper asked. He and Romano were both standing in the open doorway. John had warned them the nightmare might return. John nodded, and moved to get up. Sofia clung to him in desperation. He could see she was still lost to the dream, not yet fully awake.

"Don't leave me, John! I don't want to be alone."

John prised her arms from around his neck and spoke gently. "I'm in the next room. Go back to sleep. When you wake up, this terror will be forgotten."

"Stay with me," she pleaded, catching hold of him around his torso. If he pulled away, she might fall off the bed. While he hesitated, Sofia reached up and kissed him.

John forgot how to breathe. As his mind struggled to comprehend what was happening, his arms wrapped around Sofia. John pulled her upright from the bed and held her close. He kissed her with passionate abandon, revealing a secret desire. His loss of control was brief.

When John came to his senses, he released her and pulled away. Sofia appeared frozen in place. He took another step away from her. Her uninjured eye was open, and when she blinked, he knew she was fully awake. Without saying anything, John pushed past Piper and Romano and fled.

Heading to the kitchen, he made himself a strong cup of coffee. Romano followed him but said nothing. John's hands shook as he carried the coffee back to the living room. Sofia was waiting for him. She supported herself by leaning against the piano. The large shirt she was wearing half-covered her bruised legs. John looked away.

"We need to talk," she said. John continued to look at his coffee cup.

"Okay," he said in defeat.

"What happened to your wife, John?"

That was not the topic he expected. He glanced around to confirm the other men had joined them. He must not be alone with her. Piper and Romano were standing together near the archway. Their grim expressions added to his shame.

"You know all *my* secrets," Sofia insisted. "It's only fair you tell me yours." John hesitated, and Sofia spoke again. "I already know your opinion about divorce, so she must have been the one who took action. Why did she leave you? I can think of a dozen reasons. None of them matches what I know about you, John."

"You don't know me at all, Sofia"

"Were you unfaithful? Were you violent? Or did you abuse her?"

John shook his head in dismay.

"No? I thought not," Sofia continued, "Then she left you for another man. Why would she do that John? Did your religion stop you from satisfying her needs?"

John gasped. She thought his marriage failed because God had forbidden sexual intimacy?

"You know how to inflict pain, Sofia." His trembling hands put down his cup on a small table. "I know you're hurting, and I'm sorry for your heartache, but do you have to make everyone else miserable too?" John paused to collect his thoughts. Sofia waited for his confession.

"Arielle made a list of my failings, Sofia. She wrote them down, and I've memorised them. She left behind her two babies, declaring she never wanted to see them again. They were a constant reminder of the kind of man I am. She hated everything about me. She didn't want to be a pastor's wife anymore. She said she couldn't endure another day of watching me give God the best of everything.

"Arielle said I lacked ambition, and she was tired of being poor. She hated the way I gave generously to others when we had so little. She said I let people walk all over me instead of standing up for myself. Everything I saw as a blessing had become a curse in her eyes."

The room fell silent. Sofia nodded. "Your wife was a blind fool, John." Abruptly, Sofia headed to her bedroom and slammed the door.

CHAPTER 39
(Wednesday 25th October)

Funeral and Family

ဆဉ ✿ ଓଃ

ဆဉ ✿ ଓଃ

Sofia stood in the kitchen doorway. It was almost noon. "Where's Piper?"

Romano glanced towards her from the breakfast bar, but John kept his face turned away. John continued clearing the remnants of their late breakfast.

"Piper had to go. He'll rejoin us at the cathedral. Do you want something to eat?" Romano said.

Sofia sighed and shook her head as she settled on the chair beside him. She was wearing her long dress, but this time it was paired with one of Valentino's voluminous black shirts. Romano picked up his coffee cup, and as he took another sip, he frowned towards John.

"This is where the two of you apologise to each other," Romano said.

John turned to face them. "You think it's that easy? I could apologise a hundred times, but it won't change anything. I can't wipe out the memory of what happened. Sofia was frightened and vulnerable, and I took advantage."

Sofia quietly left her seat and approached John. Cautiously, she placed her sleeve-covered hand on his arm.

"If anyone is to blame, it's me. What does it tell you about my character? Here I am grieving one man and trying to seduce another. You were right to reject me. I'm not worthy of you."

Before John could reply, there was a loud knock at the apartment door.

"That'll be Barononi," Romano warned them, as he rose to his feet. Never had Sofia been more aware of Romano's intimidating stature. "Don't take this the wrong way, John, but it would've been better for Sofia if you *had* taken advantage of her. This man thinks she's an easy catch. He'll be looking for any opportunity."

"I'm not an easy catch," Sofia grumbled as she followed Romano.

The good-looking Italian-Australian greeted her with enthusiasm. "Sofia," he beamed. She took a step backwards, bumping into John.

"Ricardo," she responded with a sad smile, keeping her distance. "Again, I must thank you for your kindness. The weight of the coming ordeal makes me poor company today. I'm impatient to get to the cathedral. Piper's meeting us there."

The journey to the cathedral passed in uneasy silence. Sofia ignored Barononi's attempts at conversation. This time, she sat in the back with Romano, leaving John to ride in the front. As the car turned into the underground car park, a black hearse was pulling up in the cathedral forecourt.

"Is that Valentino's coffin?" Sofia asked. When Baronoini nodded, Sofia leapt from the slow-moving car. Soon afterwards, John and Romano appeared on either side of her. By the time Barononi reappeared from parking his car, he was no longer smiling as he talked into his phone.

The undertakers began unloading flowers. They were unaware of her presence until she stepped forward. An elaborate floral tribute was on top of the coffin. She reached out her hand to read the card: 'Valentino, cherished and beloved son of Doña Gabriella Marcella...'

The hypocrisy winded her. Sofia choked back a sob. Turning away, Sofia wrapped her arms across her body.

"Sofia, the priest is waiting to talk with you." Barononi had rejoined them, and again reached out to guide her. Romano pushed his arm aside and stepped between them. Sofia glimpsed a look of pure hatred on Barononi's face and shuddered. How could she have thought this man was kind? Barononi walked a few paces behind them now.

At the top of the steps, Piper was talking with the priest. Sofia recognised Father Finnegan. He was the priest who had travelled from Sydney to take part in Evie and Romano's wedding ceremony. Evie said he protected her from her vindictive aunt. The priest had inspired Evie to live a virtuous life. Sofia remembered her own shameful past. Before she mounted the steps, she glanced towards John, who was walking beside her. When she stood before the priest, Sofia bobbed a small greeting. The old priest took her sleeve-covered hand. Tears came to her eyes at his compassionate welcome.

"My dear Sofia, I'm sorry to be meeting you again in such tragic circumstances. It pleases me to see you have your brother-in-law to take care of you, but I'm surprised to see Pastor Edwards with you. Piper has explained that he's a good friend and trusted counsellor.

"I must warn you some of your fiancé's family may seem unsympathetic to your pain. In particular, his mother has expressed her displeasure at your presence. However, Valentino left instructions for you to oversee his funeral service."

Unable to find her voice, Sofia nodded her understanding. Together with her companions, she accompanied the priest into the smaller chapel. The undertakers were completing their work. Sofia looked at his mother's floral tribute and turned to Piper. She didn't have time to say anything. Piper nodded, then hurried away to talk to the undertakers. She watched as they removed the offending flowers. A cross-shaped arrangement of white roses replaced them.

"I took the liberty of ordering for you," Piper said when he returned.

"What's written on the card?" Sofia asked.

"'The river called to you, my love, and you answered with your life. The curse has broken. God takes care of those who keep their promises.' I phoned Evie this morning, and she told me what to say. I can change it if you want something else?" Piper told her.

"It's perfect," Sofia said through her tears, before turning to the priest. "What other decisions are there to make?"

"There's a small orchestra that will start playing at one-thirty. Here's the orchestra's repertoire. May I suggest Handel's *Water Music* before the eulogy?" Father Finnegan replied.

"They've listed *Amazing Grace*," John commented, looking over her shoulder. "You should remind the mourners that salvation and forgiveness are available to everyone. Even someone with Valentino's past."

"Do you have any preference for Scripture readings?" the priest asked, opening a heavy Bible on the podium.

"Can I have that one about love?" she said, and a small frown came to the old man's face.

"First Corinthians chapter thirteen: Love is patient, love is kind? That's more suitable for a wedding ceremony."

"That's not the one I was thinking of, but can we have that too? I was thinking of the one that says 'greater love has no man than he lay down his life for a friend'."

The priest seemed more comfortable with that choice.

"The Gospel of John chapter fifteen verse thirteen."

"And the one about the river, something about breaking a curse?" Sofia added. "Evie said it's in Revelation."

Father Finnegan opened the large Bible to the final chapter. "Revelation chapter 22: 'Then he showed me the river of the water of life, bright as crystal, flowing from the throne of God and of the Lamb through the middle of the street of the city; also, on either side of the river, the tree of life with its twelve kinds of fruit, yielding its fruit each month; and the leaves of the tree were for the healing of the nations. There shall no more be anything accursed.'" (RSVCE)

"Who's going to give the eulogy?" Father Finnegan asked.

"Piper, would you do that?" Sofia asked. "I know you and Valentino were once inseparable. He turned to you when he realised he was in trouble. I can think of no better way of showing them he'd changed and was no longer willing to be part of their schemes."

❧ ✲ ☙

Sofia lay in the Sydney apartment's darkened bedroom, trying to sleep. Scenes from the funeral service replayed in her mind. She remembered the haughty disdain on his mother's face. The matriarch had marched into the chapel, accompanied by a group of women all wearing black. Sofia had approached to offer words of consolation. But Doña Gabriella Marcella had turned away.

The family mourners had distanced themselves on the opposite side of the chapel. Barononi seemed undecided about which side he should choose. He stood at the rear as if waiting for someone. When other mourners arrived, Sofia heard the ancient woman loudly describe her as a whore. She suggested Sofia should have died with her son.

Gabriella's brother Augustus had arrived late, and joined his sister. Barononi had sat beside him. Afterwards, Augustus approached Sofia. She could not remember his words. But Valentino's uncle was the only one who showed any kindness. Piper's warning kept her from accepting his offer of hospitality. Traumatised by the experience, Sofia didn't go to the interment at the family mausoleum. She said her final goodbyes to Valentino in the chapel.

Sleep eluded her. Sofia looked at the ring John had placed on her finger, and thought about God's promises. Could she believe that God had a future for her, or was she destined to make one mistake after another? She thought of her ruined friendship with John, and wept.

ॐ ✡ ॐ

(Thursday 26th October)

"Home, or face the family?" Romano asked Sofia as she stared out the side window of his Maserati. It was late Thursday afternoon. The car was at a standstill in traffic on the expressway. The others had left them at the Melbourne terminal. John had been eager to return to his boys, and Piper was delivering him home. That left Sofia in Romano's care. These were the first words he had uttered since the airport.

"My heart says home, but my head says family," Sofia confessed. "I feel guilty that Piper didn't let them know we were returning. If I had only myself to think about, I would run home, lock my door, and hide. But I can't afford the luxury of self-pity."

"Your inheritance will allow you many luxuries, but that shouldn't be at the expense of your soul," Romano told her. "You need to have people around you, or you'll forget what it is to be alive."

Sofia turned to look at him. Was he sharing from his own experience?

"What did Piper tell you?" she asked.

"Enough," Romano confessed. "You met with the lawyers this morning? Valentino had already transferred a fortune into your account. Having money isn't as easy as people think it is. There will be many who will want to help you spend it. What are you going to tell your children?"

"About the money? I don't want them to think I'll finance their futures without them making an effort."

"Will you keep working in the restaurant?" Romano asked.

"Until now, I hadn't thought there was an alternative."

Sofia closed her eyes and turned away again. Romano drove the remainder of the way in silence.

"We're here," he announced.

Sofia wanted to ask him to keep driving. "You go first so I can hide in your shadow? I don't know how much Piper told them, and I know I look awful. Take me through the courtyard. I can sneak upstairs without being seen."

Romano did as she requested. Sofia slipped unnoticed up the stairs. The smaller dining room was empty. She switched on the side lamps and settled at a table in the shadows to wait. The sound of running feet on the stairs followed Marco's excited shout.

"Mum's here! Mum! Mum!" The thirteen-year-old boy burst into the room, with Romano immediately behind him. Sofia carefully stood, bracing herself against the table. Romano grabbed his nephew with one of his massive arms. He hoisted Marco off the ground and spun him around. Gratitude welled up in her heart at Romano's practical assistance. Her father Benito and her sixteen-year-old daughter Matilda were a few steps behind. They were distracted by Marco's protests. Then Mama Rosa and Leonardo appeared, with Evie on their heels. Romano barred their way. Then Romano set Marco down and stepped aside.

"Sofia, you should have told us you were coming..." Benito was saying, and then he stopped at the sight of her. Sofia took a small step and burst into tears.

"Oh Papa," she cried. Her family huddled around her. Romano hovered in the background, and Evie went to him in sorrow.

"Your fiancé isn't with you?" Mama Rosa asked, and Sofia gave a strangled cry.

Romano stepped forward, a compassionate look on his face. "I apologise for the secrecy. Our mission didn't go well. When we arrived in Bangkok, Sofia and her fiancé had disappeared. They were taken captive, and Valentino didn't survive. His funeral was yesterday, at the cathedral in Sydney. Sofia's come home alive, but alone."

Reunion Revelations

❀

Deuteronomy 12:26
Take those holy things and what you have vowed to give,
and go to the place the Lord has chosen.

❀

It had been five weeks since Sofia returned to Australia. Her lightly applied makeup concealed the lingering scars. Sofia studied her reflection in the mirror as she added another layer of lipstick. She was leaving her favourite hair salon confident she no longer looked as if she had been neglecting her appearance. The hair stylist had remarked on her prolonged absence, but Sofia had a valid excuse. She had been busy with a new project.

"You look lovely, Sofia," Patrick said, as he and Thomas came across the road to meet her. They stood on either side of her. "Do you still plan to walk to the new restaurant? Thomas can get the car if you're having trouble walking in those heels."

A small smile came to Sofia's solemn face. "I can always lean on you if I have any trouble."

"Are you sure you want to let them know you have bodyguards? Won't that make your luncheon a little awkward?" Patrick asked.

"I haven't met with the Tuesday Girls since I went to Thailand. There's going to be more awkward topics of conversation than you. As we're going to be the only diners, it would be difficult to explain your presence otherwise. I could make you wait outside, but I'd feel better if you stayed where I can see you, Patrick. Jenny reported your full recovery from your injuries, but I don't want you getting into any more trouble."

Setting a brisk pace, Sofia walked to the destination. Thomas and Patrick held back a few metres from the corner. Melissa, Kylie and Natalie were already waiting there. When her friends saw her, they started waving and hurried to embrace her. They were talking all at once, and Sofia laughed at the familiar welcome.

Melissa spoke first. "Hey, Sofia. We decided to meet early to surprise you."

"Happy birthday for last week. At thirty-nine, you look stunning," Kylie added.

"Is that another new dress?" Natalie asked.

Sofia did a slow pirouette to show off the silk dress she had bought at the *Chatuchak Market*. "I had it made in Bangkok, but until this morning I wasn't sure I could bring myself to wear it."

Her simple statement cast a shadow, and her three friends glanced awkwardly at each other. Natalie spoke. "We were sorry to hear about the tragedy in Thailand."

"Thanks for your messages of condolence, and for understanding I needed time to myself," Sofia replied. "I'm sorry I've missed so many of our luncheons. I look forward to finding out what's been happening for each of you. But one of us is missing? Where's Lauren?"

"She's going to be late. We're to send her the address of the restaurant," Kylie said.

"Where are we going, Sofia? Last month, we made the mistake of going back to where Gypsy's restaurant used to be. The food was terrible," Natalie confessed.

"I hope this new place makes a good impression, then," Sofia said as she turned towards a doorway.

"Sofia?" Natalie cried. "The sign in the window says this place isn't open for business yet. The Grand Opening is on the thirtieth of November: this Thursday."

"I know the owner," Sofia assured them. "I've persuaded the chef to allow us a pre-opening taster. Consider this my belated birthday celebration. It's also an apology for shutting you out while I was grieving."

"What kind of restaurant is this, Sofia? The windows are papered over," Natalie said.

"We'd better go in and find out." Sofia pushed the door open. A tinkling bell announced her arrival. The other women followed her. The room they entered was shrouded in shadows. Sofia moved her hand to a panel beside the door. The room filled with light.

"Oh Sofia! This is amazing. Look at the crystal chandeliers," Natalie exclaimed.

"Look at the exquisitely carved panelling for those side booths. I love the little round tables. The bentwood chairs are gorgeous," Melissa added.

"Are these plants real? And is that a water feature?" Kylie rushed across the room. "Wow, it's one of those pebbled waterfalls. Oh, and on the other side there's a lily pond with goldfish."

"Sofia, there's a white grand piano near the bar!"

"Welcome to *Valentino's*," Sofia declared with delight.

Realisation slowly dawned on them, and they turned towards her.

"This is *your* restaurant?" Natalie exclaimed.

"You named it after *him*?" Melissa said.

"Oh Sofia, I can't believe you were able to keep this a secret from us," Kylie concluded.

Again, they were all talking at once. Suddenly Lauren was standing there. She had entered unnoticed.

"Hey, girls. Sorry, I'm late. I thought you sent me the wrong address, but then I heard your laughter. Are you sure we can afford to eat here?"

"We know the owner," Kylie giggled, pointing to Sofia.

"'Welcome to *Valentino's*,' Sofia said," Natalie added.

Lauren's smile faltered. "Is everything alright? You don't seem to be yourself?" Sofia asked.

Lauren wouldn't meet her eye. Sofia felt a twinge of concern. In that awkward silence, the brass bell over the door chimed again as Patrick and Thomas slipped into the restaurant.

Why had they taken so long to make their entrance?

"I see we're not the only early diners," Natalie remarked, looking from Sofia to the two young men with interest. "Is there something else you need to tell us, Sofia? I saw you talking with them outside the hair salon earlier. I was going to call out, but I didn't want to interrupt."

"Meet Thomas and Patrick. I'm going to put them at a separate table. Unfortunately, they're not here for our entertainment. They're here for my protection. Since my adventures in Thailand, I no longer feel safe."

"You have bodyguards, Sofia? What did happen in Thailand? I thought you were involved in an accident?" Natalie asked.

"Here comes the hostess. Please leave me to make my explanation after we've had a few drinks."

An Inspired Invitation

ॐ ☼ ॐ

1 Chronicles 28:20b
Be strong and courageous as you work.
Don't be afraid or discouraged,
for the Lord my God, is with you.
He will not fail you, nor forsake you before you finish.

ॐ ☼ ॐ

The Grand Opening of *Valentino's* was in full swing. Sofia had chosen Thursday morning so her parents could attend. She planned carefully. Among the fifty guests were some of the more influential food critics.

"What an excellent idea to have a 'bruncheon' opening," one of them was saying. "You have made your independent entrance to the restaurant scene with a flourish. I was expecting something in keeping with your family tradition. But this is refreshing."

"Where did you get the idea to include the piano?" another asked.

In her speech, Sofia had announced there would be a professional pianist in the afternoons, but at other times, anyone could play. "The piano belonged to my late fiancé. I wanted to do something special to honour his memory. The concept for *Valentino's* revolves around the piano."

"His family own *Raphael Towers* and the *Renaissance* nightclub, don't they? I've been looking for his family representatives, but there don't seem to be any here?"

Sofia looked away, not wanting to say anything about the difficulties that had arisen. As his legal heir, the apartment and all that was within it was hers. She had been willing to surrender the apartment in exchange for the piano. His family had responded by delivering the smashed piano in pieces. The court case over the contested will was ongoing. A select few knew this piano in her restaurant originated from his Sydney apartment. Piper had retrieved it.

Evie unexpectedly appeared at Sofia's elbow. "Excuse me, Sofia. Papa and Mama Rosa are ready to go back to *Ristorante di Fontana*. I thought you'd like to talk to them before they go."

Her sister guided Sofia through the crowd until they were a safe distance away. "I saw the look on your face and thought you needed rescuing. More intrusive questions about why Valentino's family aren't here? Sebastian and I have fielded enough of those questions. Piper says we must maintain our silence until his family make a public statement."

The sisters made slow progress through the crowd. Their parents were near the entrance, talking with Evie's husband.

"You must be pleased with what you've achieved," Papa said with a grin. "Romano and I were talking about what your next project might be. It won't be long before your employees can manage without your guidance. It's good to see you smiling again, rebuilding your life after this tragedy. I'm sure your fiancé would have approved."

"We're very proud of you," added Mama Rosa. "You were clever to come up with this menu. The tea and coffee varieties you have chosen complement your cuisine well.

I've been in the kitchen, talking with your chef. Have you considered branching out? Our usual gelato supplier has changed hands, and the quality has declined. Chef Phillipe said he would like to experiment with more flavours. Your kitchen could handle the extra orders. He even offered to courier some over this afternoon, in time for our dinner service."

Sofia laughed and embraced her mother. "If you and Papa don't leave now, there won't be any dinner service. It's already two o'clock, and I'll have to send these guests on their way soon."

Once her parents had left, Sofia made a brief announcement.

"Ladies and gentleman, thank you for coming and making the launch of *Valentino's* such an amazing success. Please collect your gift boxes from my staff waiting at the door. I hope that I see you again soon."

The final stragglers went out the door at three. Her eldest son Leonardo had prised thirteen-year-old Marco from the kitchen. Marco was already establishing himself as a favourite with her staff. Together with Matilda, they were on their way to her parent's restaurant. Sofia planned to join them for the usual pre-dinner feast in an hour.

Sofia was more tired than she had expected, as she sat down with Evie and Romano. She watched the staff clearing away the empty plates and glasses. Next, they would reset the tables for their first public opening tomorrow. Romano went to the coffee machine, returning with three cups of coffee. Sofia smiled in thanks.

"I appreciate all you and Evie have done to support me today, Romano. I never thought you would become such a significant person in my life. What happened in Thailand opened my eyes to how wrong I was about you."

"You're well on your way to recovery now, Sofia," Romano replied. "Today we have seen some of your old confidence return."

Evie asked, "Are you still seeing the counsellor John recommended?"

"Yes, she's been helpful. I can see more clearly now the mistakes I've made all my life. She has given me some good strategies to avoid that kind of romantic disaster again," Sofia said.

"I still don't understand why you didn't continue meeting with John. Especially after he went to Thailand to help bring you home. I thought the two of you had a strong connection?" Evie asked.

"You didn't tell Evie what happened in Sydney?" Sofia turned to Romano with a frown. "I thought you agreed there would be no secrets between you."

"It wasn't my secret," Romano replied.

"What happened in Sydney?" Evie asked, looking from one to the other.

Sofia looked down and twisted the engagement ring around her finger. She was now wearing it on her right hand. It served as a constant reminder of her new commitment to wait for God instead of rushing into trouble.

"John was kind and compassionate, but I didn't know how to deal with him. There were some difficulties, and I didn't respond appropriately. John made it clear God expected better of me." Romano muttered something that Sofia didn't catch, and she frowned at him. "Let me finish. You said this was my secret and I'll tell it my way." She shook her head. "John provided me with the contact information for this other counsellor. Then he suggested I stop phoning him. I haven't spoken to him since."

"He often asks how you are," Evie replied. "Is there a message you would like me to pass on?"

"Tell him I think of him often. And I'm praying about the promises God gave me through him," Sofia responded quietly. "Does he know I've been going to church with Marilyn and Dave?" Sofia was thankful for her new friendship. She had now overcome the hesitation she felt about Marilyn because of Dave's association with Romano. "That should help settle his concerns."

ಜ ☼ ೞ

Sofia didn't work in the family restaurant that evening as she intended. Instead, she collected Matilda and Marco and headed home.

"You look tired, Mum," Matilda said with concern. "The new restaurant looks great, but it's such a lot of work on top of what you already do. Are you sure you're going to stay on with Papa Benito and Mama Rosa?"

"I plan to advertise for a manager for *Valentino's* after the summer season is over. I'm thinking of only working the dinner sessions at *Ristorante di Fontana* in the meantime."

"Mama Rosa likes your new kitchen," Marco remarked. "I heard her talking to Papa Benito about taking on another chef. Mama Rosa's thinking she'll spend less time cooking when Evie's babies are born."

There was a pause. Sofia watched her son's face. She knew him well. Marco was about to ask something awkward.

"Mum, if Valentino hadn't died in Thailand, would there have been another baby?"

"Marco!" Matilda shrieked. "You can't ask her that."

"It's okay, Matilda. No, Marco, there wouldn't have been another baby. I had an operation after you were born."

"I'd have liked a little brother or sister," Marco continued. "It's going to be lonely when Matilda and Leonardo leave home."

"We're not going anywhere," Matilda snapped.

"Marco, why do you think they are leaving home?"

"I heard them talking. Leonardo said his girlfriend wants him to move into an apartment. Then he told Matilda she must be thinking the same thing. 'There's no privacy in this house,' he said."

Sofia was still wrestling with this revelation a few hours later. Her phone rang. Each one of the Tuesday Girls had been in touch during the day. Sofia welcomed the distraction. "Hello, Lauren."

"Hi, Sofia. I've been talking to the others, and they said you're at home. Do you want to come out and have a drink to celebrate your big event?"

"Thanks for the invitation, Lauren, but I'm exhausted."

"I've never heard you admit that before. Is there something you haven't told us? You've lost a lot of weight, and your smile seems forced."

"I'm fine, Lauren. I've been busy."

"Well, if you won't come out for a drink with us, then we'll come and visit you tomorrow. You'll be at your new restaurant at lunchtime?" Lauren asked.

"Yes, I'll be at *Valentino's*. Shall I reserve you a table?"

"Yes, please, Sofia. My husband's brother is in town, and I thought you might like to meet him. It's time you stopped thinking about the past and started planning for your future..."

Secret Strategies

ಬ ☼ ಐ

Psalm 27:14
Wait for the Lord.
Be strong and courageous as you wait for God.

ಬ ☼ ಐ

"When are your sister's babies due?" Lauren asked. She had called in unannounced at *Valentino's* again, a habit that was starting to annoy Sofia. *Valentino's* had been open for three months, and Lauren visited almost every day. Lauren used to be content with the occasional phone call or text message.

"The middle of May, but twins are often early."

"And she's keeping well? You always had easy pregnancies, but your sister's not as strong as you. Do you think Evie will stop at this pregnancy or have more children?"

"She hasn't had these babies yet, Lauren. Where are you going with this conversation? I have work to do." Sofia struggled to hide her impatience.

"You never have any time for yourself, Sofia," Lauren persisted. "Why won't you let me fix you up with one of my husband's friends? You're a beautiful woman, and I hate to see you on your own. It's been months since Valentino died."

"I've already told you I'm not interested, but you don't seem to be listening." Sofia cringed at her sharp tone. "I'm getting annoyed. Don't bring this up again. If I start dating, it will be on my terms. Now let me get back to my work. I have to make sure Phillipe has finished decorating the cake for Evie's surprise party." Sofia stood up and turned toward the kitchen.

Lauren followed Sofia, still talking. "I didn't know it was Evie's birthday. What a difference a year made to her life. It must seem like a miracle she's now happily married. Even pregnant when everyone thought she was destined to be an old maid."

"God has been good to her," Sofia conceded.

"You've changed. I can't believe you've stopped hating Romano. You were so sure their marriage would end in disaster. Does it bother you that their relationship has lasted longer than any of yours?"

Sofia turned quickly. "Are you deliberately trying to provoke me?" She caught hold of a table as the blood drained from her face. "It's time for you to go. Please don't come back without an invitation."

Patrick was seated by the door. He rose noisily to his feet.

Lauren looked from Sofia to Patrick and back again. Without another word, she stormed out.

"You should have done that weeks ago," Patrick told her.

"I don't pay you to give me advice," she snapped, and he laughed.

"I'll leave you to calm down while I make a report. Your friend Lauren looked as if she could happily murder you."

Sofia glanced towards the exit in irritation. She couldn't believe she had added another fractured friendship to her problems. As she entered the kitchen, she whispered a prayer for God's guidance and protection.

ℬ ☼ ℭ

"Are you okay?" Evie's friend Marilyn Henderson asked that evening.

Sofia sat at a corner table in the main dining room of *Ristorante di Fontana*. Music, laughter and happy conversations permeated the crowded room. But Sofia's melancholy was back. She had lost interest in her sister's birthday festivities. Now she was staring at the dark wine swirling in her glass.

Glancing up, Sofia smiled at Marilyn. This homely woman was a refreshing change from her old friends. She felt at ease, and answered truthfully.

"I'm feeling a little lost."

It had been a great comfort to find Evie's friend had room in her heart for Sofia. Marilyn was the one who came up with a solution to her problem about finding another church. And she was the one who had invited Sofia to join Evie's fledgling support group for mothers and mothers-to-be. Sofia admired Marilyn's many qualities. This woman had wisdom and strong faith, two resources Sofia desperately needed now.

"Everyone else seems to be having a great time. Here I am wallowing in self-pity," Sofia said sadly.

"Is there anything I can do?" Marilyn asked, sitting down beside her. "Sometimes it helps to share what's happening so God can reveal the true nature of the problem."

"I argued with one of my closest friends today, but that's only the beginning. Matilda's sulking because I told her boyfriend he's not to stay overnight. Leonardo's planning to move out, and Marco won't stop talking about wanting a little brother or sister."

"What did you argue about with your friend? Was it the ongoing problem of another eligible bachelor?"

Sofia nodded.

"Have you realised your response to these problems comes from your loneliness?" Marilyn asked. "Your children are each struggling to find happiness in a world where casual sex and multiple relationships is supposed to be the answer. At least Marco has seen the lesson Evie and Romano have provided. He thinks you need a husband and not another lover."

Sofia flinched and looked at the wineglass again. Marilyn gently continued. "God has forgiven your past. But your life story cannot be rewritten. Your past is the foundation for your future. Your children have seen you form multiple temporary attachments. But be assured that God sees your determination not to go that way again."

"My friends have said similar things, but your words seem easier to hear. Lauren found her mark when she challenged me about Evie's marriage. Their relationship has already lasted longer than any of mine. I thought that would change when I committed myself to Valentino, but even he had a different agenda. I don't know where I'd be now if he'd survived."

"God wants you to trust Him with your future. He knows what you need. You can be sure God's about to do something to fulfil His promise. All these little problems are pushing at you. If you weren't determined to be obedient to God, it would be easy for you to give in and let the world win."

Sofia smiled. "I hope you're right. Thanks for coming to check on me."

"Actually, I had another reason for coming. Does Marco know about you and John Edwards?"

"There's nothing to *know* about John Edwards," Sofia said. "Apart from a couple of chance meetings, he's a casual friend. His involvement in Thailand was due to a misunderstanding. Why are you asking about Marco?"

"I was checking on Lilly and Rory, and I found them with Marco upstairs in the mezzanine dining room. They didn't see me standing in the doorway. John Edwards' two sons were there too. They have formed a secret society."

"What kind of secret society?" Sofia asked.

"John's boys are desperate for a mother, and Marco wa—"

"Oh!" Sofia jumped up, knocking over her glass.

"It's alright," Marilyn said soothingly. She mopped up the spill with table napkins as she pushed Sofia back into her seat. "I asked them if I could join their secret society too. Then I talked about what happened in the Old Testament stories. When people try arranging marriages without asking for God's input, trouble always follows. I've left them praying about that. They've been very resourceful. They even came up with an acronym: MMAYD – My Mum and Your Dad. I wanted to warn you they might be speaking in code if they start putting their plans into action."

"What kind of code?" Sofia asked cautiously.

"Watch out for Marco telling you he has 'MMAYD plans to spend time with his new friends'. There are five of them. So, expect invitations to birthday parties and other family celebrations. If not for the potential for this to go disastrously wrong and cause you both embarrassment, it would be amusing to watch the conspiracy."

"Are you going to warn John?" Sofia asked.

"Do you think I should?" Marilyn asked with a twinkle in her eye.

A Possible Proposal

ℰ ☼ ℭ

1 Peter 1:3b
Because of His great mercy we are reborn into a living hope
through the resurrection of Jesus Christ.

ℰ ☼ ℭ

"It's not fair!" Matilda shouted. "First you insist we go to church with you, and now you're making us look at another investment property. Sunday afternoon's the only time I get to spend with Cooper without Marco hanging around."

"The agent was only available this afternoon. Other people are viewing the property today. I want you each to have a say in this decision, because if I decide to go ahead, we'll be moving from this house."

"We're moving?" asked Marco. "Where are we moving to?"

"Nowhere if you three don't get in the car," Sofia snapped impatiently.

"I don't know why I have to come," Leonardo complained. "If you move, I'm not going with you. You told me to pray for a sign, and this talk about moving is it."

"Then having you give your vote of approval will help all of us achieve our goals," Sofia muttered as she hurried to the car. The argument continued as she drove from the city centre. No-one seemed to be paying attention to the direction they were heading.

"Where are we going? This is the way to Romano's," Marco finally remarked.

"Are you looking at property near the workshop?" Leonardo asked with sudden interest.

"How are you going to manage a restaurant all the way out here? The commute between the three locations is going to be exhausting," complained Matilda.

"Who said anything about a restaurant?" Sofia turned into a side street. She parked outside a four-storey apartment building that stretched to the cul de sac at the end of the street. The faded white paint was peeling in places, and the garden was untidy. A billboard outside declared there were apartments for sale or to rent.

"I've been here before," Marco exclaimed. "My friend Butch lives on the ground floor. His uncle Freddie works for Romano."

Leonardo walked to the corner and looked along the four-lane thoroughfare. "I didn't know Freddie lived so close to work. We're only a block away from Romano's. If you bought an apartment here, Marco could visit Evie whenever he wanted." Marco was dancing with delight. Matilda was still to be convinced.

"Let's not make plans yet," Sofia warned them. "This building looked much better online than it does in real life. If the inside is the same, it might be impractical."

A middle-aged woman wearing a crumpled suit hurried to meet them. The agent seemed anxious and was talking too fast. "Ms Fontana? The other viewer has been held up and will join us later. We'll start on this floor, which houses the communal facilities."

The agent ushered them inside. "Here's the recreation room and visitors' lounge. On the other side are the caretaker's office and apartment. The caretaker's position is currently vacant. The previous incumbent worked here for twenty years. Unfortunately, the owner was reluctant to dismiss him, continuing to employ him long after he ceased to fulfil his duties. That is why the building needs some additional work. I can provide you with the preliminary plans for renovations. The successful purchaser could transfer over the agreement or choose another contractor."

Sofia and her teenagers trailed along behind, as the agent rushed on. The whole building needed modernising.

"This is the shared laundry facility. And this hall gives access to the pool and the outdoor entertainment area. There's a community garden, under-utilised at present, but it could be a valuable asset to the property."

Finally, the agent brought them back to their starting point and paused to look at them. "Would you like to view the caretaker's apartment, or go immediately up to the second floor? There are two vacant apartments side by side on that floor. I can show you more three-bedroom apartments on the fourth floor."

"Take us to the second floor," Sofia said quickly.

Sofia was halfway through inspecting the first apartment when the agent's phone rang. The stressed woman hurried away to meet the other viewer. This left Sofia and her children to examine the space. This apartment had been well maintained. The walls were freshly painted, and there were polished floors in all the rooms. The agent said the tenant had taken particular pride in their apartment. They had only moved to take up employment interstate. There were three generous bedrooms, two bathrooms and the living space was open. The small kitchen could do with some attention. Sofia stood in the archway where two smaller apartments had been opened up to make this larger one. She eyed the connecting wall on the other side.

"The next apartment is supposed to be smaller. If we knocked out this wall, it would make a great apartment for a larger family," she said aloud.

Turning at the sound of the agent's return, Sofia froze. John Edwards stood beside the woman, staring at her in horror. Before the adults could say anything, Marco gave a wild hoot. The room erupted in the noisy delight of three enthusiastic boys celebrating their unplanned reunion. Matilda and Leonardo reappeared from other rooms.

"What are you doing here?" Sofia asked John in suspicion, remembering the secret society. Surely there was no way Marco could have known what she was planning?

"I could ask you the same thing," John said defensively. "Did Evie tell you I was looking for a new place to live? My landlord's selling our house, and I've had trouble finding another rental. Romano remembered seeing the vacancy sign here. The boys would have to change schools, but it would save me a lot of travelling time."

"No, Evie didn't tell me you were moving, and I haven't told anyone I was coming here." Sofia tried to erase her unfriendly welcome with a generous smile. "However, I have asked God to show me a sign about whether I'm heading in the right direction. Your appearance has settled my mind. I'll wait in the hallway while you inspect this apartment."

Without pausing for a reply, Sofia hurried from the room. Matilda and Leonardo followed her. Matilda was staring at her, and Sofia squirmed while her face reddened.

"Mum? Did something happen between you and Pastor Edwards while you were away?" Matilda asked.

"What makes you think that?" Sofia tried to sound unconcerned. She looked over Matilda's head towards the apartment. Through the open doorway, she could hear the three boys talking excitedly.

"When he walked in you got that 'I'm about to explode' look," Matilda informed her, "and I thought he was going to run out."

"If I thought you would listen, I'd offer you some advice," Sofia said with a sigh. "Maybe I'll tell you anyway? There are two kinds of men in this world. The first kind will promise you everything and then take what they want. They always leave you picking up the pieces. The other kind will make a promise and stand by it, even if it means they can never have what they want."

"And Pastor Edwards is the second kind?" Matilda asked. "How does that explain your reaction?"

"These men attract different kinds of women. There are women like my sister Evie who will make a man wait while she determines whether he'll keep his promise. Then there are women like me who throw themselves at any man."

"Are you saying you threw yourself at Pastor Edwards?" Leonardo asked incredulously. "Don't you care what people think of you?"

"I wasn't well," Sofia said defensively. "We both immediately understood I'd made a terrible mistake. He was kind in his rejection. Since then we've kept our distance. Please leave me to handle this!"

They both rolled their eyes and she turned away from their accusing stares. She could hear Matilda and Leonardo whispering together. Sofia held the banister rail to steady herself and looked down into the stairwell. Her children thought she was about to make another terrible mistake.

Is this Your answer to my problems, Lord? John didn't seem happy to see me, and yet Evie insists that he's always asking about me. What if I say something to make things worse between us?

You came to buy a house with many rooms, and John finds himself without a home.

Is that what this is about? I get to have John Edwards as my neighbour! You know how I feel about him, how I can't stop thinking about what happened in Sydney. I have pleaded with You to take away this longing. How much harder will it be if I have to see him every day?

You have asked me to provide him with a wife.

But Lord, I didn't mean me! You know he has small children. You know what kind of woman I am!

A loving mother, an obedient wife, a steadfast friend.

Okay, Lord. But You have to let him know this is Your idea.

You can tell him.

Sofia heard voices, and turned as John and the agent came from the apartment.

"What do you think of this apartment?" Sofia asked, trying to sound in control of her emotions. She glanced at her older children. "In gratitude for all that you've done for me in the past, I am willing to give you first option on this apartment. Before I realised you were interested, I was planning to take both this one and the one next door. It should be easy to knock a hole in this connecting wall to create a parents' retreat. That would create more living space for energetic boys. It would add another bathroom, and provide both a master bedroom and a study. I could still do that, if you think it would be a good idea? We both know I have plenty of money and the work could be done quickly. Let's go and see the next apartment to determine whether this idea's viable."

"Wait a minute, Sofia," John insisted. "You're talking as if you're planning to buy both apartments. I can't ask you to buy me an apartment, and I certainly can't afford to pay the kind of rent you would be asking."

"I'm sorry, John. I thought you knew the whole building is for sale. There are other vacant three-bedroom apartments upstairs. If you don't like this apartment, there are other options. I am sure we can work something out. You can see that your children would love having Marco for company."

Sofia took John by the arm and led their group next door. The inspection of the second apartment was brief. It was neither as large nor as well maintained as the first. After an excursion upstairs, they returned to the first apartment. Sofia led the group into the centre of the living room to make her announcement.

"I've decided I'll purchase this building. I need to talk with John about which apartment he'd prefer. There is no reason this can't be a win-win situation for all of us."

The three younger children were ecstatic. Matilda and Leonardo looked at each other but remained quiet.

Sofia told the agent she would meet her in the downstairs visitors' lounge in fifteen minutes. That should be enough time for the flustered woman to prepare the documents Sofia needed to sign. The agent hurried away to inform the vendor the building had sold.

"John, with your permission I would like to send our children away with Matilda. I want to talk to you without being distracted by their excitement. Matilda, here's my credit card. Take the boys down to the shopping centre and find them something to eat. Try to avoid too much sugar.

Leonardo, please go with them. On your way, you'll pass a dark blue car parked near mine. Please stop and tell my bodyguards that one of them is to accompany you. When the children have finished eating, take them to visit Evie and Romano. We'll meet you there."

"What's going on, Sofia?" John asked, when they were alone.

Sofia practised her sweetest smile. Her heart was racing, and she felt faint. She prayed silently, asking God to give her the right words. There might not be another chance.

"I have missed your friendship, John. I'm hoping enough time has passed, and you will give me the opportunity to show you I've changed."

"I haven't asked you to change," John replied. "You're beautiful, just as you are. But we crossed a line in our relationship, and there's no going back."

"That's what I want to discuss with you. I've been praying for a solution to my problems, and you turn up. When this happened before, you said God was at work. I have a proposal for you. You need somewhere to live, and God has told me to buy an apartment building."

John crossed his arms across his chest and nodded for her to continue. "I'm listening."

"Matilda and Leonardo are struggling to make good relationship choices. They are talking about moving in with their respective partners. We both know the problems ahead of them if they make that choice. I want to show them it is possible for two people to love each other and continue to live separately while they wait for marriage. Before you say anything, you have to know that it was Marco together with your children who came up with the idea of merging our two families."

"What?" John looked stunned.

"I can understand your reluctance. We both know I have many failings, but God is changing me. I would be a faithful wife, and a good mother to your children."

John looked as if he was ready to run. He took a step backwards. "Are you asking me to marry you?"

Sofia tried to hide her disappointment at his reaction.

"If you find the idea of marrying me too difficult, I'd settle for having you as a neighbour. Naturally, I'll give you some time to make up your mind," she said.

"I don't need any time," he said quickly, shaking his head. "People will say I'm only interested in your money."

"What do I care what people think? My old friends will say I can't stand the idea of being alone, and I'm looking for someone safe. They'll think I made you an offer you weren't able to refuse."

"And are you?" he asked.

"Making you an offer?" she asked, as hope bubbled up inside of her.

"There's no doubt about that. But are you asking me because you're looking for someone safe?" His direct stare revealed his interest in her answer. Sofia took a deep breath, determined to be bold.

"There was nothing safe about you in Sydney, John Edwards," she told him. Sofia closed the distance between them. She reached out and straightened his tie, and then placed her right hand on his shoulder. "I thought I'd awakened a passion greater than I've ever known. Your hunger threatened to consume me."

John glanced at her hand, noticing the ring she was wearing. He looked back into her eyes.

"You did awaken a passion," John said with a grin, and he pulled her closer. Sofia held her breath. He kissed her lightly on the lips then loosened his embrace. Taking her hand from his shoulder, he removed the ring he had given her and swapped it to her left hand. "Now that you've proposed and I've accepted, I'd like another kiss." This second kiss intensified, and Sofia didn't want it to end. She sighed when John released her.

"The agent's going to wonder where you are," John said with a playful laugh, kissing her quickly. "You'd better hurry downstairs and sign away your future. I'll lock the doors and join you soon. I need some time alone to thank God for answering my prayers."

CHAPTER 44
(Monday 2nd April)

The Commitment Celebration

ஐ✿ஐ

Zephaniah 3:17
The Lord your God is with you, mighty to save.
He delights in you. He calms you with His love.
He sings over you with joy.

ஐ✿ஐ

"Hurry up, Leonardo. How long does it take to put on a jacket and tie?" Sofia shouted through the closed door.

"Why do I have to wear a tie?" Leonardo grumbled. "We're only going to brunch at your restaurant."

"We've talked about this before. I'm hosting John's fortieth birthday party, and I want this to be a memorable occasion. And it's Easter Monday. And his family will be there, as well as most of his church congregation. You know this will be our first official outing as a couple. It's only natural I want my children to look their best."

"I don't understand why you've kept your relationship a secret," Leonardo said as he wrenched open the door. "Why haven't you asked him to move in? Why is he any different from all the other men you've had?"

"For your information, young man, this is one man I haven't 'had', and I don't intend to have until we're officially married. It's taken me a long time to discover there's more to a relationship than sexual attraction. Now I want my happy-ever-after wedding. I have found a good man who loves me enough to wait until we've exchanged promises in front of a room full of witnesses."

"Do you love him?" Leonardo asked, watching her closely.

"I love him more with each passing day. The signs were there right from the start. But I was blinded to the truth. Now, if you've asked enough questions, could you please drive me to the restaurant? I've already sent Marco and Matilda ahead to help finish the table decorations. I wanted to have some time alone with you before the party. You'll be moving into your new apartment this afternoon, and we won't see as much of each other from now on."

"I'm only moving into one of your apartments. We'll be neighbours when your renovations are complete."

"I know, but it won't be the same. You did remember to invite your girlfriend? You complain about how John and I have kept our relationship a secret when I haven't met her yet."

Leonardo grimaced. "She can't come. We haven't had much time together since her grandfather died."

Sofia hadn't known about the death in the girl's family. Why was he so reluctant to talk about this young woman? But there were more important concerns today. Sofia prayed for patience and peace. Today was going to be significant, and she didn't want to make the mistake of forgetting God was in charge.

Arriving at *Valentino's*, Sofia felt a twinge of doubt about this venue. But it was essential to their secret holiday plans that they treated their guests to an early meal, and brunch was *Valentino's* specialty. John and Sofia needed to escape in time for their afternoon flight. Only Evie and Romano, and John's mentor Max Foster, knew of their plans.

"Do you think you've ordered too many flowers?" Sofia asked herself as she walked in and saw the floral display. There were bunches of flowers wherever she looked. Colourful ribbons adorned the chairs. Each table had floral decorations with the stubby candles already alight. A few early guests had arrived. Three of the Tuesday Girls had gathered near the grand piano, and they waved to her in greeting.

"You look stunning, Sofia. Where did you find your dress?" Kylie asked.

"That shade of blue suits you," Natalie added.

"The invitation didn't say what the occasion was? Can you give us a clue why you're having a formal brunch?" Melissa asked.

Sofia laughed. "You know I like dressing up. If I didn't make the dress code formal, when would I get to wear lace and satin in the morning? Now I'd better go and greet some of the other guests."

John and his family had arrived. Marco raced her to them, taking charge of Peter and Matt. She watched as the boys headed straight for the lily pond. Sofia detoured to remind them not to get their good clothes wet. She raised her hand and signalled to Patrick. She asked him to station himself near the water.

"What a pity if you miss out on the feast," Sofia told Marco, "when I send you home to get changed."

"Did you know it's our Dad's birthday?" Peter asked her, looking up with his big brown eyes. Sofia resisted the urge to smother him with a motherly embrace, as she bobbed down to talk to him. There would be time for that when her relationship with their father was official.

"Yes, I did know," she said with a grin.

"Did you get him a present?" Matt asked.

"You'll have to wait and see. It's a surprise," Sofia told him and held her finger to her lips. She stood up and walked across to where John was standing with his parents.

"Hello, John," she said as she gave him a gentle kiss on the cheek. "Happy Birthday." John smiled in welcome and turned to introduce his parents.

"Mum and Dad, this is Sofia. She's the owner of this restaurant and responsible for organising my birthday brunch."

As he spoke, she felt John slip his arm around her waist. Sofia lost herself to the wonder of having him publicly declare his affection. She could not remember afterwards what his parents said in reply. Nor could she recall the names of his other relatives. Her total focus was on his loving reassurance and the words of adoration he whispered in her ear. The restaurant filled with guests. John continued to hold her close. Evie and Romano arrived with Sofia's parents. Evie had already warned them about the new relationship. Her parents acted as if seeing John embracing Sofia was commonplace.

Romano walked over to the piano and spoke to the pianist, who had been playing softly. The musician struck a series of dramatic chords, and the room fell silent.

"Ladies and gentleman," Romano's booming voice declared, "please find your places at the table. There will be a few formalities, and then brunch will be served."

It took a few minutes for everyone to find their allocated seats. John reluctantly released Sofia. She was seated on the opposite side of the room with Marco and a heavily pregnant

Evie at her table. Matilda and Leonardo were at a nearby table with her parents.

"When you've filled your glasses with the fruit juice on your table, please join me in a toast to the birthday boy. Happy fortieth birthday, John," Romano declared.

An echo swept across the room. John stood up and bowed. "Thank you, Romano. For those who haven't met this intimidating giant, I can assure you God has given this man a huge heart. My friend has the wisdom to know when to shove me in the right direction. You're like a brother to me. I pray God will continue to bless you, and your wife Evie, as you await the birth of your twins.

"I must confess it's a little daunting to stand here before you, without having the pulpit to hide behind. Thanks for accepting my invitation to help me celebrate today. I want to especially welcome my parents, my sisters and their husbands, and my nephews and nieces. Thanks for putting up with me, and for coming to help me celebrate. Thank you to the members of my church family. Your support and encouragement make it a pleasure to serve you. I want to acknowledge the presence of my friend and mentor Max Foster. He will be saying a few words after we've eaten.

"Finally, I want to say a special thank you to my dear friend Sofia. She has opened her restaurant on this Easter Monday holiday to host my celebration. There's an old proverb that says the way to a man's heart is through his stomach. Sofia has done more than enough to capture my attention."

"We love pancakes," Peter called out, and the crowd laughed.

"Because you're so eager for pancakes, I should ask you to say grace," John quipped. Unexpectedly, the little boy jumped up on his chair.

In a loud voice, Peter shouted, "Dear God, thank You for pancakes for breakfast. And bacon. And eggs. And all the other yummy things we're about to eat. We're especially thankful there's going to be cake. Please make it a big one. Thank You for my Dad, and for making him forty so we can have a party. I'm thankful You MMAYD this happen. In Jesus' name, AMEN!"

Sofia glanced across to where Marilyn was sitting, and they shared a smile. Marco was grinning at his co-conspirators, and Sofia's smile broadened.

Romano spoke again. "With such an enthusiastic blessing, I declare breakfast served. Sofia's staff will come to your table, and if you are in need of anything, all you have to do is raise your hand."

Marco's hand was up in a flash. Another round of laughter followed. Soon the guests were devoting their attention to the delicious food. Sofia watched her guests, and when most of them had finished eating, she stood up and walked over to the piano. The pianist played another resounding series of chords. The servers delivered champagne to the adult guests.

"Unlike our friend John," Sofia began, "I'm unaccustomed to public speaking. I ask my sister Evie and her husband Romano to come and help me with the next formality. Without them, I'd never have met John Edwards. He was the minister at their wedding. I know he still remembers our first conversation. I must confess I behaved badly. From then on, it seemed he only saw me at my worst. Being a faithful Christian, he promised to pray for me. I don't think he understood what God was going to do with that promise. John, please come and stand with us. I want to show you my appreciation for all you've done for me."

John arose from his table, and his two sons jumped up to accompany him. Sofia bobbed down to the same height as the smallest boy. Romano brought out a small parcel from behind a mountain of flowers, and Sofia gave it to Peter. There was a similar present for Matt.

"Go and ask your grandmother to help you open them," John told them, and the boys hurried to obey. Exclamations of delight could be heard as the boys opened their presents.

Sofia smiled as she waited for John to turn towards her. Romano had taken a small object from his pocket and slipped it into her hand.

"John Edwards, there aren't enough words to express my gratitude for your love and acceptance. You showed me how to live my life again, by teaching me about God's patience and forgiveness. I give you this ring as a token of my love, and I pledge to devote myself to caring for you and your sons. I make this promise in the presence of God and with our assembled guests as witnesses."

Sofia reached out and placed a gold band on the ring finger of John's left hand. He looked deeply into her eyes, as he fumbled in his pocket.

"Sofia Fontana, I receive this ring as a token of your love. In return, I give you this ring as the fulfilment of God's promise. From now on, I claim you as my wife, and I will be your husband. May God teach us how to honour and obey His commandments and grow stronger in our obedience to His will."

Unnoticed, Max Foster had come to stand beside them. "Ladies and gentlemen, you have witnessed the giving and receiving of these rings and heard their declarations of love to each other. By the power vested in me by the Commonwealth of Australia, I pronounce John Edwards and Sofia Fontana husband and wife. What God has joined together may no man put asunder. John, you may kiss the bride..."

Sofia closed her eyes as John wrapped his arms around her. He held her as if he intended never to let her go, and the crowd began to cheer. Their lips met, and joy exploded in her heart.

Character List

Sofia's family
Sofia Fontana (38) – manager at *Ristorante di Fontana*
Leonardo Fontana (19) – Sofia's son, Romano's apprentice
Matilda Fontana (16) – Sofia's daughter, part time waitress
Marco Fontana (13) – Sofia's son, part time kitchen hand
Benito Fontana – Sofia's Papa, owner of *Ristorante di Fontana*
Mama Rosa Fontana – Sofia's mother & Benito's wife, chef
Evie Romano – Sofia's sister, office manager at *Romanos*
Sebastian Romano – wealthy business man, Evie's husband
Ristorante di Fontana – Fontana family restaurant
Romanos – automotive workshop, home to Evie & Sebastian
Nicholas – Sofia's first husband, Leonardo's father
Sven – Sofia's ex-boyfriend, Matilda's father
Theo – Sofia's second husband, Marco's father, bigamist
Cooper (20) – Romano's apprentice, Matilda's boyfriend
Phillipe – chef at *Valentino's*
Valentinos – new Melbourne restaurant

Sofia's family associates
Danielle – Sofia's friend & deputy at *Ristorante di Fontana*
The 'Tuesday Girls' – Sofia's friends:
      Melissa, Lauren, Kylie and Natalie
Gypsy (Guiseppe) Amorosi – Sofia's friend
La Vita è Bella – Gypsy's restaurant
Marilyn Henderson – Evie's friend & matron of honour
Dave Henderson – Marilyn's husband
      Romano's business partner
Lilly Henderson (5) – Marilyn's daughter, Evie's flower girl
Rory Henderson (8) – Marilyn's youngest son
Alex Henderson (18) – Marilyn's eldest son
François – friend Sofia met on holiday
Father Finnegan – Sydney Catholic priest

Character List con't

Valentino's family & associates
Valentino Horatio (43) – businessman, Piper's cousin
TDH – Sofia's nickname for Valentino
Tiny – Valentino's childhood nickname
Raphael Towers – Horatio family headquarters
Masterpiece – restaurant in *Raphael Towers*
Renaissance – Enzo Horatio's *Raphael Towers* nightclub
Doña Gabriella Marcella Horatio – Valentino's mother
Enzo Horatio (73) – Valentino's elder brother
Theresa Serpios (72) – Valentino's eldest sister
Beatrice Paulini (60) – Valentino's second oldest sister
Cecilia Ferro (58) – Valentino's second youngest sister
Diana Abatangelo (54) – Valentino's youngest sister
Sabrina Horatio (60) – Enzo's wife
Raymond Serpios – husband to Valentino's sister Theresa
Luigi Paulini – husband to Valentino's sister Beatrice
Orazio Ferro – husband to Valentino's sister Cecilia
Fabio Abatangelo – husband to Valentino's sister Diana
Augustus Gallo (78) – Valentino's Sydney uncle
Ricardo Barononi – an associate of Augustus Gallo
Roger Silvania – pilot for Enzo's private jet
Hillary Silvania – Roger's mother
Jezebel (34) – fugitive, Evie's enemy

John's family associates
John Edwards (39) – church pastor, Evie & Romano's friend
Matt Edwards (9) – John's eldest son
Peter Edwards (7) – John's youngest son
Max Foster – retired minister, John's mentor
Lucinda and Fergus McLachlan – friends of John's parents
Arielle – John's ex-wife
Lisa-Jane – John Edward's secretary

Character List con't

Piper's associates
Piper Maxwell – Romano's friend, Valentino's cousin
Maximum Security – Piper's business
Pietro Gallo – Piper's childhood name
Jenny Prescott – *Maximum Security* operative, Evie's friend
Patrick Sims – *Maximum Security* operative, Evie's friend
Thomas Demistrani – *Maximum Security* operative
Nelson Felmingham – *Maximum Security* operative
Oliver Johnston – *Maximum Security* operative

ঙ ✿ ಚ

Thailand characters and locations
(*real locations, imaginary characters and events)
Chatuchak Weekend Market
Bumrungrad International Hospital
Maena Sakhay Bangkok Hotel (translation = Important River)
Phuhying Swy – a shop at the Market
Mr Wattana – *Maena Sakhay* Hotel representative
Chaisai - *Maena Sakhay* Hotel employee, Sofia's butler
Prija – *Maena Sakhay* Hotel employee, Chaisai's sister
Kirikait – *Chatuchak Market* tour guide
Dr Pin Baelmuntrisuma - Doctor at *Bumrungrad Hospital*
Tang – jungle militia leader

Timeline

August 25	Sofia meets John at Evie's wedding

This book is the second in the River Wild Series.
Evie's wedding takes place in Book 1: Chapter 25

August 29	Sofia meets Valentino; & meets John again
September 4	A luncheon date for Sofia and Valentino
September 5	Valentino flies to Sydney
September 6	Sofia's new friendships are tested
September 8	Valentino is missing
September 12	Sofia begins to question everyone's loyalty
October 14	Sofia and Valentino are reunited
October 16	Valentino invites Sofia on a business trip
October 20	Sofia and Valentino travel to Thailand
October 22	John is recruited for a rescue mission
October 25	A family funeral in Sydney
November 28	A new Melbourne restaurant opens
February 22	Sofia faces a difficult decision
February 25	Sofia hosts a family celebration

Acknowledgements

This book could not have been written without the support and encouragement of many people.

Firstly, I am grateful to God for giving me the inspiration, the time and the persistence to bring this story into life.

My writing adventure has not been a solitary one. Since my first book was published earlier in 2019, I have been greatly encouraged by the support of my faithful Facebook followers. Tameka Devlyn, Lisa Haynes and Donna Bullen accepted my offer to suggest character names. I hope you enjoy seeing your suggestions in print.

I continue to thank God for my supportive reader team. Each one brings a different contribution. They always ask challenging questions, and when I have too many ideas, they point me in the better direction. They have also helped spread the word about my writing adventure. Thanks to Gillian Perrett, Naomi McGlone, Belinda McGuire, Donna Bullen, Tim Berry, Glenda Charles and Lisa Haynes for your help with *When Promises Are Broken*.

A special thank you to Belinda Pollard, publishing mentor and editor, for taking me under her wing and for the professional advice that has pushed me to improve my skills so I could bring Sofia's story to my readers.

Last but not least, thanks to my husband Tony for his constant encouragement and ongoing support.

Chrissy

A Note From the Author

Greetings from Tasmania, Australia.

Thank you for reading Sofia's story. If you are able, please leave a brief online review, as this will help other readers find my work. Please contact me if you require more information on how to leave a review.

To receive updates about when other books in the **River Wild Series** will become available, please visit www.chrissygarwood.com and complete the form.

Links to social media can be accessed from my webpage.

Publishing a novel was a childhood ambition, one that I set aside a long time ago. Since then, I have added wife and mother, student, childcare educator, visual artist and chaplain to my list of achievements. To help me appreciate the brighter moments, God has guided me through dark days in the wilderness, where my faith has been tested.

I have learned a lot about myself and my ambitions while writing the books in this series. The confidence I have gained as a storyteller has enriched my character. I believe it has made me a humbler disciple of Jesus Christ, a more determined encourager, a better friend.

When I first lost myself to the rediscovered joy of writing, my horizons expanded. This was how *The River Wild* series was born. This fictional world is populated with characters who whispered their stories to me. This is the second in the series. While each book can be read alone, many of the main characters appear in other books.

Chrissy

Have you read Book 1?
White Rose of Promise

A prophetic dream she can't remember. A shameful past she can't forget. An impossible future she dare not cherish.

Maria Evangelina Fontana comes home from twenty years in exile. She is looking for reconciliation but her family refuse to acknowledge the secret that keeps them apart. They cannot accept that the lost years have changed her forever. Her hope for a new beginning fades.

Sebastian Romano has no time for women and abhors weakness. The wealthy businessman is uncertain why he offers Ria a way out of her dilemma, but it is too late to change his mind. If only he had understood the risk.

Ria's innocence turns his orderly world upside down. Her faith challenges his values as she steps into her destiny. He thought he was done with his violent past, but his enemies have found her. Romano watches helplessly as the prophecy unfolds...

Active links are available at www.chrissygarwood.com

River Wild Series books scheduled for 2020publication
Book 3: What Price My Freedom?
Book 4: Which Promise This Time?

Fantasy River Series

(scheduled for 2020 publication)

Phoena's Quest: First Spark

The quest begins with a first spark. It flares in isolation, untended and unknown. Too late, the darkness tries to smother it...

The Westernbrooke Academy for Young Noblemen has always been Phoena's home. An orphaned servant without a past, the teenager lacks magical talent and protections. She is often targeted for magical experiments. After years of torment, she longs for invisibility. The other servants think her luck is running out.

Lord Karilion, the Academy's best magic-user, has beaten all challengers. The wealthy heir is also the champion swordsman. Viscount Baraapa, secure in second place, has no magic but his scientific mastery outweighs that disadvantage. The foreigner, Lord Oramis, threatens the balance when he refuses to be tested. What is the Ambassador's son hiding?

The quest selects its champions: a servant girl and three noblemen who think winning her loyalty is a game. And there's a dragon in the back garden...

Other titles in this series:
Phoena's Quest: Second Flame
Phoena's Quest: Third Fire

Chrissy Garwood

9 780648 543428